C000319601

AC

Act of Exposure

Cathryn Cooper

HEADLINE
Liaison

Copyright © 1996 Cathryn Cooper

The right of Cathryn Cooper to be identified as the Author of
the Work has been asserted by her in accordance with
the Copyright, Designs and Patents Act 1988.

First published in 1996 by
HEADLINE BOOK PUBLISHING LTD

A HEADLINE LIAISON paperback

10 9 8 7 6 5 4 3 2 1

All rights reserved. No part of this publication may be reproduced,
stored in a retrieval system, or transmitted, in any form or by any
means without the prior written permission of the publisher, nor be
otherwise circulated in any form of binding or cover other than that
in which it is published and without a similar condition being
imposed on the subsequent purchaser.

All characters in this publication are fictitious and any resemblance
to real persons, living or dead, is purely coincidental.

ISBN 0 7472 5400 1

Typeset by Avon Dataset Ltd, Bidford-on-Avon, Warks

Printed and bound in Great Britain by
Cox & Wyman Ltd, Reading, Berks

HEADLINE BOOK PUBLISHING
A division of Hodder Headline PLC
338 Euston Road
London NW1 3BH

Act of
Exposure

Chapter 1

It was eight-thirty on a Sunday morning when Lance Vector took his mother the newspapers and her first cup of tea of the day.

'Just open the curtains about twelve inches dear,' she said as he drew back the brown brocade.

He did not comment that he knew exactly how she wanted them. Every Sunday her instructions were the same. So was the routine. Tea and papers in bed at eight-thirty precisely, curtains drawn back so that one third of the window let in the light of another Sunday morning. Any more and the violets on the dull beige wallpaper would have looked more faded.

Blinking rapidly, he watched as his mother placed her glasses on her nose. Her breasts heaved as she pulled herself more upright against the mountain of pillows. He leapt forward to help her. She took his assistance without smiling, without speaking, but she seemed pleased. Everything being in order, she reached for the papers.

Behind his back, Lance clenched his fists so tightly that his fingernails dug sharply into his palms. He could stand the pain. It was waiting for her opinion on the latest sex scandal that he found difficult.

As she began to read the most lurid of the Sunday tabloids, the very paper for whom he reported, Lance stood completely still. Would she like it? He hoped she would.

At last, it happened. She smiled, laughed, and tossed her head.

Lance laughed too. Tension left his shoulders, his arms and his fists. He saw her nostrils flare as she took a deep breath, half closed her eyes, and tipped her nose towards heaven.

'Smite and smite again!' she cried, and clapped her hands. 'Expose the fornicators, the sinners, those who fall to the lure of the flesh!'

Lance clapped too – just once – then rubbed his neat, white hands together. His fingers were cold, his palms clammy. He beamed brightly. She liked it. She really liked it. Even though he was in his mid-thirties, his mother's opinion of his work mattered very much.

'Do you like the article best, or the photograph?' he asked, though he didn't really need to. He could see that she liked them both. Her face, then her words, said it all.

In a tone reminiscent of a Bible belt priest, her voice rang around the bedroom. 'Your words are forthright and righteous! Your pen is the sword of truth. As for the photograph, see!' she exclaimed, tapping her finger on a spot where one Carol Anne Flowers held her hand in front of her face in a futile attempt to hide her identity. 'See how she tries to hide her face as though she can hide her shame the same way? The woman's a slut, a modern-day Whore of Babylon!'

Lance sighed with happiness. His shoulders became less hunched, his body more fluid. 'I'm glad you like it, mother. I put a great deal of effort into that particular piece of work. The editor was pleased too.'

He kissed her cheek, and as he did so, glanced over at the front page article he had written and the photograph he had taken.

"CAUGHT IN THE ACT," screamed the headline. Carol Anne Flowers, a pretty girl with dark brown hair and darker eyes, was still recognizable despite her raised hand and spread fingers.

Oh yes, he was good at his job; good at rooting out the wrongdoers, the sinners, the fornicators – no matter their status, no matter their wealth. No one was safe from his probing, his pen or his camera. Like a worm, as flexible as plasticine, he could get in places where no one else could get, see things no one else could see.

Straightening up, he sighed happily. An urge had come upon him, an overwhelming desire to go down to the basement where he kept all the other evidence about his particular case and many others.

Besides the article and the photograph, there were video machines down there, and piled beside them were tapes of all the other sex scandals he had reported on. He taped all his assignments. That way, he got to know his subjects' movements, their whereabouts, and their habits. From these tapes he could also lift stills if need be.

Of course, his mother didn't know too much about what he did in the cellar. She never went down there on account of her hip operation. It was just as well, otherwise she might take a different view of her son if she saw what some of the more explicit material actually contained. His mother only

3

took pride in his achievements on seeing the end product, the damning evidence across the front page as another public figure was exposed as a sexual sinner.

'This, my son, is your crusade. It is for you to expose those who swim in the cesspool of fleshly sins. It is for you to find them out and expose them in their true colours. The more high and mighty they are, the greater are their sins!'

Of course, the newspaper Lance worked for didn't look at things in quite the same way as his mother. All right, they did their best to present themselves as upholders of public morals, but basically their intention was to increase circulation and make money. But of course, Lance never corrected his mother's view of them or of him. Lance revelled in the praises of both his mother and his editor. In his deep, dark soul, he was satisfied that work that brought such praise from others, was rightfully a delight to him.

'More tea?' he asked. Another useless question. She always had a second cup.

Whilst in the kitchen making another pot of tea, Lance could not resist opening the door that led down to the basement. A soft shiver travelled over him as his gaze settled on the first two steps which were picked out by the light from the kitchen. Beyond that, there was only darkness, a soft, velvet, beckoning darkness that filled him with excitement.

He reached for the switch that would turn on the light lower down the stone steps and light up the mix of grey flagstones and red tiles on the basement floor. Before his fingertips could touch it, he curled them into his hand; retreated.

'Not yet.' He said it softly. There was sweet regret in disciplining himself; the pleasure of visualising that floor, and the contents of his own private realm. Restraint and patience, would ultimately result in greater pleasure. Once he had delivered the tea to his mother he could indulge himself to the full. For now, he would enjoy the delicious tremors that spread like fine needles beneath the surface of his skin.

Already, in anticipation of what lay below, his throat was dry and his breath seemed to grate across his tongue. 'Not yet,' he said again. 'Do your duty. Wait.'

Dutiful son as he was, he took his mother her second dose of tea, then told her he had work to do down in the basement.

'On a Sunday, my son?' Her eyebrows rose high. Behind the thick glass of her spectacles, her eyeballs seemed larger and closer, as if they were separate from the rest of her head.

He knew she would say that. Was ready for her saying that. Once he had explained that he had a new subject to study, new sins to uncover, she smiled and gave him her blessing.

Odd jobs around the house, even gardening, was not allowed on a Sunday, yet anything to do with his job as a scandal sheet journalist *was* allowed. After all, he was exposing the wicked, the fornicators, and what better day than Sunday to reflect on his achievements and contemplate his next subject for exposure.

Lance had no qualms about exposing other peoples' sex-lives. To his mind, those in high places, in public life, had an example to set. Because they were in the limelight, they had no real right to a private life – especially a sexual one. They were the confident people, the people who had been born to status or had achieved success. They smiled from photo-

5

graphs, talked with authority on television, and mingled with others of comparable status and wealth. But they were all the same to Lance Vector. They all had feet of clay, and deserved their weaknesses to be made public.

To his mother his work was a crusade. To him, it was the most rewarding job he had ever had, and to his editor, he was catering to the age-old view that sex, no matter in what context, sells anything – especially newspapers.

Although his mother never came to the basement, Lance bolted the door after him. With mounting excitement, he switched on his latest video.

There she was. Carol Anne Flowers. And there was her partner in sin, Nigel Porter, the head of a huge public organization. Both were naked, their limbs entwined around each other, their breaths noisy as they sucked and licked at each other's bodies.

Porter was a man of humble background who had worked his way to the top. He was an icon to some and a shrewd representative of the capitalist system to others.

Carol Anne was an actress from some peak-viewing TV soap opera. Both were married, famous and therefore fair game for media exposure.

'Sixty-nine,' said Lance, tilting his head like an inquisitive sparrow as he studied the heaving bodies. '*Soixante-neuf.*' He chuckled, then said it again, only this time more slowly as if he were both savouring the words and experiencing their meaning for himself. But, of course, he wasn't. He was only watching.

Fascinated, he ran his tongue over his lips as the man on the screen ran his over the famous starlet's sexual divide.

How did her sex taste? he wondered. Enlightenment came as the salty wetness of his upper lip transferred to his tongue. Like the sea, he decided, she would taste like the sea.

In the manner of a child intent on aping its parents, Lance poked out his tongue. As the tip of Nigel Porter's tongue tapped at the small bud of flesh within the woman's sex, Lance tapped his against one of his fingertips.

How was Nigel feeling? How was Carol Anne feeling? He did his best to imagine and was well satisfied with the result. Over the top of Nigel's head, he could see the rise and fall of the man's buttocks as his member slid in and out of Carol Anne's mouth. How would *that* feel?

He undid his zip and let his penis fall into his hand. It was not exactly soft, and was getting harder. He knew from watching other videos he'd taken of people's sexual antics, that his penis was of decent proportions. The only difference between his and those of like size on the screen was that they were getting something he'd never had. Lance, despite his age, was still a virgin.

As best he could, he formed his thumb and forefinger into pretend lips. His other fingers became her mouth and her tongue, hot and firm against his erecting flesh.

He raised his other hand before his mouth, and again tapped the tip of his tongue against the tip of his forefinger which had now become her clitoris.

In his mind, he was with them on the screen. True, he could not feel the softness of her belly against his, her breasts against his loins. But he could imagine it. Oh yes, he could imagine it very well.

He shuddered with them, groaned with them as Carol

7

Anne's flesh pulsated against Nigel's mouth, and Nigel's hips spasmed against hers.

They had come, and so had he.

Relief spread over his body as his semen spewed forth from the head of his member and lay in a milky pool on the floor. He sighed. It was over – at least for him. After tucking himself away, he zipped up his flies.

Something on the screen caught his eye and made him wonder anew. Nigel, a slim, graceful man of forty or so, was standing up now. So was Carol. They were gazing spellbound at one another as they ran their hands in sweeping caresses over each other's bodies. There was real affection in those looks, real emotion.

Lance undid his shirt and ran his hands over his own chest. He frowned. No matter how well he copied their movements, he could not feel so moved that his expression reflected theirs. For the very first time, he wondered how it would truly feel to run his hands over a woman's body and to have her touch him that way. To his own great surprise, he had a tremendous urge to escape his celibate state and once, just once, taste the fruits his mother warned him against and his newspaper decried.

His mind was made up. He would find someone to suit him. Someone aloof from the seduction of others; a cool, confident woman. Not an actress. Not a television personality. Someone professional, intelligent and as engrossed in her work as he was in his.

Leaning forward, the light from the screen accentuated the hollows above his deep set eyes, the grooves on either side of his nose and mouth. He screwed up his eyes and studied the dark-haired, dark-eyed woman.

No, he decided, *he didn't want a woman like her*. For some reason, the fact that she was dark and the fact that he had watched her seemed to go hand in hand. *No. Not a dark woman*. He would go for a fair one, the fairer the better. And she would have to have blue eyes.

Now, where, he asked himself, *would he find her?*

Prerequisites raced through his head. Not a prostitute, he told himself, not someone who had to be paid for it. The woman he would give himself to had to be beautiful, but she also had to be willing to have sex because *she* wanted to, and not because she was paid to have it.

On the other hand, he had to be aroused by her. So far, no woman had had that effect on him. True, he took these secret videos of women having sex with willing partners, but, in all honesty, he was not exactly turned on by the women themselves – not in the flesh anyway. He took his pleasure from them purely through the video screen, at a distance, so to speak.

Yes. He had to find someone who aroused him, who appeared impervious to the approaches of others – almost as if she were waiting purely for him.

Chapter 2

Besides the white wig and black gown of a Queen's Counsel, all the dancer wore was a pair of thigh-high black boots, and a mask that covered her face. The mask was made of something pale mauve and had a faint sparkle. The boots were suede, the gown – naturally – was of silk.

She carried a black rod that was about two inches in diameter, and four feet long. At first, she passed the rod behind her back, and hooked her arms over it so that her naked breasts pouted forward like two round and ripe grapefruit. The crowd roared their approval. Then she wriggled her hips as though she were getting out of some item of clothing that was loath to leave her flesh. The audience fell to an instant hush. A few groaned or mewed as if they too would like to shed their clothes.

Satisfied she now had their full attention, the dancer turned her back on the glistening faces, slid the rod up under her gown and pushed the black silk up towards her shoulder-blades. Then she bent over so that those watching could appreciate the firm curve of her behind and the sultry shadow that peeped so provocatively from between her legs.

Judging that they had seen enough of her rear, she turned

to face them. To a roar of approval, she slid the knob of the rod over the lips of her sex, then clasped it between her legs. Folding her arms behind her back, she held the black gown away from her body.

As she exposed the extraordinary perfection of her high breasts, her narrow waist, and her flat belly, she swayed her hips from side to side; backwards, forwards, slowly, then more quickly. As she moved, so did the rod, and as the rod moved, she ran her tongue over her lips, and moaned deeply, throatily into the microphone.

The effect was electrifying, and she knew it. She knew also that mentally, each man there was making love to her, embedding his own rod in her as she writhed beneath him. He wouldn't be asking whether she liked what he was doing to her, or what her personal preference was: missionary, rear approach, oral or anal. He wouldn't even be asking her if she liked her nipples being rubbed. Selfishly, he would notch her up as just another hot pussy he had screwed who had gyrated like crazy on the hardness of his giant – no – to him, unique erection.

Because of the mask, she was only a body. Each individual could indulge in his personal desire to his heart's content. The wig and the gown added an extra dimension; a belief, even, that the law itself was not above the delights of the flesh.

To the woman who danced beneath the discerning gleam of a dozen spotlights, the mask was something else. Behind its anonymity, she took in the florid faces, the fish-bowl eyes, and the slack, open mouths of her spellbound audience.

They see my body, and that is all they see. But I see them clearly. I see them at their most lustful, their most foolish, and their most vulnerable. I see them for what they are, but they never truly see me.

Eventually, to tumultuous applause, her dance was over, the lights went out. Like something that was not quite real, a fanciful apparition existing only in over-ripe imaginations, she melted into the shadows, just as dreams vanish at dawn.

She stripped and refreshed herself in the privacy of her room, warm streams of soapy water taking her sweat and her dance from her body. After showering and dressing, patting her coal black hair, and reapplying her make-up, especially her bright red lipstick, she slid back the bolt on her dressing-room door.

Immaculate in pale blue suit, paler shirt, and white satin tie, Archie Ringer, who owned the Red Devil Club, walked straight in. His mouth smiled. His eyes were the same colour as his suit, but less solid, less appealing. His voice was slow, monotonous – like a car engine on tick-over.

'Carmel, darling, I do not know why you bother to lock the door. You know I am not interested in your body, and the boys will stop anyone more vulnerable to your charms from barging in.'

The boys were Trev and George who were in their late thirties, wore satin shirts, split to the waist, and had bodies that were far more to Archie's liking than hers was. The fact that their predilections were not heterosexual suited the sort of establishment this was. They were effective because, with their sexual preferences, they could stand apart from the more general clientele. Added to this, they gave impeccable service, and paid outstanding attention to detail.

'I like my privacy, Archie.' She didn't look at him as she spoke. Instead, she surveyed herself in the mirror, then patted into perfection her glossy black hair, which was cut in a neat page-boy style that swept her shoulders. With her small finger, she neatly scraped a smudge of red lipstick away from the corner of her mouth, then pursed her lips as if she were kissing the mirror, or the reflection of herself.

Archie shrugged, his shoulder pads bunching as if they had minds of their own and were nothing to do with the narrow shoulders beneath them. 'Please yourself, darling. I take it you will be coming into the bar before you go?'

She smiled. Not at him, but at herself – the one reflected in the mirror. 'Once Jezebel Justice has left the stage, I always come into the bar before I go.'

She didn't need to do that. Archie's place was no sordid hole where the exotic dancers were also expected to sell their bodies. That particular choice was their own. It was a club of rich fabrics, immaculate service, and richer clients. The woman Archie knew as Carmel enjoyed that part of her night almost as much as she did her dancing.

From her favourite spot, she could watch those who were wealthy enough to be admitted, watch them as, sometimes nervously, they enjoyed their drinks, the floor show, or the company of people with similar minds, and similar bank accounts. These were the people who came in through the front door which was down a narrow set of steps below black-painted railings and a crumpled pavement. Building, railings and pavement had all been there since the eighteenth century.

Upstairs was another part of the club, a place reserved for the more favoured and famous members of the Red Devil

14

Club. It was a place only whispered of. Entrance was granted only to a few select people. So far, the graceful young woman with the black hair and bright red lips had not been invited up there, though she wasn't really sure she wanted to be.

Upstairs remained something she only knew of, and from all that she had heard, she felt for the moment satisfied enough to gaze at the crowd on the lower level.

Some faces were familiar. Some too familiar. These she kept away from, although, like her, they would not want their two lives mixing – their professional life and their life of pleasure. She knew who they were, but they did not know her; such is the benefit of a double disguise. She was the dancer, Jezebel, who was also Carmel. But she was also someone else, someone she wished to keep hidden from those at the Red Devil Club.

Because she had worn a mask during her act, no one could be sure of who she was – that Jezebel Justice was Carmel. Someone extremely beautiful, but remote. But they did look, they did admire. The more heroic ventured to ask her if she wanted a drink, company, or a late supper in one of the rooms upstairs – and perhaps to join the 'special' club up there.

'I never go upstairs,' she told them, and they retreated before the crispness of her voice, the hard look from her coal-black eyes.

But still they stared. Still they came and asked the same questions. But then, how could they resist?

To match her hair, she wore a small black dress that barely covered her breasts and only skimmed the cheeks of her behind. Black suspenders crossed her creamy flesh and bit into the tops of her sheer, black stockings. They showed and

15

were meant to show from beneath the hem of her dress. Her legs seemed to go on forever. The whole effect could have been cheap, blowsy, but instead there was a girlish, almost innocent quality about it.

As she raised her glass to her bright, red lips the girl known as Carmel to Archie Ringer, and Jezebel Justice when she was behind her crystal-bright mask, eyed the men – and the women – who jostled for drinks, conversed, laughed, and looked her over. And all the time, she looked for a face, a physique that would make her evening perfect.

Carmel was Abigail by day, but although Abigail was successful in her chosen profession, there was a side of her that needed release, needed adventure of the more sordid kind. But then, the Red Devil Club catered for people like her. All the same, she never came here as herself. Most people trusted the club's reputation for discretion. That's why the rich and famous went there. Being a barrister by day – and by inclination – made her more wary, more apprehensive of the turn such a climate could take. Not content with changing disguise once, she was Jezebel behind the mask, and then Carmel of the black hair, black eyes and crimson lips when she sat at the bar. By day, as Abigail Corrigan, herself, she was fair-skinned, her hair silvery blonde, her eyes very blue, and her lips, cleaned of any trace of lipstick, were a pale, enticing pink and of a shape that had no need for outline or colour.

Within the Inns of Court, she was regarded as single-minded, highly professional, aloof and cold. It was said, and she knew it, that she had nothing to do with men because she was frigid. Such knowledge amused her. Their attempts to seduce her were perfunctory. Not for her the candle-lit dinners at some bijou restaurant, a weekend away at some Torquay hotel, a sweating, noisy copulation with a soft-fleshed colleague. Sex, to her, had to be laced with excitement, even danger. And she liked powerful men with hard bodies and a yen for variety of venue and partner. But experience had taught her to be careful.

Slowly she cast her gaze over those assembled. What would her friends and colleagues think, she wondered, if they knew that for one night a month she was Jezebel, the woman behind the mask, and Carmel, the dark beauty who radiated sexuality?

Because she was so single-minded in her work, her natural sexuality was stored up. It bubbled inside her as it got hotter until it reached boiling point and she half expected steam to start shooting out of her ears, her nostrils, her mouth, but most of all, out of her sex organs, so hot, so demanding it was.

The dance excited her. She left the power of law and the precision of court address and the politics of chambers behind her the minute she stepped up onto that stage. From then on, she was as much at the mercy of her dancing as her audience was. This was a world and an occupation in which she needed to release her own emotions, exploit her own weaknesses.

Her nipples were hard against the constraint of her bodice; the frilled lips of her most secret place were slick with the juice of arousal. Her body was goading her to live out the rest of her fantasy, a role she only enacted on one night in every month. She needed a man. She needed passion.

A twirling orb positioned above the bar threw shafts of light over those who lingered in the shadows. There was a smell of expensive perfume, heady wines, and headier cigar smoke.

Carmel saw faces she knew; men's faces. Some were bankers, others were 'something' in the city. Others were 'something' in uniform, mostly generals and admirals. Some had titles, most had a fortune. Some she avoided. Only one other person knew her little secret. Valeria, a dark-skinned beauty of Anglo-African parentage.

There she was now among the crowd at the end of the bar. Carmel waved, and Valeria waved back, then turned and said something to someone behind her. Carmel craned her neck and tried to see who it was. Valeria had a friend with her, a tall, blonde friend who seemed reluctant to step into the limelight.

Just at the moment when Carmel was about to leave her perch and join Valeria and her friend, a hand landed on her shoulder.

'Carmel, darling. There's someone I want you to meet.'

Recognizing Archie's voice, she turned round to face him, ready to hurl a sharp rebuke that she had entertained enough. Her time was now her own. For the moment, she buttoned her lip. Like chips of broken coal, her eyes went from Archie to the man beside him. He was tall, blue eyed, his facial features irregular, but not unattractive.

'Do you really?' Her voice was noticeably hostile. Archie ignored it, his smile still plastered on his face.

'This is Olly, darling. He specifically asked me if I could introduce him. I said you wouldn't mind.'

Archie barely winced as her glance hardened.

'I'm not a whore, Archie, and I'm not something you bandy around like a snort of coke.'

For the umpteenth time since she'd first asked Archie for a job, shivers of revulsion crept up her spine and burst into frosty twigs across her shoulders. Not that Archie was disgusting to look at. He was smooth, polite, shiny and sleek; just like the satin of the shirts he sometimes wore. But all that glitters is not gold, and the shine of satin can hide the most obscene, the most hirsute of bodies. That was Carmel's feeling about him; that the sleek outer casing hid something more bestial, more dangerous.

Archie smiled his most carefree smile, turned on his most winning charm.

'Darling, I would never presume such a thing.'

His lips were damp on her cheek, his breath moist upon her ear. 'For me,' she heard him whisper. 'Please.'

Through half-closed eyes, she studied the man who stood next to Archie as though he were some schoolboy applying for his first job, his first step into the adult world. But this was no adolescent, and by definition, he was not likely to be inexperienced in the ways of a wicked world. He was tall, and his eyes twinkled when the shafts of light from the twirling orb caught them.

'Oliver Hardiman, Miss Carmel.'

She let him take her hand, raised her eyebrows when he kissed it. His lips were cold; from his last drink, no doubt. *Gin*, she thought, *with ice*. His head hovered above her hand. She took in the glossiness of his hair, the slightly thinning spot in the middle, and the large mole just behind his left ear.

Once he raised his head, his eyes looked intently into hers. They shone with admiration; almost with awe, but more so with lust. 'Miss Justice. Jezebel. Or may I call you Miss Carmel – I am told that is your true name. Your performance was incredible. I have truly never seen anything like it in my life. Perhaps we could have supper tonight?'

'No. I'm sorry. We can't.' She caught the wary, almost fawning expression on Archie's face, and wondered what his relationship was with this man. Why had he betrayed her identity to him? Normally, he respected her privacy once her act was over. Anger replaced her loathing for him.

The look on Oliver Hardiman's face told her he was not used to being rejected. It also said that he did not much like the experience. 'Then lunch?'

She tossed her head. Held it high. Her eyes looked past him to the mix of people, silk suits, and designer dresses. She took a deep breath and almost got high on the mix of expensive perfumes.

'No. I never mix business with pleasure, Mr Hardiman. I regard collusion with my audience as detrimental to my professional performance.'

Fair eyebrows rose sharply towards the gleaming blond hair. Now there was no denying the annoyance in his voice. 'Good grief, Miss Carmel. Spoken like a lawyer. No wonder they named you Jezebel Justice!'

'That was the reason,' said Archie. 'I noticed the way she spoke. And the clothes, of course. It was my idea to call her that. In fact I . . .'

His attention suddenly seemed to drift. Carmel looked to where he was looking. The light from the glass orb had stopped and settled on the group of people at the other end of the bar.

Valeria was among them, but did not notice that Archie was looking her way. She appeared to be in deep conversation with her friend who had shoulder-length blonde hair, was very tall, very angular, and wore a dark grey trouser suit.

Oliver Hardiman attempted to regain her attention. 'If that's the case, perhaps I could buy you a drink.'

'I'm sorry,' said Carmel as she slipped off her stool. Suddenly, an idea came to her. She smiled sweetly up at him. 'But perhaps you'd like to meet my friend, Valeria. I'm sure she'd like a drink with you – perhaps even supper.'

She ignored Archie's look of annoyance. How dare he presume she would accommodate this man. How dare he betray her privacy.

Oliver eyed her sidelong. He looked puzzled, but Carmel – Abby – gave him no time to question her actions. Grabbing his hand and dragging him firmly through the crowd, she led him to where Valeria still stood with the tall blonde stranger.

Valeria's dark eyes opened wide when she saw her friend. 'Darling,' said Valeria in that husky voice of hers. 'Marvellous to see you.'

Abby introduced everyone.

Valeria was all attention, all gushing enthusiasm. Her eyes raked Oliver Hardiman's body as though he wasn't wearing the Armani suit and Gucci shoes. As though he wasn't wearing anything but a big smile and a large hard-on, and Valeria did like big erections!

Her long dark fingers were grasped by his. 'Charmed, Mr

21

Hardiman. My word. Where did Carmel find such a gorgeous man as you?'

Abby took charge of events. 'Here, darling. Now do try and get on together. Get closer. Get to know each other.'

As she said it, Abby, in her guise as Carmel of the black, shoulder-length hair and bright red lips, caught hold of Valeria's hand. Accompanied by such words, anyone else would have placed it inside Oliver's hand. But Carmel was not anyone else. She was something very different, something far more special than those who saw her could ever realize.

With a haunting smile around her bright red lips, she guided her friend's hand to Oliver's crotch; then laughed at his sudden intake of breath and the shocked look on his face. All the same, she knew he would not refuse to let that hand go further, to let it undo his zip in some darkened place, and let Valeria do to it whatever she pleased.

'Well . . .' Valeria's breasts swelled with excitement. Her dark brown eyes were wide, and her generous, plum-coloured lips glistened after her tongue had run over them once or twice.

Like a panther, thought Carmel, like a sleek, black panther about to partake of a meal.

'Carmel . . .' Fingers touched her shoulder. 'Hardiman is a very special man. I wanted you to . . .' Archie's voice was low, but coldly angry. Carmel slid from his grasp. Now, she decided, was the time to leave. She had no wish to hear why Archie wanted her to ingratiate herself with a 'personal' friend of his. The shadier side to Archie's world was something she carefully steered clear of. There were rumours that he was involved in other rackets; drugs, prostitution, dirty films. She wanted to know nothing about them.

Taking the view that there is safety in numbers, and a certain security in like reaching for like, she grabbed the arm of the big blonde who had come with Valeria.

'Come on,' she said quickly. 'Valeria can manage him without our help.'

Valeria, she could tell, still had the man's crotch in her hand, her body leaning against him so he was trapped between her and the bar.

The blonde began to protest, but her voice sounded croaky, as though she had a cold. Carmel ignored her protests.

'Don't be a gooseberry,' she said crisply. 'Val likes to have guys to herself. Don't worry. She's set up for the night. She won't miss you.'

Outside, the night air tingled and throbbed with the sounds of civilization. A thousand lights twinkled from the night-time city. The sky blearily reflected its brazen light.

'Taxi!' shouted Abby, and raised her hand.

'No!'

Strong fingers gripped her arm.

'I have a car.'

'And a cold?'

Either the blonde did not hear, or she ignored Abby's obvious comment about the deep croakiness of her voice. With heels clacking along the cracked, uneven pavement, the two figures threw long shadows as they passed beneath the yellow glare of an NCP sign. They took the stairs, the blonde consistently taking them two at a time. Abby did a pretty fair job of keeping up.

'This way.'

Now it was the blonde's turn to grip Abby's hand and guide her among the parked cars.

'This is mine.'

They stopped and the blonde rummaged in a small patent leather handbag. 'Keys are in this bloody thing somewhere. Oh, shit. How can anyone find anything among all this bloody rubbish!'

With that the blonde tipped the contents of the bag onto the ground. Lipstick rolled one way, mascara another. Clunk went the keys as they too hit the ground. With knees spread wide, the blonde bent to retrieve them.

'What about your make-up?' Abby caught the rolling lipstick under her sole as she said it.

The blonde straightened up before she responded. 'Stuff the bloody make-up. I won't be needing it any more. Quick, get into the car.'

Abby shook her head in amazement and smiled. 'You must have money to burn. That stuff's going to take some fair money to replace.'

'I won't be replacing it. I told you, I won't be needing it any more.'

Glad to escape the fridge-white coldness of the car park's fluorescents, Abby slid into the front seat of a sleek, black car. The car smelt of leather and expensive tastes. Her companion switched on the interior light.

'Thank God for that!'

That is not a woman's voice, thought Abby. At last, the penny dropped, and as if her head was perched on a spring, she turned quickly and stared at the person beside her. Her heart skipped a beat. A blonde wig flew into the back seat. A pair of high-heeled shoes followed.

'How the hell do you women wear these things?'

Should she laugh, or should she scream and get the hell out of here? A male face; female make-up, female clothes, broad, male shoulders. No. There was no danger. Valeria had something to do with this, and if this guy was a friend of Valeria, he could not possibly be suspect.

'Never mind how women wear such things, what explanation do you have for wearing them?' As she spoke, she took a deep breath and recognized the scent of a man among the warm leather smell of the car seats.

'It was Valeria's idea.' He smiled. His teeth looked very white, though comical, against the peachy brightness of his lipstick. 'I dared her to do something. And in return, she dared me.'

He paused. She was aware of his eyes studying her face, her eyes, her hair, and her lips.

He had brown eyes, dark eyebrows. Even in old age, she thought, his eyebrows would still be dark. His hair, although flattened tightly to his head from wearing the wig, was also dark and expensively cut.

Should I stay, she asked herself, *or should I go?* It was a stupid question. She already knew the answer.

Unblinking, she studied the firm contours of his face, the smile that played around his mouth and in his eyes. The seat beneath her buttocks felt suddenly warm, suddenly mobile. Her body was beginning to move, to demand. She sensed this man was unusual, as unusual as herself. She also sensed his sexuality. Strong forces were at work between them; complex

25

chemical reactions that neither could fully understand, but both were responding to.

A woman of your profession, she thought to herself. *How could you do this? How could you?* But the need was too strong, and anyway, it wasn't the first time.

Once more, she told herself, *I'll take a taste of the wild side just once more, and then I'll leave this life for good, stick to the day job, perhaps even get married and have a family. But for now . . .*

She smiled, leaned forward, kissed his cheek.

'So, my blonde bombshell, you have exposed your gender. How much more is there to expose?'

He laughed, reached out, and cupped her cheek in the palm of his hand. He might just as well have cupped her breast or forced his fingers between her legs. The effect was the same. One touch, and her body was on fire.

His lips touched hers as he murmured his answer.

'Only my body. What about you?'

She did not hesitate.

'The same,' she lied.

The editor had told Lance not to spend any more time spying on the Red Devil Club, but Lance did not always do what his editor told him. Earlier he had seen the two women come out, had thought of how beautifully one of them moved – so seductively that he gave scant attention to the other.

He would have followed them if he'd been off duty, but to his mind, he was on duty, and that duty was in making notes about who went up and down the stairs that were lined with black painted railings and led to the dark red door at the bottom.

His editor might have ordered him away, but he knew his prey well, knew their habits, knew where to find them. Until his editor or the man above him gave explicit instructions as to whom he was to expose, he would do his own thing, and at this moment in time that meant hanging around the entrance to the Red Devil Club, searching out sinners.

Chapter 3

The man who was dressed as a woman parked his car in a place he told her would be safe from radio bandits and joy-riding drogues. Abigail looked around her. Empty streets, a few brick buildings, a railway arch that looked as if someone had scooped it out of the embankment with a soup spoon. Sodium street lights garnished the pock-marked road and pavements with hints of tangerine. *This*, she thought, *is an odd place to leave something sleek and shiny, but it's his car, his problem*. All the same, she couldn't help but comment. 'There's no one around here.'

'Correct. It's empty of people.'

He's right, she thought as she slammed the car door and cast her gaze over their immediate surroundings. There were no buildings; no pubs, clubs, houses, or blocks of concrete flats. The road was lined with fences of corrugated tin, spiteful wire, and crumbling stone walls. Behind such dubious compounds, wrecked cars were piled in rusting ziggurats, and around their base, guard dogs barked and howled.

'I know a place,' he told her. His fingers were warm and firm on her hand, and she trembled. It was as if the warmth and the firmness were heralds of his masculinity, and that masculinity was diffusing into her flesh. A host of familiar feelings gathered between her legs and hung there like molten lead. Later, that heaviness would disappear, that thrill of illicit fear would turn to sensual excitement. Later – when they got to where he was taking her.

She stumbled, so he let her hand go and slipped his arm around her waist. He led her over wet cobbles. Their footsteps, even their breathing, sounded hollow, echoing in the emptiness. Long and black, their shadows fell across the streets, the tin and the yards. Behind their makeshift barricades, the dogs in the scrap yards barked more excitedly.

Excitement was also in Abigail's mind. *Who was this man to assume she was his for the taking in some dingy, dark hotel room?*

Sidelong looks at his face, his height, revealed nothing. Good looking, dark haired. Was it blue eyes? Sodium street lights were notorious for mutating natural colours. She thought they'd been brown in the car. But then, he thought hers were black. She smiled to herself. A mask. Another mask.

None of it mattered. He looked good, he smelt good, and her body was on fire. She wanted him, this man who had been dressed as a woman. Another mask.

Thinking about that and wondering at his reasons for being in disguise, she glanced down at the silk trousers that skimmed her companion's feet. Instead of high heels, he now wore a pair of white trainers. They looked new. All the same, they did nothing to enhance the rest of his outfit.

He seemed suddenly aware that she was studying him. His

gaze met hers. Yes, his eyes were brown. Her thoughts went back to the white trainers. She laughed.

'What are you laughing at?'

'I hope they don't object to your dress in the place we're going.' She glanced pointedly at the offending articles sticking out beneath the swirling silk of his trousers.

He took her point and laughed too. His eyes sparkled as they passed beneath a street light that leaned at an odd angle. She liked the way he laughed, liked his eyes and the way his hair left his forehead. He squeezed her waist, his hand moist and warm. Then he kissed her as one friend would another. 'I doubt it. Clothes might maketh the man in the Red Devil Club, but round here, it's money alone that opens doors – and no questions asked.' His voice was as warm as the palm of his hand, its moistness diffusing through the fabric of her dress.

The neon sign that creaked above the door said Railway Hotel. The sign was ugly in design, and garish in colour; the transparent pink of plastic sandals.

A round man with a bald head took the money and slid them the key. He did not look up from the paper he was reading.

By craning her neck slightly, the woman who was Jezebel, Carmel, and Abigail, could see it was open at a picture of a busty blonde. Below it the caption read "Tracy Figures Big".

A mathematician? she wondered, *or has she just passed her maths A level? Neither,* she decided with a wry grin. *She just happened to have big tits and was probably screwing the editor, an editor who purported to be the upholder of public morals if his front page headlines were anything to go by.*

The room was clean, but basic; a bed, a table lamp, dressing table, one chair. The bathroom door was slightly ajar.

As the net curtain billowed before the open window, a goods train rattled by, its wheels squealing as it inched slowly along the huge loop that happened at that particular place in the rails. The noise it made drowned out any other sound. Neither spoke. It was pointless to try.

The train passed. The man bent and switched on the table lamp.

'Turn it off.' Abby said the words softly, but hinted at passion. *This is Carmel's voice*, she said to herself. *This is the voice of Jezebel Justice, a woman with black hair and black eyes who only comes out at night.*

The room would have been completely dark, completely mean, except for the amber glow of a sodium streetlight just outside the window. Just the hint of its golden light lifted the decor of the room and made it look a little richer than it really was.

But her surroundings were of no real consequence. It was this man who intrigued her. Who was he, what was he?

Not that he had been the first she had accompanied to a seedy hotel room. Indeed, wasn't that the attraction of this side of her life, this escape to the unknown, the improbable, the dangerous?

Memories of other such occasions came to her mind and aroused her body. She had opened her legs in the back seat of a car, felt the coldness of a glass window against her backside as a hot tongue had licked her to distraction in some dark shop doorway. They were memories to cherish in the other side of her life, the side that was far straighter and far narrower than the one she lived as Carmel.

Her eyes locked with the man who had been dressed as a woman. There was passion in them, a dancing excitement.

At that point, she could have asked his name, but she did not. Like her, he had another life, another world that he would not wish to divulge in a shabby room at the Railway Hotel. They were here for sex, and the night was fading fast.

'So,' she said in a low, husky voice. 'Let's see if you really are a man. Expose yourself, whoever you are. Take off your clothes.'

The words seemed to hang in the amber darkness of the room, then were drowned as another train rattled by. Sounds were not needed anyway. Vision was enough. One by one, item by item, his clothes dropped to the floor. No matter that the remains of make-up still clung to his face. As his earthy, masculine smell reached into her senses, she shivered. Even without that smell, his body and his rigid erection proclaimed what he truly was.

Everything was exactly as she wanted it. The night had been right, this room was right, and this man, she decided, was worth having.

A faint hint of diesel drifted through the open window, but was drowned in his scent, the chemical eruption that was drawing the female body to the male. It was as if small, invisible hooks were piercing her flesh, pulling her closer to him. But those hooks did not hurt. They only tingled, only tantalized.

Slowly, as if she were peeling the skin of a fig away from its sweet, soft flesh, she eased the black dress from her body, let it fall to her ankles, then kicked it to one side. As the last rattle sounded from the passing train, her other clothes lay with it.

Strange, she thought to herself, *that only his eyes are exploring me, and yet, I feel pinpricks of sensation running over my skin. My nipples are hardening, and a warm juiciness is pouring from my vagina – like melting jam, toffee, or honey – anything that melts when it gets warm.*

With eyes shining, and her breath racing in short, sharp, impatient gasps, she stared at his penis. Made golden by the orange light that sliced through the window, it reared, like a magic wand from a bed of dark, tangled hair. Large, thick, virile. A pleasure to hold. A pleasure to have.

She gulped, swallowed, tingled from breast to knee bone. She did not want to rush this.

Slowly. Slowly. Savour each moment, she told herself. *Memorize each detail; sight, smell, and touch.*

Her fingers followed the curve of his muscles, the soft, scattering of body hair, the dark indent that ran from his chest to his penis.

'You have very dark pubic hair,' she said, her voice hushed, her gaze resting on his springy, tangled curls.

His look mirrored hers.

'And yours is very fair. Strange, when the hair on your head is so dark.'

His comment jarred; sounded a warning note. Normally, she shaved her pubic hair off completely. But of late, she had been busy. Under pressure to perform, and perform well, she had let it grow. After all, her legal career came first. Her erotic dancing was purely a sideline.

Wary of what he might be thinking, she was immediately alert to the question in his eyes, the slight frown denting his eyebrows. She must not allow him to dwell on that feature. It could so easily give her away. Much against her inclination, she had to speed things up.

The gap between them narrowed until the tips of her nipples brushed the hardness of his chest. As his lips met hers, she ran her hands from the thickness of his neck down along his shoulders. How good they felt, how hard as the blood of his desire rushed through his veins. Belly met belly as the warm firmness of his palms swept down her back until he held her behind in his hands. His fingers curved and dug into her buttocks at the point where they met the tops of her legs. Breath mingled with breath as tongues danced in a parody of courtship. She clasped her hands at the nape of his neck as he lifted her by her buttocks and carried her to the bed.

His closeness, his smell, sent a shock wave through her system. She nuzzled her nose against his armpit and drew in the scent of maleness. She had a need to drink it, drink him, eat him, even. She also had a feeling of wanting to drown in his warmth, of wanting him to fill her, to crawl into her, penis first, and make love to every organ in her body.

On the bed, his mouth left hers. Not to stray. Not to speak, but to explore her body with his lips and his tongue.

There was no sound except for hushed murmurs of pleasure from him and from her; the whisper of his hands and body passing over hers, the sound of the net curtains rasping in the breeze.

He sucked her nipples, tickled their sensitive nubs with his tongue, traced circles around their halos of pale, pink flesh. She mewed with regret when his mouth left them, showed her regret as she covered them with her own hands. His tongue licked long, and pleasurably over her belly; tantalized her navel, then swept in slow but enticing circles down towards her open legs.

He paused, his thumbs caressing her clutch of silvery hair. She sensed he was looking at it, wondering again at the stark contrast between that and the hair on her head. He must not wonder too long, must not be allowed to guess.

Tensing, she wriggled her hips, moaned, and heaved her buttocks up from the bed so that her scent would rise and veil his face. The strategy worked. As his tongue divided her most hidden flesh, she arched her back, closed her eyes, and truly became Carmel, the woman with coal-black eyes, black hair, and an appetite for sex on the wild side of the city.

Her mind, as well as her body, wallowed in the sheer sexuality of it all, the sordid surrender to whatever this man wanted to do to her, because whatever he wanted, she wanted too.

'No,' he said at last, and pushed her hands away from her breasts. 'Let me do it to you. You need do nothing to me. Nothing at all. Tonight, you are my toy. By receiving pleasure, you will give me pleasure.'

She did not argue. Somehow, the words fell deep inside her and interlocked with her basic nature. Shivers of excitement ran through her body. She was vulnerable, but willing.

Even though her heart was beating fast in her breast, she let him tie her hands to the headboard, her ankles to the base. This was what she wanted from a man. This was what she had always wanted, but had never dared allow – at least – not willingly.

Not because the man she was with might not have been willing. Oh no, it wasn't that. It was just that she had never quite trusted such casual acquaintances, and somehow, this once, she had trusted.

As he looked into her eyes, he traced the lines of her face with his fingers.

Softly, he followed the arch of her eyebrows, the straight perfection of her nose, the select drama of her cheekbones. He let his finger fall beneath her chin, then brought it up to explore her lips, to dip between them, and – like something much hotter, much more demanding – force it between her teeth and onto her tongue.

Murmuring, writhing with pleasure beneath his body, she wanted to drown in him, wanted to fuse with him like one hot metal to another.

She cried out as he nipped her nipples, sucked her breasts. It was as though he were eating her through a straw; like an ice-cream sundae. No. More like coffee cream, laced with brandy. Smooth, sweet, and incredibly heady.

In the half-darkness of the room, the weight of his body pressed her to the bed.

She was only vaguely aware of the roughness of the bedspread against her back.

She was intimately aware of his pubic curls crushed against hers, the dewy wetness of the head of his penis as it ploughed through her sex, its strength and size as it penetrated her; the heat of his stem against the soft suck of her pubic lips.

'You like being tied up, don't you?'

His body thudded against her.

'I might.' Her voice trembled with passion.

'Say it. Go on, say it.' There was power in his voice. He was willing her to do this.

'I can't.'

It was true. Somehow, to say such a thing would be to expose her innermost self; the person she really was. Or was it that she didn't want to say it? That she wanted him to force the words out of her?

His features hardened. His body banged heavily and fiercely against hers. The sound of belly slapping against belly filled the tiny room.

She cried out.

'Say it. I know you like it.' He continued to fuck her as he said it. His face was intense, his jaw set like iron.

'I won't!'

Her cry held more than defiance. It trembled with pleasure.

God – she liked what he was doing to her, liked this feeling of helplessness with a man she instinctively trusted!

All the same, she was aware of the grim line of his mouth, the tight grip of his hands. The tips of his fingers dug into her hips.

'You,' he said, as he skewered her more deeply, then paused, 'are not what you seem.' He withdrew a little, then plunged again. She cried out.

'You,' he said as he repeated the ramming, the pausing as he asked her the question, 'like what I'm doing to you, but will not admit it.' Again he withdrew, held himself back like an archer about to fire.

38

Abby, lost in her own sexuality, her own fantasy, sucked in her breath. Each time he thrust her enjoyment increased. Each time he paused, harbingers of climax radiated upwards and outwards from the centre of her pleasure. The coming climax was like the feathers of a fan. First it was only slightly open. With each thrust, each pause, it opened a little more, tantalized a little more. But it was increasing. The fan was gradually opening into one fantastic statement. One fantastic climax.

'You,' he exclaimed again as he rammed himself into her, 'like to be in control of your life and of men, yet, when it comes to sex, you need to submit to the more sordid side of your nature. Is that not right?'

The sensations increased. The fan of sexual feathers went that much further towards its fullest opening.

Moaning through gritted teeth, Carmel thrashed her head from side to side, burying her face and her cries in the pillow. At the same time, she arched her body so that she might better meet the fierceness of his thrusts.

He retrieved his cock, then rammed it in again.

'Is that not right?' he demanded again . . . and again, and again, her juices slurping as he pumped himself into her in time with his question.

'Yes!' she cried. 'Yes! Yes!' The ostrich-feathered fan of her own sensations was now fully open.

As her climax ranted through her mind and her body, she would have said anything, would have done anything, and would be anything he wanted her to be.

Even once the orgasm was completely over and he lay snuggled close to her side, he did not untie her. Strangely enough, it did not seem to matter. The way he stroked her breasts as they talked made her forget she was still tied to the bed and to his wishes. The warmth of his voice against her ear, and the way one hand stayed trapped beneath her behind, gave her a strangely secure feeling.

But why am I allowing this? she asked herself. It was a question she had asked herself before. The answer was there, and she knew it was there.

In her other life, she was powerful, successful, and unapproachable. It was her that led the way, made the headway, and dominated her field in a way few women ever got to do. Here, in this other world, this twilight where people indulged their wildest excesses, she was someone else, and wanted to be someone else. She needed him to dominate her, to draw her sexuality and her fantasies out of her.

She yelped like a puppy as he pulled on her pubic hair.

'Why is your hair down there so white, and yet the hair on your head is so black?' he asked.

Her response was quick. 'I dye it to match the wig I wear in my act. Black gown. White wig. White pubic hair.'

'I see.'

He believed her. She was glad of that, but she didn't want any more questions. She could not afford to let him know the truth. She took the advantage.

'So why were you dressed as a woman?'

He laughed against her shoulder. 'I dared Valeria to come out with me one night dressed in nothing but her stockings and a coat.' He laughed more loudly. 'I take my hat off to that woman. She loved doing it.'

'Where did you take her?'

'We went for a drive in the country. Found a lovely old pub with thatched gables and dark beams – you know the sort of place.'

Carmel nodded as best she could. Such an effort made her breasts wobble like firm jellies.

'We had a drink, had a bar meal. Then we drove into the forest and I made her take off her coat and fucked her over the bonnet of my car.' He kissed her ear. 'Lovely, don't you think? Just imagine, the warmth of the bonnet against her naked breasts and belly, and me plunging into her from behind. And all by the light of the moon!'

Carmel murmured a response, and mewed appreciatively as his fingers rolled back the flesh of her pubic lips. The fingers of his other hand probed between the cheeks of her behind.

'Then what?' she asked, her buttocks wriggling against her exploring fingers and a new climax rising between her pubic lips.

'Then,' he said, after kissing her neck, 'I refused to give her back her coat. I made her climb naked into the boot of my car.'

'Like a piece of luggage.'

'That's what she said too. Said I shouldn't treat women that way, that I had no respect for them. I told her she was wrong, told her how much I loved them, worshipped them, would do anything, be anything they wanted me to be. So, put your money where your mouth is, she said. Be a woman.'

'Good for her.'

They laughed, kissed, and talked more. He asked her if she made a habit of picking up men at the Red Devil Club.

'Only if they meet my very high standards,' she replied.

41

'So I'm honoured?'

'Not really. I thought you were a woman. Archie was trying to get me to go upstairs with that man I left Valeria with. I did not wish to do that. I thought I would be safe if I went off with another woman. I went off with you on that understanding, and that alone.'

'Well, what a surprise you got.'

'Yes,' she said, and pressed her leg against his member which was now flaccid and huddled against his thigh.

His lips then his voice became warm against her ear. 'Tell me about them.'

'One of my lovers?'

'Yes. It turns me on.'

It was her first instinct to say no, but his cock was still flaccid and she had a few more hours to kill.

'There was one in particular. He was American. I think he was in oil. Either that, or he was a gangster.'

'Why do you say that?'

She shrugged. 'Looked like one. He had a good body, nice face, but had a scar down one cheek. Perhaps it was that that made me wonder. He was staying at the Savoy. The suite was expensive. That night, I lay between silk sheets.'

In the mean light of the Railway Hotel, the man she was with cuddled closer. She felt his penis hardening. He nibbled at her ear.

'How did he take you?'

She told him of how he had asked her to walk around the room as she undressed, as though she were familiar with undressing in front of him. As though watching her was a familiar habit.

He asked her to sing as she did it. She had asked him what song. He had said any – no – 'Move Over Darling' or 'Move Closer'. Either of those, he said.

So she'd obliged.

'Was it good with him?'

'Yes,' she answered, remembering that it had been good. She was also aware that this man lying next to her had hoped she was going to say it hadn't been. What an ego boost that would have been for him. *It's almost,* she thought, *as though we know each other well. Already, he is showing jealousy.*

Jealousy, like being recognized, was something else she could do without. Yet somehow, like him, she was enjoying listening to what she was saying. She was also enjoying remembering.

'I remember he had that scar on his face, and another on his chest. It was just beneath his chest hair. It was barely covered by it. Strange,' she added thoughtfully, 'but I had forgotten that.'

She didn't add that the guy, who she vaguely remembered was called Dwight, had wanted to set her up in an apartment in Knightsbridge. That was her business.

'I'm stirred,' he said against her ear. 'I'd get you to tell me about all your other loves, if we only had time.'

She enjoyed the delicate touch of his breath on her face before his lips and tongue again sought hers. His penis had hardened, and as he rolled over onto her, it dug into her belly.

Abby enjoyed his dominance, the harsh tone he adopted when he ordered her to turn over and be re-tied to the bed. Her sex quivered with excitement against the crumpled bedclothes as he pinched and slapped her bottom. Then she cried out as he raised her hips, steadied them, and pushed himself back into where he had already been.

Alert to the sound of his breathing, she waited until she was absolutely sure that he was sleeping before she slipped out of her loosened bonds and went to the bathroom.

She washed the smell of him from her body, then stared at herself in the mirror.

Who was this woman who stared back at her? How could she do the things that she did?

For the first time that night, fear at what might happen burned in her chest.

'But it didn't happen,' she said quietly to herself. 'You enjoyed everything that happened tonight. Leave him now. Leave him to the bed, the bill and the fact that you are gone and he will never have you again.'

For the first time ever, she did not quite believe what she was saying. There was a nervous knot in her stomach about this man. There was also the premonition in her head that she wanted to see him again and have him again.

She glanced at her watch. Almost four. Time to be gone; time to cross the divide between this life and her other one.

Praying that the water pipes wouldn't be too noisy, she turned on the chrome tap that haphazardly sprayed cold water into a cold white sink. With yellow soap and a frayed flannel, she washed what remained of the red lipstick from her mouth and the black make-up from her eyes.

Keen to cleanse her face of Carmel and the night, she was too vigorous with the water and the rough towel. Eyesight blurred as a small circle of plastic tipped out onto her cheek, then fell downwards.

'Damn!'

Squinting slightly, she felt around the basin for the stray contact lens. Her fingers failed to locate it.

Exasperated, she threw her head back, and clenched her fists. *No. This mustn't happen! The floor! Perhaps it fell on the floor.*

Naked, she dropped on all fours to the cold vinyl. Her actions were more rushed now. She could not chance him seeing her like this. With or without the contact lens, she had to get away before he awoke.

Her fingers failed to locate it. Hopefully, so would anyone else's. She stood up and looked one last time in the pitted glass of the frameless mirror.

A pair of dark-lashed eyes looked back at her; one black, and one blue.

'Damn!' Her exclamation was vehement, but no more than a whisper.

Quietly, she crept back into the bedroom, gathered up her clothes and her handbag, then left.

Not until she was safely tucked up in her own bed in a room with grey and yellow wallpaper and furnished with Queen Anne style reproductions did she think about him and wonder who he really was. After all, she hadn't even known his name.

The funny thing was that somehow, it hadn't seemed to matter. Despite his strange garb and the remains of his make-up, there was something familiar about him, almost as though she should know him quite well.

She let it go. She had met him in the Red Devil Club where her name was Carmel when she wasn't dancing, and

Jezebel Justice when she was. Now she was home, and now she was Abigail Corrigan and had a right to a black gown and white wig. In her other life it truly was part of her profession.

Chapter 4

John Humphries, QC, had lately been honoured to receive the red cloak of a high court judge. Like many professional men whose acquaintances cross the social divide, he had an eye for the main chance. Public image was as important to him as the woman who was still his wife, the sons at Cambridge, and the elegant mistress whose pedigree was far superior to his own. Therefore, many were invited to celebrate his success in the auspicious surroundings of Trendleham Court, his magnificent Elizabethan house that sat ringed with yew trees near the Cotswold village of Blockley.

Besides his colleagues in chambers – judges, high ranking barristers, solicitors, and police commissioners – his guest list also included politicians, celebrities, and last, but by no means least, those employed in broadcasting and on newspapers.

Television presenters and journalists mingled with those whose weekly income could keep a traditional journalist in booze and birds for the rest of his life – almost.

John Humphries did not know the sprinkling of media people either socially or professionally. A less astute man would have considered their presence unnecessary. After all, their masters were there, so why invite the boys from the engine room? But John Humphries had got where he was by being shrewd and using what he had and what he knew. Part of that knowledge was that one whisper of scandal at ground level in a newspaper office, and the rich newspaper proprietor would grasp the chance of getting richer. Accordingly, he invited the boys from the engine room, placated them with good food and fine wine. He also presented them with the picture of a successful man, a family man, and best of all, a highly moral man.

On such occasions, his mistress, a very understanding woman in her late thirties and with a private income, stayed firmly out of the picture. His wife, bless her, did not allow mention of his mistress's name, but did know of her existence. Sex, she philosophized, did not necessarily mean love.

Within the oak-panelled room, where lead-paned windows looked out towards the Severn, voices brimming with authority, knowledge and general gossip blended in a rich chorus that lay heavy on the ear.

Commensurate with such gatherings, some people drew more attention and admiration than others. Some also drew offers to have lunch, have dinner, and much, much more.

Abigail Corrigan, QC, a colleague in chambers of the honoured gentleman, was such a person.

Not only did she turn heads because of her legal track record, which, in all honesty, was outstanding for someone of her age, but Abigail was stunning to look at too. Clear blue eyes gazed from above high cheekbones. Her nose was straight, her lips, so adept at delivering verbal broadsides, looked capable of planting the most luscious of kisses. They were also very pale in colour, which made her eyes look even bluer, her cheekbones even higher.

Perhaps inherited from some Scandinavian ancestor, her hair was silvery blonde, her figure long and lithe, her skin creamy rather than icy white.

Many who knew her nodded genially whenever they met her, respect glowing on their faces, their admiration further revealed by the way they spoke of her.

'Youngest ever called to the bar. And a woman at that!'

'I've heard her in court. Cutting in her cross examination, and enigmatic in her summing up. Deadly. Very deadly.'

'They do say the female of the species is deadlier than the male,' mused a learned man with bushy grey eyebrows and an expressive twinkle in his eye. 'And if I was twenty years younger, I'd make it my job to find out just how dangerous she might be.' This last comment was made more softly, to himself, rather than to anyone else.

Those who did not know her presumed that despite the sombre blackness of her outfit, this sleek young woman could not possibly be what she was: the most successful young barrister in the city. Because they did not quite believe that someone so beautiful could also be so brilliant, they tried their hand and their luck. At the same time as propositioning her, they could not help but imagine her generous mouth on theirs, her breasts bare and heaving gently beneath their gaze and their groping hands, her legs parted. At first, of course, they would ask a mundane question; something low-key, something legal, and with the most sensual of mouths, she would reply, speak of the law, of her views on the latest judgements, of her opinion on the outcome of the case of financial double-dealing now being played out at the Old Bailey.

Those who might have asked her to lunch balked at their own crassness in even thinking that she was the sort of woman to be regarded as anything other than a professional. Abigail Corrigan was a glittering example of what women could be if they did not let their sexuality weaken their resolve.

If those who conversed with her ever noticed that her eyes never quite looked at them and that she was always searching for something or someone among the crowd, they did not comment on it. It was enough that she had spoken to them and they knew what sort of woman she was.

Abigail Corrigan glided serenely on her way. Her nocturnal adventures of just a fortnight ago were consigned to some secret corner of her mind, as they usually were. But usually was a slipshod word now, after her last encounter. Aspects of the man she had lain with in the Railway Hotel kept seeping into her mind.

She thought repeatedly of the darkness of his eyes, the warm pressure of his lips on hers and the firmness of his tongue as it had pushed into her mouth. And of how willingly she had let him in. Unknown before that night, he was now drifting around her mind like a familiar shadow. Even while sitting in court these sweet memories evoked delightful sensations that ran like shivers over her flesh. Beneath her robes she was bare from stocking tops to waist. Abby never wore underwear. In her professional life, it was her only concession to sexuality.

Pleasurable thoughts were put away when someone she knew spoke to her.

'Abby, my dear. How nice to see you here.'

She smiled at the tall man with the shoulder-length grey hair that was so smoothly tied back in a ponytail at the nape of his neck. He had another guy with him, a pink-cheeked young man who had the scrubbed-clean confidence that only a public school education can achieve. He looked at her with obvious interest.

'Christopher.'

He shook her hand in a thoroughly businesslike way, but his eyes held meaning. He was one crown prosecutor who had felt the sharp edge of her tongue, the tight precision of her legal defence. All the same, she could recognize the lust in his eyes. She had also seen him with his mouth hanging open, his eyes glazed as he beheld her in another place and as another person. Oh what marvellous inventions are masks, coloured contact lenses, black wigs, and bright red lipstick, she thought to herself.

'This is Lance Vector,' he said. 'Freelance journalist. He's following my star assignment at the moment. This, my dear Vector, is Abigail Corrigan, a woman who is wed entirely to her profession and has never been known to accept the offer of a date unless it's in court. She's our very own Snow Queen, and the sharpest legal defence around. If ever you need a lawyer, she's the one you should ask for.'

Abigail shook the young man's hand. Immediately, she knew she had had an effect on him. Whatever expression had been in his eyes altered. His jaw dropped ever so slightly, his handshake lingered longer than necessary. After pulling her hand out of his, she turned her gaze firmly back to Christopher Probert.

'And how is the Rheingold case? Is Reuben Rheingold likely to wallow inside the Scrubs for his manipulation of other people's wealth?'

Christopher Probert took a swig of dark, red wine before he replied.

'If I am successful, my dear Abigail, he will wallow there for a very long time. Wallowing will suit him. He's fat as a hippo, has no hair, and has an odd penchant for wearing grey suits, and grey only. He's a very grey man. Wallowing was made for the likes of him. Besides, he made away with a lot of people's money.'

'A lot of *rich* people's money,' Abigail countered. 'And rich people can afford to – shall we say – make you push a little harder for a conviction?'

She saw him wince, knew for sure that he had only been talking law, not thinking it. As usual, he was imagining what he would like to do to her, what he would have her do to him.

The journalist was still staring at her. She managed to avoid looking directly at him. Like Christopher, it was easy to see what was on his mind.

Christopher continued. 'He's guilty, Abigail. I'm thoroughly convinced – not just as a professional, but also on a personal level. I had money in Swan and Swallow Investments myself.'

'I didn't know that. However, can you really say that the evidence you have is conclusive? Do you really believe that this one man – a manager as opposed to a financier – could alone be responsible for the mistakes made? Give,

Christopher. Tell me the names of those you think are really responsible. You must have some idea.'

Christopher tossed his head and hissed slightly. His tone became more intense. 'You're an idealist, Abigail. More so than you think. You're looking for the cavalry or the white knight to come riding in and put everything to rights.' He leaned nearer to her. She could smell the wine on his breath. 'Well, it won't happen. Rheingold will go down regardless of what one certain member of Parliament is saying.'

Abby shook her head and eyed Christopher with amused pity. She'd heard that an MP named Stephen Sigmund was asking awkward questions. 'I had heard he was crusading for an investigation by the SFO.'

'Crusading! Is that what you call it?'

'Yes. Crusading. Like a white knight. You know. The sort that gallops to the rescue of those that can't help themselves.'

Vector the journalist had so far remained silent. Now, inspired by what he had heard, he awoke and spoke.

'Crusading – that's a wonderful term, Miss Corrigan. What a lovely thought to have a white knight riding into battle, to save the holy scriptures from the infidels, the law from the lawless, the sacred from the profane!'

It was hard not to be speechless, but Abby hid her sudden cough with a mouthful of wine. *What the hell was going on in this guys' mind? Why did he turn so pink as he gazed adoringly at her?* – she looked to Probert, who just stared blankly at Vector, blinked, then quickly and clumsily changed the subject.

He began to tell Abby all about his own investments and the fifty thousand he had lost at Swan and Swallow. Now, she judged, was the time to take her leave. She made her excuses, smiled at each man, then walked away. Aware they were both watching her, she did not look back.

Recently arrived, Stephen Sigmund watched the tall, graceful woman with the silvery blonde hair. Being a politician, of course, he could carry on the most convoluted conversation as he did this. He talked of the latest scandals, the rumour that more than one politician had had his fingers in the Swan and Swallow Investments fiasco. He also repeated his own boast that he would make every effort required to expose the offenders.

'You could run into trouble,' someone said.

'So could they,' he countered. 'I dislike power making scapegoats of the weak, and Rheingold is weak. He's only a manager. There's someone else behind him.'

'All very well, my dear Stephen, but how the devil are you going to prove it, man?'

Stephen looked casually at the man who had spoken, but took in the nervous tick beneath his right cheek – a sure sign of guilty tension.

'I'm making enquiries. I'll get there in the end.'

'Aren't you just making unnecessary ripples to bring attention to yourself, Mr Sigmund?'

'Ah!' Stephen forced himself to look pleasantly at the fresh-faced journalist who had just latched himself onto the group of listeners. 'But you would say that, wouldn't you, Mr . . .' he paused as he let his eyes skim over the journalist's yellow name tag, 'Mr Vector. Your newspaper doesn't appear to want any grey areas to this case. By the tone of your journalistic prose, I get the distinct impression that your editor would hang the old man if he could.'

The young man's thick lips half-smiled, half-sneered. 'We reflect public concern, Mr Sigmund. That's our job. Public concern, public morals.'

'And I, Mr Vector, believe in justice. I do not believe in manipulation of facts. Neither do I believe in manipulation of moral thought. I believe everyone has a right to privacy and to justice. Obviously your paper thinks otherwise, judging by the lurid attention to detail over Mr Rheingold's private life.'

Vector looked as if Stephen had just slapped his face. His defence was flustered. 'Are you saying that him paying for the sexual services of two young women one night, and two young men the next, is acceptable, Mr Sigmund?'

Stephen's facial expression hardened. His eyes glittered, and only the strong jaw moved as he spoke. 'What I am saying, Mr Vector, is that Mr Rheingold is unattached, wealthy, and perhaps even lonely. His tastes are his own and break no laws. All those involved did so out of choice and were all above the age of consent.'

'But they were paid . . .'

'Yes. They were paid by him to participate. But let us remember that your paper also paid them for the honour of publishing the story. Who's to say which of you are immoral, Mr Vector? Who's to say which of you is the procurer, the pimp or the prostitute?'

Eyes almost black with fury, Vector sniffed indignantly. 'All we did was reveal how suspect his morals are. We only reported the truth – that he's a dirty old man.'

Stephen Sigmund's eyes narrowed and his jaw tightened

visibly. 'The morals of your newspaper are suspect, Mr Vector. You *cater* for dirty old men – young ones too. You, your newspaper and your ilk are nothing more than hypocrites!'

Although Vector's face went from pink to red, his voice became icy. 'Your sympathies are noted, Mr Sigmund. We'll expect no quarter from you, and you can expect none from us!'

Sigmund was unmoved. His jaw, his expression were as strong as ever. His chin jutted defiantly forward as he responded, 'Then we understand each other, Mr Vector!'

Hairs bristled on the back of the journalist's neck as he stomped off. Inside, he boiled. *Just you wait, Sigmund. Just you wait. You'll see who's likely to scream for quarter. You'll see!*

His jaw relaxing slightly, Stephen watched him go. Outwardly, he still looked calm, controlled. Inside, he had an urge to rush up behind the smug little sod, grab him by the neck, and thump his stupid, self-satisfied head off his shoulders. But he didn't. Instead he took a deep breath as a restraining hand landed on his arm.

'You've made a dangerous enemy, Stephen. That man makes a living from ferreting out the most intimate details of people's lives. See what he did to Nigel Porter. His wife's suing for divorce, and Carol Anne Flowers has been sacked from her job – at least for the moment.'

It was John Humphries, a man whose own reputation was impeccable. No matter that he kept a wife and mistress. Neither, he had told Stephen, affected his ability to stand in judgement of others, and each knew of the other's existence.

Stephen shook his head. His expression still held anger in it, and even disgust.

'I couldn't help it, John. My God, that paper has no right to preach moral ethics at anyone. They spout about guarding public morality when in truth they are pandering to suburbia's fascination with the erotic.'

'You're right. Years ago, you'd have been put in the pillory as an adulterer or gone to beg absolution from the church. Nowadays you get the front page and public indignation which is really just the public's fascination with your sex-life and an insatiable lust for detail.' John shook his head mournfully. 'And if it's not lurid sex they're peddling, it's horror – the more grisly the murder, the more editorial.'

Both stood silently for a moment and watched those about them. Both were thinking of how they would react if their sex-lives became public knowledge. The Rheingold, Swan and Swallow case also preyed heavily on Stephen's mind. His brows knitted in a frown. John Humphries was first to break the silence.

'Have you strong enough evidence to get you to the true instigators, the powerful people who are really behind this debâcle?'

Stephen's eyes continued to study those gathered even as he answered the question. 'There is a witness. We have yet to agree a meeting however. That's all I can tell you at the present time.'

John Humphries nodded and looked down into his glass. He liked Stephen. There was no humbug about him, he uttered no mealy-mouthed platitudes about what an upright man he had been since his first wife had died. Even the press knew of Stephen's brief liaisons with beautiful women. Time and time again his picture had appeared in the press, some pretty face smiling at his side. But like him, Stephen had a darker side, a side that needed a real woman and not just the sort who only came out to play if a dinner party was in evidence, or her picture was likely to appear in some society magazine.

Pity, he thought, *that women were divided into two camps; the lady of the house, the dinner party, and the holiday home in Provence, and the woman who was sexy no matter where she was or who she was with. It was an even greater pity that he had never encountered a creature who could be both of these things, but such women were few and far between.*

'I would advise you, Stephen, to get together with your witness as quickly as possible. I would surmise that those involved will do everything they can to stop you getting to the truth – *if* you get to the truth. I'm not entirely sure anything good will be gained from it, but I admire your persistence.' John Humphries patted the younger man's shoulder in a fatherly way. His dark eyes looked darker as his brows lowered in a frown. 'I personally would advise you to desist from this witch hunt. They could easily destroy you before you destroy them.'

'And leave Rheingold to carry the can?'

'Open prison. Five years, maybe seven. He won't be uncomfortable.'

Stephen frowned. John Humphries' comments came as something of a surprise. He'd always viewed him as a man who truly believed in justice.

'I don't believe I'm hearing this from you, John.' He

looked more intently into the face of the older man, almost as if he were seeking something he might have missed earlier.

Humphries shrugged and looked away. 'I'm just being realistic. Who is this witness?'

'I can't tell you that.'

'No. No. Of course not. But if you should need my help, don't hesitate to ask.'

Stephen thanked him, but refrained from explaining further. Such detail was for him to worry about.

Unfortunately, the witness who was scheduled to supply him with the necessary evidence was being elusive. But Stephen could not divulge this fact, not publicly. He had to be patient, had to try and persuade this man to meet him in a mutually acceptable place. But the man was being stubborn in his choice of such places. Soon, very soon, Stephen would have no choice but to comply with his wishes, and the thought of that lay heavy on him.

Forget it for now, he told himself. *Think of something pleasant. Think of the Railway Hotel and of her; the first time with her.*

The first time? Why did he refer to it as that? Why did he assume that he would see her again, make love to her again? Thoughtfully, he fingered the transparent fragment that nestled in his pocket. For two weeks he had carried it around, transferring it from one jacket pocket to another. In his mind it had become a talisman, a part of her that had to be returned to the whole.

But what was the whole?

The contact lens was black. Why wear dark contact lenses unless they were meant to disguise the true colour of her eyes? Like her eyes, her hair had been black – on her head, that is. On her pubes, it had been light blonde, verging on silver. Her true colour had to be that, and the colour of her eyes had to be blue or grey, perhaps, at a push, even hazel or green.

He touched the hidden lens again. As he touched it, his gaze followed the effortless movement of the tall, slim young woman who gathered so many admiring glances from older men as well as those in her own age group. The way she carried herself, the set of her head, the proud chin, the self-confidence, stirred his memory and caused a tightness to gather in his groin. His heart began to beat that bit faster, his blood flowed that much hotter.

He narrowed his eyes and followed her as she moved around the room. Commensurate with her profession, her suit was black, her cuffs and collar white. Wrong versus right. Although seamed and fitted to the lean lines of her body, the suit did not cling but merely hinted at what was beneath its expensive touch. Her face was the sort he dreamed of, and there was more in those bright blue eyes than the letter of the law could ever account for.

I know her, he thought to himself. *I know what her body looks like beneath that suit. I know that movement, that face, that expression, yet I see it with black hair, black eyes, and bright – very bright – red lips.*

He smiled to himself, then absent-mindedly slid his hand into his pocket again.

Stephen Sigmund didn't just remember faces. He remembered form, structure, and movement as well. No matter that this woman was fair, had blue eyes, and dressed in the black, though attractive, conformity of a barrister's business suit: the blackness in itself gave her away.

Perhaps it was the contrast of her suit with her silky skin. It might even have been the unforgettable structure of her face, and the easy movement of her body, but he knew instinctively that he had met Abigail Corrigan before. He also knew she was more than she made herself out to be.

However, being the adept speaker of words that he was, he continued to talk with those who wanted to know more of what was happening in Parliament. As he talked, he fingered the small, fragile thing that nestled in the pocket of his pure wool jacket. His stomach muscles tightened as just the feel of it ignited the sensations that had been so overpowering on that night in the Railway Hotel.

No matter how much he talked, how interested he appeared to be in everyone's conversation, his gaze wandered occasionally. He made sure he knew exactly where she was in the room at all times. Eventually, he saw Abigail Corrigan grow tired of the gathering, and seek a quiet place to hide. His chance had come.

One of the opulent windows had a seat built into it. She had used the bathroom first so that any prevailing eyes might lose track of her and had then quietly made her way to the window seat and sat right next to where the thick tapestry curtains were tied back with thick green rope. While sitting there no one could see anything much of Abigail Corrigan, though her long, shapely legs were protruding just beyond the fringes of the heavy curtains.

She was just taking her second sip of wine, when her solitude was interrupted.

'May I join you?'

The first thing that struck her about him was his eyes. The second thing was that she knew him.

'Stephen Sigmund.' He smiled and offered her his hand.

'Abigail Corrigan.' She smiled back at him, memories of that night running through her mind.

As their palms touched, her heart quickened as if it were recognizing something her eyes had failed to do. A hungry ache arose in her pussy as though she had been starved for ages, and a feast was being set before her. A shiver streaked down her spine, and not just because of one night in the Railway Hotel. A few days after that meeting, she had seen his face smiling out from a photograph on the front page of a newspaper, and realized who he was.

Now, she pretended otherwise. Her two-pronged life was too precious to surrender recognition to a man – any man.

'The MP! Of course. I'm very pleased to meet you. My name's Abigail Corrigan.'

'I know.' He smiled. His teeth were very white, very notice-able against his tanned skin. Small wrinkles of something like amusement played around his eyes. 'I understand you're a superstar in the legal world. A real performer. Are you the same in private?'

His comment threw her off balance. Despite knowing him more intimately in the guise of Carmel, she had, as usual, been preparing to talk law. As he sat down beside her, his thigh hard against hers, she became wary, and determined to throw him off the scent. She tore her eyes from him, stared out of the window towards the rolling lawns and clusters of maple, birch, and beech, but saw absolutely nothing. Her voice remained even.

'I have worked hard for success, Mr Sigmund. I swore I would make it despite my sex, and I have made it. I have achieved exactly what I wanted to achieve.'

'In your public life?'

'Yes.'

'And what about your private life? Have you achieved everything you wanted in that?'

She thought of snapping a suitably tart reply about him minding his own business, but some echo of her other life caused her to temper her response.

'I am happy, Mr Sigmund. Happy in my work. In fact, I am completely engrossed in my work. I have little time left for a private life. My career is very important to me.'

'Regardless of sacrifice?'

She turned to look at him, her chin high as she did her best to adopt an expression of cold detachment. Usually, it was easy. With him, it was difficult.

He was resting his elbow on his knee, his chin in his hand. His eyes were so warm, his smile so knowing. It was as if he were daring her to tell the truth. But the truth was hers and she was keeping it. She took a deep breath before she replied.

'Sacrifice of what? My life is my work.'

'So you gave your sex and your sexuality the old heave-ho, is that right?'

'We all have choices to make, Mr Sigmund.' Her voice was tart.

He smiled. 'Stephen. Call me Stephen.'

'We all have choices to make. I made mine. If I wanted to get to the top, relationships had to take a back seat.'

'That doesn't mean sex has to take a back seat too.'

63

Aware that her jaw had dropped, she stared at him. For someone who was a Member of Parliament, he was being very unguarded in what he was saying. How could he be sure she wouldn't betray his words to the carnivores of the tabloid press?

'What makes you so sure that I have no sex-life?'

'Your colleagues call you the Snow Queen.'

Abigail refused to be ruffled. This name was not unknown to her. In fact, she quite liked it. Scorned women resort to fury; scorned men to malicious sarcasm.

'It is of no consequence to me, Mr Sigmund. As I have explained, the law is my life. I am devoted to it, and I expect everyone I work with to adhere to its principles and disciplines just as I do. Besides which, my sex-life is my own affair.'

She made as if to rise and leave him. To her astonishment, he gripped her arm and ordered her to sit down. To her further amazement, she obeyed. Vaguely, she was aware of a warm tingle running up her arm and across her breasts. His lips were near her cheek. She could see his eyes from the corner of her own. His breath was warm, and his close proximity made her want him. His voice moved her.

'You like giving orders, don't you, Abigail Corrigan? You like laying down the law to everyone else, using your sharp words and your convoluted arguments to persuade a jury that what you say is gospel truth; that you are like the Statue of Justice herself, blind to anything but what she sees behind her mask.'

Her heart thumped so hard. *Could he hear it? Could everyone hear it?* She tried to get up. 'I don't need to listen to this!'

He held her tightly. Strong hands looped one of her wrists into the tie-back of the curtain. He pulled on its long tassel so that the rope tightened. A controlled whimper escaped her mouth. There were people on the other side of the curtain. She could not – would not – allow them to hear her. Her breath came quicker, and her breasts heaved in mute apprehension. He held onto her other hand with his own.

His face, his mouth came near her, his breath warm upon her cheek, his lips soft against her ear. *Why couldn't she move? Why didn't she* want *to move?* His voice seeped into her brain.

'The statue above the Old Bailey wears a blindfold, Abigail Corrigan, but you wear a mask at night – and little else.'

His dark eyebrows and dark hair blurred as she looked into his eyes.

'Why are you doing this?' she whispered. The answer was irrelevant. She knew why, knew that by this small action, he was replicating one night in a seedy hotel room beside a railway shunting yard.

'Because I am like you, Abigail Corrigan. I am someone who lives two lives, not just one.'

Strength turned to weakness. She stopped struggling. She stared, half-knowing what he knew, what was about to happen. His fingers left her wrist, went to his pocket. He held his hand against her chest, his palm uppermost. Dare she look down? Fear of what might be there made her head swim, her pulse race. She swallowed, took in the roguish expression on his face, his smell, the expensive cut of his hair and his suit.

65

At last, she had to do it. She had to look down.

'Yours, I believe. Left at the Railway Hotel.'

Sitting in his palm was one black contact lens.

Behind the privacy of the heavy hangings, his lips were on hers, his hand on her breast, and her hand on his erection.

No one within the polished panelled room saw them when, some moments later, they emerged from their temporary privacy.

And yet one person had seen them kiss and embrace.

Lance Vector had excused himself from the gathering on the pretence of needing fresh air.

Hidden from the house by a shiny-leaved bush, he had retrieved his cellular phone from his pocket, dialled an ex-directory number, and spoken to the man who paid his salary. Word by word, he played back his conversation with the MP, Stephen Sigmund, by way of a miniature tape recorder.

'Good work, Vector.'

'Thank you, sir. It's a pleasure.'

It was a pleasure. He was being paid well for this assignment. All that he could find out about Sigmund would be carefully reported. Except, that is, for the episode in the window seat. That was an incident he wanted to use for himself. Three weeks ago Sunday, he had made an acute observation about the video he was watching and about himself. He had promised himself he would lose his virginity when the right woman came along, and now, he decided, she had.

Being a man who studied people's behaviour for a living, he had watched the bright young barrister from the moment she had entered the room, and prior to being introduced, he had asked questions about her and found out that she was a lady who held herself aloof from sexual encounters. Snow Queen. He liked that. It said it all.

Some, perhaps those who had been the victim of rebuff, swore she was either lesbian or asexual. Some just said that her work was her lover. She loved her work as some women love men and that was the way of it.

And that, he decided, was the way it was. Stunned by her looks, her voice and her reputation, he had listened to her talking to Probert. There was a fire in her eyes when she spoke of the law, and a crispness to her voice as though justice was the only thing she truly adored.

He told himself there were similarities between them. She was a seeker of justice. He was a seeker of truth, and the more sleazy it was, the wider its appeal. Yes, he decided, she was definitely the woman he needed.

Already in his mind, his hands were sweeping over her firm breasts, her flat belly. Tingles of pleasure swept over him as he imagined her hands on his chest, her blue eyes gazing up into his, lost in adoration.

Oh yes, he could imagine, all right. What a day that would be when he got her to himself, when she lay beneath him, the scent of her sex wafting up into his nostrils as his tongue licked her pussy, and his penis pumped in and out of her generous mouth.

Seeing her kissing another man made him feel jealous. Suddenly, Stephen Sigmund, the man he had been ordered to expose, had done him an awful wrong and he wanted revenge. As yet, he had no file on him, no smutty statements from call girls or rent boys to mould into an article. But that, he reckoned, he could easily rectify, and rectify it was something he desperately wanted to do.

For the first time in his life, Lance Vector wanted a woman, and the woman he wanted was Abigail Corrigan.

Chapter 5

Abigail and Stephen left the celebration separately. It wasn't something they agreed to do in words. Neither did they exclaim that they wanted each other, but also wished to preserve their public image. They just knew by the sparkle in each other's eyes, the parted lips, the subtle movements that only they perceived and only they could interpret. Then, once they were certain that they were not being seen or overheard, they agreed to meet up later that evening.

Stephen suggested an old inn just off the main A4 – probably, thought Abigail, the same place he'd taken Valeria.

Without him having to spell it out to her, she knew what she was going for, knew what he wanted from her. That didn't mean she had to go. It didn't mean she had to submit herself to whatever he wanted her to do. But in some strange, intriguing way, he had snared her. By some invisible thread, he was pulling her along the dark road, drawing her closer to him.

A coldness trickled down her spine as she thought of his hands on her body, his solid, male weight pummelling her against the bonnet of his car, just as he had Valeria. The coldness spread from her spine. Like water turning to ice, it seeped over her body and made her flesh tingle. And yet, between her legs, there was only the heat of desire.

Like a piece of driftwood being tossed by the sea, she was going with the flow, but in doing so, was breaking her own rules. Her personal life was gradually merging with her daytime career. Until now she had enjoyed complete control over both her professional life and her private one. Everything had been clear, everything had been neatly, perhaps even coldly, divided between the two compartments of her life. Stephen Sigmund had changed all that.

Lascivious thoughts had given rise to lascivious dreams in the two weeks since she had danced at the Red Devil. Two weeks, just two weeks, since she had left that place with a man wearing a blonde wig and high-heeled shoes. Two weeks since she had allowed herself to be bound to a rough bed in the Railway Hotel. And now she was with him again, but this time in an old inn, which was surrounded by the Savernake Forest.

Except for the flickering of a large log fire, and the odd coach light hanging a little lopsidedly from a dark oak beam, the inn was dimly lit, a fact that suited them both very well.

There were few people in the bar. Some huddled protectively over their drinks, or whispered attentively to women who were clearly not their wives.

Stephen kissed her cheek. He smelt expensive, and felt warm. His hand covered hers. Like his body, she thought. Just like his body will cover me.

'How did you recognize me? Was it just the wig, just the contact lens?'

In a sweetly affectionate manner, Stephen flicked his fingers at a few strands of hair that had escaped the velvet bow holding it back from her face.

'Your hair was coal black. So were your eyes. But your pubic hair was incredibly fair – too fair to be fake.' He winked mischievously. 'Then I found the contact lens. And there was something about the way you spoke, the way you moved. The moment I saw you today, I knew immediately. Anyway. Takes one to know one. I know the pressures you have. I sympathize.'

'Yours are worse.'

'Much worse. If you think it's the MPs running this country, think again. The civil service is loath to lose the power of centuries. Their internal politics are more convoluted and more vindictive than those of the House of Commons.'

He smiled, paused; seemed to be enjoying just looking at her, just stroking her cheek. In turn, she enjoyed looking at him, stripping him off in her mind, feeling the heat of him against her, his hardness in her.

His voice caressed her thoughts. 'No matter what anyone says or thinks, Abigail, we all have to have a private life. Some of us – you and I – have to indulge in things a little more way out than others. We have to walk on the wild side of life; taste the sordid as well as the sublime.'

All in that one moment, what he was saying and what had happened between them seemed strangely unreal. A kindred spirit had flown into her life. A very public man and a very successful woman had met, fused in the tumbling heat of sexual ecstasy, and acted out their most secret fantasy.

'You're right.' As she spoke, her body seemed to confirm her words. She tingled as if she were outlined in a crisp layer of sugar, sugar that as it warmed, slowly began to melt. 'We cannot help but expose ourselves to danger in order to taste excitement.'

He smiled. She smiled with him and edged that little bit closer; enjoyed the feel of his thigh against hers. Their eyes met, and an unspoken message flashed from one to the other.

'Shall we expose ourselves here?' It was her who voiced what they both were thinking.

'Yes.'

Beneath the privacy of the rough wooden table, she unzipped his trousers and pulled his weapon from its lair.

Already, it was hot, hard, and rearing in her palm. *Like velvet*, she thought, *like a piece of warm, soft velvet that has lain before a fire.*

As his hand settled on her knee, she opened her legs.

The sweet juice of her desire seeped from her vagina. Swollen with longing, it awaited his touch, his entry, the pink, delicate flesh already coated with a sheen reminiscent of satin. Although her thighs were hidden beneath the table, she felt the progress of his fingers, heard them rasp over her stockings before being silenced by the smoothness of her thighs.

With one finger and thumb, she squeezed the head of his rod. With her fingernail, she dug into his opening. She smiled as she did it. He groaned, his lips curling away from his mouth. His teeth were clenched firmly together. No one would hear him.

'You bitch,' he said through clenched teeth. 'I'll make you pay for that later.'

His fingers travelled higher. After travelling the smooth expanse of naked thigh that divided her stockings from her body, his smile turned to surprise. He gasped with delight.

'You hot little bitch! You're not wearing any knickers! And you're soaking wet. How delicious!'

She squeezed his penis. 'I never do. Not even in court.'

'Tell me about it.' His voice sounded strained, almost as if he were in pain, although the prime mover was pleasure.

As Abby squeezed his erection, she rubbed her body against him, her lips close to his ear. 'Can you imagine what the judge would think if he knew my quim was naked beneath my neat suit, my black silk gown?' She paused, gave him time for the words to sink in, for his body to respond. 'Can you imagine what the prosecution would think? But they don't know. Only I know I am almost naked beneath the trappings of the law, beneath the watchful eyes of some seedy old judge who spouts law at me, but would much sooner have his penis spout into my mouth, my cunt, or my ass. It's just to remind me that no one, absolutely no one, is without a darker side to their life. It's just to remind me of my other life as Carmel – and Jezebel Justice. Just as the wig and gown I wear in my act reminds me of this side of my life and of the fact that I am Abigail Corrigan. Both temper my passion for the law and my passion for sex – in their own way.'

In order to control his voice and his urges, Stephen took a deep breath before shaking his head and smiling. It was a boyish, innocent smile, one that made her want to suck his lips between her own, invade the wet cavern of his mouth with her tongue.

His voice was low, hushed. 'So in one life you are an icon

of respectability, conformity, and the process of law. In the other, you are still an icon, but one of fantasy, myth, desire. So far you've been lucky in your choice of men to temper those desires, to give you what you want – what you know you want. Now you need someone more permanent, more in tune with your desires.'

'Are you offering?'

'Would you accept? A role play. A scenario to infuse and excite both our libidos?'

It took her no time to answer.

'Yes.'

The word trembled on her tongue. Her desire was mounting. Vividly, she recollected all that had happened at the Railway Hotel – and all that could happen.

They left the inn and drove along a forest track. Black battalions of fir and pine on either side of them divided the ribbon of sky from the ribbon of road.

'Is this where you took Valeria?'

He didn't answer. Something in the air, something in themselves had suddenly changed. The division that separated their professional lives from their private ones had crept silently into play.

Apprehension made her sit rigidly in her seat, made her stare out of the window into the darkness and see two naked bodies etched in the glass of the car window and in the dense blackness of the trees.

Stephen could almost taste her anxiety. He also knew that shortly it would turn to desire.

His inclination was to smother her with kisses, and yet he knew she would expect more from him – much more. This was no back-seat Venus, no clinging vine who craved security, domesticity, or the humdrum sexuality of a pink bedroom in a red-brick semi. This was a woman of dramatic tastes and infinite imagination. He had to give her what she wanted.

The car pulled to a sudden halt. Stephen turned to face her.

'Take off your clothes.'

The tone of his voice was noticeably harsher.

Abigail experienced a thrill of excitement as she first removed the seat belt. An item of restraint. The first item to leave her body. Her businesslike shoes, her black suit, her white blouse, and her underwear followed.

'Give it here.'

He took it from her, and got out of her car.

Looking over her shoulder, Abby saw the car boot open, then felt the car shake as it banged shut.

'Get out,' he said to her.

She did as he ordered, the earth soft to the soles of her bare feet, the night air raising goose bumps on her naked body. She noticed Stephen was holding some sort of straps and buckles. What was his intention? For the first time that evening, she felt very vulnerable again, and a little afraid.

He saw her wary look, drew her close, and sucked her lips into his.

As the feel of his body warmed hers, any fear she might have had disappeared. Again, fierce vibrations stirred deep within her. Her nipples shot forward into the palms of his hands as she arched her back and thrust her belly to his.

'Don't be afraid, Abby. Let yourself go. Let all your

professional restraint crumble away. Leave it to me to give you what you want.'

'What do *you* want?' she asked him, her lips a mere kiss away from his.

He smiled again like a small, but very imaginative boy. 'I want a mascot for my car.'

His mood was infectious. A playfulness, a careless abandon came upon her. Like him she became a child again, excited and happy to be losing herself in her own imagination and a shared fantasy made reality. Just like a mocking child, she laughed in his face, poked her finger into the centre of his chest.

'So you want a mascot, do you? Well, you'll have to catch me first!'

Catching him unawares, she sprang from his arms and ran into the dark shadows of the trees.

The earth beneath her feet smelt rich and felt soft. Ferns and small bushes brushed against her thighs, her hips, her legs and her naked breasts.

She heard him behind her, his shoes heavy upon the ground. Judging by the sound of his footsteps, he was gaining on her, but then she meant him to.

'Got you!'

Strong arms gathered her close to his body. She struggled, a naked, helpless struggle against the hardness of his chest. The advantage was his.

'No!' she cried out. 'Let me go!'

But she didn't want him to let her go. This game had been devised by him, yet she instinctively knew the rules, knew what she was required to do and to be.

'Certainly not.'

He tied her hands behind her which made her breasts jut forward just as they did in her act. Then he hobbled her ankles so she could only walk, not run.

'Get going,' he ordered. A strip of the leather that bound her hands and also formed a leash, landed on her buttocks.

She yelped like a puppy, started, then began to stumble forward. Lacking the freedom of movement that had made her feet fly over the damp earth earlier, her step now was less confident, her eyes wary of the dark that surrounded her like a chill cloak. All the same, she was still shivering with excitement as she stumbled on.

'Keep going!'

Stephen's voice was accompanied by another stroke from the leather leash.

Back at the car, he had her sit on the bonnet. It was warm, pleasant beneath her bottom. Each leather leash remained fastened to her wrists. He pulled the ends back and fastened them around the wing mirrors. He undid the strap that hobbled her ankles, then tied it to something on the front wing so that her right leg was spread out to one side. He found a new piece of leather and did the same to her other ankle.

Abby's breasts heaved with excitement when she heard the car door slam. What was he planning to do with her? Her arms were stretched out behind her, her wrists secure. Because her legs were spread out to each side, the breeze trifled with her pubic hair and the delicate inner lips of her sex.

In her mind, and probably in Stephen's, she was the Spirit

77

of Ecstasy – but improved. The original was made of metal and chromium plated. She was real. She was flesh and blood. She felt something the original had never felt.

As the car moved forward, the breeze whipped her hair back from her face. The black velvet bow had already fallen off in the car.

Because the breeze was cooler on the move, the goose bumps returned to replace the warmth she had enjoyed during the chase. Her nipples hardened and swelled to three times their normal size. Partly due to the breeze, and partly excitement, her stomach muscles tensed.

The track through the forest became more bumpy.

Behind the wheel of the car, Stephen watched as her body which was held so tightly by the restraining leather, swayed from side to side. Her bottom bumped up and down on the shiny black car, her flesh jiggling slightly as the engine intoned its monotonous note.

The sight of her like that delighted him. From behind, he could imagine her breasts jiggling gently then more vigorously as he purposely drove over the deepest pot holes, the roughest gravel. Every so often, the odd patch of fine gravel would be sure to fly up and pepper her with its tingling sting. How exquisite that would feel to her; how delightful the thought of it felt to him.

He was aware that his erection had reached superb proportions. However, he knew better than to stop the car and immediately push himself into this woman.

Abigail Corrigan was sophisticated, a woman of unusual tastes. It would not be enough to slam into her and say thank you afterwards. She was the sort of woman who needed someone to draw into her deepest well and extract the last droplet of erotic arousal.

Stephen Sigmund had no trouble admitting to himself that he had an imaginative taste when it came to sex. The trouble was in convincing someone else that such experiences could be mutually enjoyable.

Valeria had gone along with his fantasy, but only because he had presented it as a dare.

To Abigail, it was not just his fantasy, but also her own. For the first time ever, he had not needed to explain himself. Incredibly, he had met a kindred spirit.

When the car came to a halt, Abby's breasts stopped trembling. Stephen turned the headlights off and got out of the car.

It took effort to keep to the part he was playing. For a moment he gaped as he studied her. The moonlight made her hair seem more silver, her body more unreal.

She turned to look at him and he felt like drowning in her eyes. Such a feeling made him want to pounce on her there and then. But this was Abby and he could not allow that to happen. If he did, if he stepped out of the role play and became merely a lust-filled lover, he might never see her again, and that was something he could not bare. He forced himself back into his role.

'Look straight ahead and keep still. I want to look at you.'

She did as he ordered.

For one sweet moment he had seen the brightness of her eyes, and knew she was enjoying playing her part, that nothing he could say or do would offend her.

She trembled as he reached out and cupped one breast.

Her flesh was cold and covered in goose bumps. And yet, beneath his touch, it warmed, responded, her nipple pressing into the palm of his hand.

He could not resist.

She moaned as he bent his head and ran the hotness of his lips from her ear to her shoulder. A wake of warmth blossomed wherever his mouth travelled.

How soft her skin feels, he thought to himself, *yet how firm*.

Abby tingled with pleasure, and in her mind, a door slammed shut on her professional life that was spent among law books and oak-panelled courts. With Stephen, her sexuality was freed from constraint.

Hungrily, she sucked on his lips as his tongue entered her mouth. Her flesh, which had been cooled by the night breeze, now warmed as his hands covered her breasts, slid downwards over her taut stomach, then firmly grasped her slender hips. His lips travelled from her mouth to her breasts, his tongue darting out to lick at her flesh, his teeth nibbling at her nipples.

Lost in a sea of sensations, she groaned, closed her eyes, and threw back her head.

As his tongue coursed over her pubic hair and gently tickled her most sensitive flesh, she opened her eyes and saw thousands of stars. *Not all*, she thought to herself, *are up there in the sky. Some are in my head, and some are set to explode*.

Slowly, softly, his mouth travelled back up over her body, his hair brushing her skin before his lips warmed her flesh. He kissed her throat, her chin, and the very tip of her nose before he kissed her mouth.

The weight of his body forced her backwards onto the bonnet of the car.

His hands fumbled between her open legs. She heard his zip open, and was aware of something warm and hard nudging at her open sex. He steadied himself, pressed her down onto the bonnet of the car, then pushed himself into her.

She cried out, and would have cried out again as he thrust fiercely, his length and breadth filling her slippery flesh. But her second cry was muffled by his lips and lost in his mouth.

Still bound by the leather straps, Abigail lost herself in enjoying what he was doing to her.

His hands explored her breasts, did as he pleased with them; stroked, pinched, kneaded. It was as though they were made of something as pliable as fresh dough.

Hot breath mingled with half-strangled words as he moaned sweet exclamations into her ear, kissed her cheeks, her lips, her throat, and sucked on her breasts as if he were feeding from them.

And all the time, the car bounced on its springs as he thrust against her.

Sometimes he thrust slowly, drawing himself half out then leaving only his very tip in her and lingering. He gazed at her, gauging her reaction, hearing her moans of pleasure – and of regret that he could leave her so – before pushing back in.

She could see the fascination in his eyes, the pleasure of watching her, of enjoying her mews of delight, and the desire that burned in her eyes.

Once she was purring with the slow, sensual tempo of his loving he altered pace, surprised her with deep thrusts that brought loud gasps from her throat, and caused the car to rock more vigorously.

But the point came when he was no longer in control of his own urges. Sensations as old as time, as powerful as the force of life itself, took over his body. Hot blood ran through his veins and hot semen up his stem.

Abby could feel it in his flesh and in the stiff organ that was now embedded so deeply within her. She too was being taken by it.

No matter that civilization had made her into a woman that could survive in a man's world, a woman that spouted law so very precisely and won far more cases than she lost. Modern aspirations and values were swept away by the primeval, the most basic drive of all.

Threads of nervous energy spiralled throughout her body, cork-screwing downwards to accumulate around her tingling clitoris.

Veins stood out in stark relief around Stephen's neck as he threw back his head, closed his eyes, and filled her with his essence.

Abby cried out, arched her back and thrust her hips up to meet his. As she climaxed, she gasped at her breath and at the sky. It seemed as though the stars above were bursting, flying, falling around her in one glorious explosion.

In the darkness of the undergrowth, Lance Vector watched, his eyes wide, his penis pulsating in his trousers. His breath caught in his throat, his heart thudded like a hammer in his chest. Finally, he opened his zip and allowed his semen to spurt into the low shrubs behind which he hid. Despite his release anger boiled inside him. Stephen Sigmund had sullied the women he desired. He had convinced himself that his first time would also have been hers, and Stephen Sigmund had stolen that moment from him.

As the two of them had performed, he had quietly recorded everything they had done. Normally, he would have rushed it home, and taken notes as he played it back before rushing it off to a press ever hungry for tales of horror and lust. But this time he would not do that. This tape was for him alone. He had no wish to sully Abigail's name.

It might be said by a romantically-minded observer who could not look into his twisted mind that Lance was in love with her. Perhaps he was, but he was also obsessed with a sudden desire to lose his virginity. It was as if his pubescent yearnings had finally arrived. He had a desperate need for carnal knowledge, and the object of his desire was Abigail Corrigan.

Chapter 6

Just as Abigail could not get Stephen out of her mind, Lance Vector could not get Abigail out of his. Sitting in front of the video screen, he pretended he was Stephen and that it was his tongue licking her slippery pink flesh, his penis sliding in and out of her welcoming pussy. Pretending was not sufficient to quell his hunger for sex. For the first time, he wanted the real thing.

On the morning following the celebration at Trendleham Court, Lance picked up the phone and dialled Abigail Corrigan's number. He adopted the casual, confident tone that he'd heard other men use when attempting to seduce and beguile the fairer sex. 'How about you taking me to lunch?'

Abby remembered the fresh-faced man who had stared at her as though he were viewing his very first date. Her response was immediate. 'How about you taking yourself?'

It stung, but he wouldn't be put off.

'Don't be dismissive, counsellor. Think what I can do for you. Consider also what I can do *to* you.'

In his mind, he was running his hands over her naked body, burying his nose between her breasts and sucking in the smell of her sex. *Imagine*, he thought, *the silky curls of her pubic bush rubbing against my face.*

Perhaps it was the tone of his voice that triggered similar imaginings in Abigail's mind. Of course she was thinking of Stephen, but it didn't hurt to use another man's voice, another man's suggestions to rouse her desire. However, the tone of her voice remained even.

'And what, Mr Vector, could you do for me?'

Vector's voice lowered an octave or two. 'I could wine you, dine you, help you throw off the dust of all those affidavits, all those legal briefs. I don't ask many women out, Miss Corrigan, only those that are special.'

If she closed her eyes, Stephen became that much clearer in her mind. If she concentrated very determinedly, she could almost smell him.

Unknown to Lance Vector, Abigail uncrossed her legs. As she did so, the nylon of one stocking rasped sensually against the other. The sound was as provocative as the action.

Briefs. Lance Vector had mentioned briefs. She smiled as she trailed one finger over her inner thigh and between the shaved lips of her sex. Briefs were something she never wore. Of course, she knew the man was referring to legal briefs, but to hear him spar around what he really meant, amused and excited her.

She adopted her most professional voice. 'And how would you do that, Mr Vector?'

She heard him sigh, and wondered if her unseen caller was masturbating as he spoke to her.

'I could massage your temples. I could have you sit in front of me – press my thumbs into the very corners of your forehead where your skin meets your hair. You could close your eyes. Then I could fan my fingers around your face, massage your cheeks and your jaw. If you approve of me doing those things – as you become more relaxed – I could move my hands to the nape of your neck, roll my thumbs over your tense muscles, spread my fingers along your shoulders.'

Although her clitoris was hard beneath her thumb, and her body was responding to the vision in her brain and the finger in her vagina, Abby spoke precisely, indeed almost coldly, into the telephone receiver.

'Really, Mr Vector. Would that indeed be your intention? I'm intrigued. Tell me, where would you go from there?'

She heard him sigh again.

'Lance,' he said almost plaintively. 'Call me Lance.'

'Lance.'

'Could you call me "darling". I'd love to hear you say that.'

Abby hesitated. She was going to say no, but if she did, he would probably hang up and at this present moment, she didn't want him to do that. Her fingers were doing such delicious things. Once aroused, she preferred desire to reach its ultimate conclusion.

'Darling.' She said it in a low, husky voice, the sort she knew he was dying for. 'Darling,' she said again. 'What would you do then, Lance, darling. Tell me what you would do?'

He moaned. 'I would have you lie down.'

'Naked, I presume.'

Her blatant declaration and the vision it conjured up in his mind brought him up short. What would she think of him going on like this? He should stop, but her likeness was still

87

in his head. He imagined her naked, her bottom swaying gently from side to side as he played with her breasts.

He gulped as he tried to eliminate his lust and not say anything further. It was no good. He had started something he had to finish.

'Yes! Naked! I would have you lie face down and naked. Then I would run my hands down your back, massaging all the tension out of your body.' He paused for breath as ever more lurid pictures formed in his mind.

'And then?'

Triggered by the reality of Lance Vector's sexual suggestions, fantasy had fashioned Stephen in Abigail's mind. Never had such a lover been so easy to construct from pure thought, memories of sight, sound, touch and smell. Never had she been so affected by a man. Usually, her sexual longing would have abated after one night. Images of other men had not lingered so long. But Stephen was not other men. Her body had had plenty of him, and yet she still needed him, could still go one more climax before her mind was completely attentive to her work. The young man on the telephone was doing a very good job of arousing her.

She was climbing a cool, green wave. A little more of his voice, a little more of her finger, and she would reach the highest crest of that wave, then come crashing down in a swirling, rippling climax.

'Then,' his voice faltered as his thoughts became clearer and his tongue thickened with desire. 'Then, I would run my hands over your naked buttocks, divide them with my thumbs, press them and roll them with my palms and my fingers.'

'Oh really.' Her tongue licked her lips. It was her turn to pause, the moment for her voice to tremble. 'And pray, Mr Vector, Lance, darling, what would you want *me* to do as you are doing this to me?'

Say it! Say it! She threw back her head, bit her bottom lip. Her thumb tapped against the centre of her arousal. One finger, then two, dipped in and out of her vagina. All she needed were those few words that would send her over the top of that wave and crashing down the other side.

Say it! screamed her mind, her being.

Lance Vector was sweating. He had an enormous hard-on that he wanted to touch. But although he was on his mobile phone and no one could hear what he was saying, he was in a public place. But oh, if only he wasn't! He licked an over-abundance of spittle from off his lips before he spoke.

'I would have you open your legs so I could massage your thighs, tickle the backs of your knees, rub your calves, and manipulate your toes, your soles, your heels.'

He paused as his breathing became more laboured and much quicker. He licked his lips, imagined her in all her naked glory. He hardly seemed to notice that she was saying nothing, that all was silent on the other end of the phone.

'Then I would push one – no – two fingers into you, press my thumb against your clitoris and jerk into and against you again and again until you shuddered and shouted for me to stop.'

In the privacy of her office, a room lined with cherrywood shelves holding row after row of legal tomes, Abigail Corrigan murmured her climax.

Lance Vector did not know this because at that very

moment, Abigail made sure that her chin was pressed tightly to the mouthpiece.

As Lance began to describe how he would then mount her and push his wayward penis into her open portal, she at last spoke.

'No thank you.' She said it curtly, and put the phone down.

She was grateful for him phoning, but at this moment in time, she was not interested in meeting him for lunch, dinner, or anything else.

Stephen Sigmund was still in her mind and was the man she preferred to be in her body. She felt a certain loyalty to him, a loyalty that could not possibly last, but was, at the moment, extremely strong.

All the same, she rested her chin on her hand for a moment, and let her eyes flit over the shelves of green, red, and black books with their spines of gilt-etched lettering. She smiled. Lance Vector sounded as if he were a child in a sweet shop and she was all that was on sale – or the only item he was interested in.

Although he had made her shiver when she had first met him, he was a pretty young man. Who knows, perhaps if he was as innocent as he seemed, she could initiate him into his first sexual encounter. The thought made her wet again and regretful that she had brushed him off so quickly.

Enough of that, she told herself. The intercom was buzzing. Her next appointment had arrived.

She opened the file marked libel. Medina Frassard versus Valeria Spendle.

Val was a senior police officer and, as always, looked the part. Her hair was neat and dark and framed her face like a small cap. Twenty-two carat gold stars shone from her earlobes. Her skin gleamed like polished mahogany, and despite the charge against her, her dark eyes and her overall bearing still pronounced her confidence.

'Darling.' They both said it, both kissed the other's cheek.

Once Val was sitting, one stocking lisped against the other as she crossed her long, dark legs.

'Well? What's the score?' Val's eyebrows arched a little higher as she asked the question.

Abby shook her head. 'No go. Medina Frassard wants more than an apology. She wants recompense.' Abby interlocked her fingers and tapped her index ones against her chin as she viewed the woman who was both a friend and a client. 'She's after your heart, Val.'

The police commissioner, whose sexual appetite equalled her professional ambition, shook her head. 'Not my heart, Abby, honey. That chick's after my black ass!'

'Your words obviously opened a very deep wound.'

'Shit no! My words referred to her very open legs. You know me, Abby. I hate people trying to pretend they're something they're not. Anyway, I was a bit tipsy at the time, and that woman is a racist cow. Do you know what she said to me?'

'Certainly. I have it here.' Abby flicked to the relevant section in the buff folder. 'You allege, and I quote, that Medina Frassard hinted that you had got your job purely by the colour of your skin and not by your ability.'

'That's right!' Val's eyes lit up as she recalled the swiftness of her retaliation. 'And I said to her that her wealth and position had been acquired by how wide she had spread her legs, and not by the width of her intellect.' She shook her head. The brown eyes took on a soulful look before a smile came to her lips. 'Shit. If she won't accept my apology, then I retract it. I'll see her in court.'

'You could still refer her comment to the CRE.'

Val shook her head. 'No. I got this far in life on my own two feet, so I'll stand or fall the rest of the way on them.'

'It might be a definite advantage to have a black ass if you do fall. It could get bruised.'

Val smiled and shook her head. There was a knowing look in her eyes. 'I won't change my mind, Abby. There's nothing you can say that will do that, my darling girl.'

Abby sighed and leant back in her chair. She crossed her hands in front of her waist then smiled. 'Not even if I threatened to expose your sex-life to the press?'

Val threw back her head and burst out laughing. 'Me, you and Stephen too!'

Abby chuckled into her hands. Val stopped laughing and looked at her friend a little more seriously. 'Have you two been having a good time? Or shouldn't I ask?'

Abby nodded and lowered her lashes. 'You can ask, but I won't go into detail.'

Val raised her eyebrows. 'Wow. Could this be love?'

It was an effort not to blush, but Abby managed it. Somehow she couldn't answer this at the same time as looking Val directly in the face. Normally they would have discussed it like two giggling school girls, compared notes, feelings, and made personal comments about the man's assets and technique. This time something stopped her.

Val was perceptive. She reached across and covered her

hand. 'This ain't just sex, Abby. You two got more about you than that. You two are made for each other. Do the right thing, girl.'

Abby looked at the hand then looked directly at Val. 'And what about you doing the right thing. What about you going to the CRE?'

'No!'

It was at times like these that Abby wanted to shake some sense into her best friend. Val's comments to Medina had been heard by a room full of people whereas Medina's own remarks had not been heard at all. Val was on unsafe ground, but she was a stubborn woman.

Abby loved her and had known her a long time. They had met at Bristol University where both had explored the intricacies of law and the delights of the flesh with equal enthusiasm. They had awoken one morning in the same bed with a man between them, and after he had left they had discussed how much they enjoyed sex, and that no matter how successful they might be in their chosen careers, they would never stint themselves when it came to sexual pleasure.

'I will give my heart and soul to the pursuit of justice,' Abby had said, 'but my private life will be my own.'

'The public won't let you have a private life,' Val had responded.

Abby would not be beaten however. 'Then I will divide my life. In one I will be one woman, and a different woman with a different name in my private life – and ne'er the twain shall meet!'

That agreement had been common ground between them.

Both had been successful. In disguise and with the utmost discretion, both had maintained their private lives. And now one would be defending the other in court.

Abby left orders with her clerk to inform the Plaintiff's legal representative that they withdrew the apology and awaited their response. A court date obviously. It was unavoidable.

She and Val went off to lunch at a nice little Italian place with pink tablecloths and pale green walls. It looked a little like an ice-cream parlour, but the food was good and it was always packed.

Observant at all times, a necessity in the double life she led, Abby's eyes skimmed the lunchtime crowd. 'Well, well!' Her eyes narrowed and Val's gaze followed hers to where Medina Frassard sat with Christopher Probert. Medina, sleek in olive green with hints of gold, looked controlled and slightly aloof from the man opposite her. Probert, one of Abby's colleagues in chambers, stared into Medina's eyes, unaware that they were watching him. It was not difficult to deduce that he was mesmerized by the woman.

Val's eyes kept drifting in their direction as they sat at their table, and eventually she asked, 'Is that guy in love with her?'

'Might be. Is it possible that Medina might be in love with him?'

Val shook her head and thrust her bottom lip outwards. 'Doubtful. Not powerful or rich enough.'

'True.'

Abby studied her friend. Their eyes met. *You know I want you to tell me*, said Abby to herself. *I want you to tell me who Medina's lover is, but you won't.*

94

Val raised a long brown finger, shook her head, and shook the finger in front of Abby's face.

'Don't look at me like that, Abby. I can read your thoughts, but I'm not going to tell you who her current man is.'

'It could help. Confront her with that information, hint that you might show it to the media, and she would back down.'

Val's head-shaking was now emphatic. 'A matter of principle. I dislike the gutter press more than I do Medina.'

Lance Vector's telephone call was still fresh in Abby's mind. Her nod of understanding was abrupt. Their conversation ceased as the waiter came to take their order.

Chapter 7

Lance Vector did not give up easily. On average, he telephoned every two or three days. She let him, glad of having someone talk dirty to her when Stephen was not around. It was not yet their time to meet, and besides, he was working hard both in his constituency and at his enquiries into the Swan and Swallow affair. Not that Stephen would mind her having another man. On the contrary, they had both agreed that neither would hold the other to any false promise, any half-meant declaration of love.

Both went on respecting each other's privacy. Both had made a promise that this affair would not affect their public lives, or, indeed, their private ones.

Days, weeks went by without them meeting. Perhaps it was as well, because when they did meet, their lovemaking was more demanding, more energetic than anyone who knew them in their other lives could possibly have imagined.

After making love in every position known since the world and sex had begun, they lay apart, panting, their eyes open or closed, their thoughts converging just as their bodies had done.

Lust, each thought as they lay together, was bad enough.

Neither admitted to the other that they harboured an overpowering wish to see each other, that one particular look, voice, body. But love too? Was this what was happening to them?

Being new to such an emotion, neither could admit to it. They didn't ring each other like lovers do. They didn't meet for lunch or dinner. They made set arrangements from one meeting to the next, and kept strictly to those arrangements. They each clung stubbornly to their need to lead their own lives, to keep to their own space. It was enough that they met like that, each using the other as an instrument for sexual pleasure, a pressure valve on their very hectic and very public lives.

They had promised each other that outside the sex, their lives would not cross – not even at the Red Devil Club when, once a month, Jezebel Justice would again incite the audience to gasps of ecstasy and stunned silence. Everything would stay as it was because neither would admit their emotional attraction to the other.

But Stephen was worried. After making love, he would presume she was asleep and lie there beside her, a worried frown on his face and a thoughtful look in his eyes. Instinctively, she would tense, knowing that he was burdened and that his burden was making him angry.

As though being closer to him could help, could make him feel that much more secure, that much less alone, she curved her body against him, and stretched her leg across his.

'What's troubling you?' As she asked him, her fingers traced circles, squares, and triangles among the drift of hair that clung to his chest and spilled down his belly.

She was almost afraid to hear his answer, but also knew she had to relieve the pressure he was under. Of course, it had occurred to her that sharing each other's worries was tantamount to admitting that their relationship was more than just sexual.

He kissed her forehead, mumbled sorry, and told her that sometimes he thought he was drowning in parliamentary sleaze, furtiveness, and cover-ups.

'The Swan and Swallow case?'

He sighed. 'Old man Rheingold is taking the rap – as the Yanks say. To my mind, he's afraid to speak out, but soon I'll know more. Soon – somehow – I'll persuade my witness to meet me and talk.'

'Why is he so shy, do you think?'

Stephen shrugged. 'I'm not so sure that he is, it just seems that he picks the worst possible places to meet, places I don't want to be seen in.'

'Go in disguise.'

His face brightened. 'That is a possibility.'

Infused with an urge to make him forget his worries, she kissed him, and once again, their bodies came together. Temporarily, his worries were buried in the soft folds of her flesh, the tight embrace of her vaginal muscles.

Theirs was too great an alliance to crack asunder, too intense a relationship for the outside world to shatter. But neither could truly say where it was going, or where it would end up. As though it were a bed of bright red roses, they revelled in the look, the scent, the enticing feel of its petals. Neither wished to contemplate its development which could end in fulfilment, or could end in oblivion.

At his request, she went with him to Leys Open Prison to meet Mr Rheingold.

He was of Latvian Jewish descent and had come to England with his parents immediately after the war. Pale eyes gazed from a fat, jowly face. Loose lips drooped and exposed his bottom teeth. As Probert had said, he was fat, and his fat fingers moved continuously as he gazed like a drowning man at the only person who seemed willing to believe him.

Stephen introduced Abby.

'I hope you don't mind her listening in?'

'Pleasure,' he said, and dipped his head politely in her direction. 'What gives?' He said upon turning his gaze back to his potential saviour.

'If I can nail this witness down, I might be able to get your case reopened. I might also be able to nail the true culprits behind this. Are you sure you don't know their names?'

Rheingold shook his head. As his jowls flopped and made a slapping sound, Abby was reminded of an aged blood hound or, as Probert had said, a hippopotamus.

'Once the investment went abroad, the particulars were passed to a middleman there. Even in this country, I was only given a contact phone number and occasionally I met a representative of theirs. As I told you, his name was Mike Smith.'

'Not John?' Stephen was half-joking.

'No.' Rheingold shook his head. He was in too deep to notice or care about jokes. 'No. It was not John. It was Mike.'

Abby leaned a little further forward. 'What did he look like – this man Smith?'

Rheingold shrugged. 'Average man. Tall. Not special.' He

paused, frowned and pinched his lips between his thumb and forefinger. 'Except for the mole. Yes. A very big mole behind his ear. Left, I think, though I can't be sure.'

Stephen was sitting beside her, so she touched his hand, glanced at him sideways. 'I think I might know who that is. I can't be sure, but I think it's worth checking out.'

Stephen stared at her spellbound. 'Who . . . ?' he began.

'Let me look into it first.'

He nodded.

Following a telephone call to Miss Simpson, her own pet private investigator, Abby rang Stephen.

'Oliver Hardiman has a large mole just behind his ear. He is also something in the city – a will-o'-the-wisp type financier who brokers deals for people who don't want to get their hands dirty. He's not easy to get hold of, but I'll see what I can do.'

She didn't tell Stephen that she'd almost had Oliver pushed on her at the Red Devil Club by Archie. Neither did she tell him that she'd pushed him onto Valeria.

She and Valeria were sharing Val's Jacuzzi when Abby asked her about Hardiman.

'What was he like?'

'Pleasant. Good body, good dick, good lay. Why? Fancy having him yourself? You with that good looking Stevie baby in tow?'

'No. But I would like to ask him a few questions about a few million dollars, pounds, and deutschmarks going astray.'

Val raised her eyebrows. 'The Swan and Swallow thing? Is he involved?'

'Might be. Did you get an address for him?'

'Sure. The Ritz.'

'No home address? No contact number?'

Val shook her head. She had short hair but in her private life she wore a long dark wig, false eyelashes, red lipstick and very high-heeled shoes.

Abby frowned thoughtfully. 'No fixed abode. But someone knows where he lives.' Her face lightened. 'And I think I know just the person.'

She made a mental note to go along and ask Archie Ringer some pertinent questions. At present he was abroad, but she would certainly catch him when he got back.

In the meantime, she and Stephen still had their sex-lives. Totally lost in their longing for each other, she hoped, and he did too, that everything would go on in the same vein – perhaps until their passion was tempered either by marriage or old age. But neither told the other of their hopes and their fears. They drank of the wine, but had no need to prove whether it was run-of-the-mill or *premier cru*.

On an October day, when the city was rapidly embracing the imminent arrival of a grey November, everything changed.

The first thing Abigail knew about it was Stephen phoning, then being cut off as though someone had grabbed the phone from him. Before she could phone him back, the newspaper landed on her desk. A stark headline glared up at her.

The telephone went down. Coldness churned in her stomach. Two photographs accompanied the article. One showed a grim-faced but defiant Stephen. The other showed him in similar garb to that he had worn on the night she had met him. Wide-eyed, her throat dry, Abigail scanned the paper.

Neither the headline nor the article made pretty reading. According to the report, Stephen had been found dressed as a woman in public lavatories. According to a man named Carl Candel, he had been buying his sexual favours.

Even before she finished rushing from the first paragraph to the last, the telephone rang.

'I have a call for you, Miss Corrigan. The man refuses to give me his name, but he says it's urgent and you'll know who it is.'

At first Lance Vector entered her head. *No*, she said to herself, *don't let it be him. Let it be Stephen!*

'Put it through.'

A small click signified that the call had been connected. Abigail waited for the caller to speak.

'You've read it, I suppose.' It was Stephen. His voice sounded shaky.

'Yes. I have.' It wasn't easy, but she kept her voice steady. Confidence, she realized, was something Stephen would need badly.

'Abby. Someone is trying to smear me. I'm positive it's all to do with the Swan and Swallow affair. Effectively, they've put me out of the picture. By questioning my private morals, they're automatically questioning my public integrity. Innocent I may be, but I need your help to prove it. I feel trapped, Abby. I need you.'

Her heart and her body ached for him. For the first time since she had known him, Stephen sounded a little lost. He had cause to be. Public outrage had been stirred and it would take a lot of courage to face his accusers. Friends and acquaintances would fear for their own reputations if they were seen to defend him. Liberal thought and deed would drown in a flood of homophobia. He would need her. He would need her badly. Nothing would stop her from helping him.

'What do you want me to do?'

'I need to see you, but I don't want to come to chambers. That chap Vector's still snooping around. So are a host of others. Will you come here?'

Vector! Abigail bit her lip. She came to a decision.

'All right. Give me your address.'

So far in their relationship, neither had ventured into the other's territory. Their meetings and sexual adventures had mostly been outdoors or in the more seedy parts of town. That was the whole point of their games. Such surroundings heightened arousal and the sense of danger, of being found out. But danger had come from another direction, and Stephen had been accused of something that was not true.

Now, without caring about the consequences, she was going to meet him in his town apartment.

'Seven. This evening?'

'Yes. Yes. That's fine.'

Just after putting the phone down, there was a knock on the door and Christopher Probert walked in.

'Abigail. Good morning.'

As she answered his greeting, Abby folded up the piece of paper on which she had written Stephen's address, and pushed it into her pocket.

She had the distinct impression that Christopher's eyes had followed her movements. The chill smile of his thin lips widened as his gaze transferred to the newspaper that still lay on her desk. He came behind her, his arm deliberately brushing against her breast as his finger tapped on the face of a surprised-looking Stephen.

'Another bites the dust, I see.'

'Another what, Christopher?' Her voice hinted at disdain. She held his eyes with her own.

'Another MP. Can't keep their hands off nubile buttocks and hard dicks, can they? All tarred with the same brush, they are. All keen for a bit of bum breaching in stinking lavatories. Serve him right, arrogant bastard.'

Abby rose to her feet. Her head was high, her eyes were bright with battle.

Recognizing the familiar stance, Christopher took a backwards step.

'Why is he an arrogant bastard, Christopher?'

Her voice was strident and as firm as the one she used in court when cross-examining a particularly tight-lipped witness. *Ask questions. Keep them short, succinct. Let them do the talking. More lucid talk gives way to more sharp questioning.*

Christopher blinked. Instinctively, she knew he would try to be evasive. It was too late. Her steely nerve was intact, but his was blunt and cracking. Christopher could not help saying things that would enable her to assess the sincerity of his answers.

'It's him that keeps pressing for a public enquiry into the Swan and Swallow affair. The case would be blown out of all

Cathryn Cooper

proportion if he had his way. As it is, justice will be done, Harold Swallow and Gustav Swan will be exonerated, and . . .'

'The taxpayer will foot the bill, Mr Rheingold will stay in prison, and those behind the whole sorry affair will get off scot-free.'

Christopher, whose eyes flitted between her breasts and her face, now blinked and looked nervously towards the door.

'Justice will have been done.' A smirk came to his face. 'Well, there's no chance of a public enquiry now, is there? It was only Sigmund pushing for it, and he's likely to be too busy preparing his own defence to meddle in other affairs.'

Abby's blue eyes blazed. 'Is that why you were at lunch with Medina Frassard? Is she pulling your strings, Christopher, or is she pulling something nearer your heart but below your waistline? Are you fucking her, Christopher? Is she giving you pussy in exchange for favours?'

Probert's pale face went paler. His eyes seemed to sink deeper into his eye sockets. 'That's none of your business. She just wanted some advice.'

'You can't give her advice. We're in the same chambers, and I am acting for a client in a libel matter. It's not ethical.'

'It was personal, not professional.' His retort was hot and snappy. He didn't linger after he'd said it – *in case*, she said to herself, *I ask some more pertinent questions*.

Abby sat down. She frowned. Probert's nervousness troubled her. She'd never liked the man. He was slimy, he was toady. She recalled some sleaze about him from his college days, something about an affair with a senior lecturer and the death of her husband. They had called it an accident, but sometimes she wondered . . .

Abigail looked again at the lurid headline, and tapped her fingers against the face in the photo.

In that instant, and following what Christopher had said, she knew why Stephen wanted her to come and see him, knew what he wanted her to do.

As confirmation of her disgust, she would have thrown the paper and its offending story into the bin if the name beneath the headline hadn't caught her eye.

"*Our man in the know*," it said. "*Lance Vector*."

Him! Vector, who had had the nerve to ring her and ask her to lunch. Now she wished she had accepted his invitation, if only to pour soup over his head or drop hot coffee into his lap. She imagined the whiteness of his penis turning red, glowing as the hot coffee stung the skin, trickled through his pubic hairs, and licked like tongues of fire at his balls.

Cruel, she thought, *you're being cruel*. She had not thought herself capable of such vicious thoughts. But for Stephen she would be anything. Proving Stephen's innocence was paramount. She would do whatever it took to prove that innocence. She would sell her soul, sell her body. Anything.

Sweet words came to her mind when she thought of him. Descriptions of how he looked came to her. Tall, dark haired, brown eyed. Hard, well defined muscles, a tight, flat stomach, strong thighs. Between those thighs hung the silky sacs that made him male, the twin generators to that rod that rose so hard and so proud when he looked at her, when he

touched her. Lust, need, desire. Those three words came
to mind. So did love. She loved him. So far, such knowledge
had stayed hidden in her mind, reined in like a prancing
horse. But soon, very soon, she would have to tell him,
the world and everybody. She would have to admit it to
herself. Their first night together at the Railway Hotel
came easily to mind. So did visions of his body. So did the
memory of his penis entering her body – *her* body – a
woman's body. Could she really imagine that beautiful penis,
so obviously male, so obviously made for fucking women,
entering the body, the anus, of some spotty, diseased rent
boy?

The boy concerned was lying. He was a blackmailer. He
had to be.

She felt sore. Sore inside from all her sex with Stephen,
and sore now at the youth who had blighted their arrangements and what they felt for each other. She could not –
would not – believe it.

In the cold greyness of the multi-storey car park, Lance
Vector swung his dark blue Lotus out of the parking bay
and in behind a buff-coloured Mondeo. Ahead of the
Mondeo, Abigail Corrigan sat at the wheel of her light grey
Mercedes.

It wasn't in her mind to worry about who might be
following her. There were too many other problems, too
many questions in her mind about what had happened to
Stephen for her to concern herself with what lay behind
her. All she was worried about was what might be facing
her.

Lance swung out of the car park behind her, following her through the city.

She drove quickly away from streets where concrete slabs of offices sparkled with squares of brightly-lit windows. Out on the motorway, the sun-bright orange of lines of snaking sodium lights blinked past as they moved from one part of the city to another.

A light drizzle mutated what Lance was seeing out of the windscreen. The vision of her, naked, helpless, was clear in his mind.

In a street that spoke of stockbrokers, lawyers, and six-figure salaries, he saw her pull up and park. Quickly, he turned off his car lights and slid into the kerb behind her parked car. Ducking down as low as he could, he watched to see where she was going.

White pillars fronted the door of the Regency-style house where Stephen Sigmund lived. Abby's heels were the only sound in the street. Her head was high as she sniffed the evening air. Not so many car fumes now, not so many smells of a city at work. Night and excitement were approaching with the darkness.

Some might have surmised that in the circumstances it was only to be expected that such an eminent QC would be visiting him. But Lance knew otherwise, and such knowledge angered him. She was his. He had earmarked her as his from the very first time he had seen her. But Sigmund had got there first, and Sigmund, he told himself, had to be destroyed.

He smiled to himself. The plan was already in operation. A little inside information about his legal defence passed to the people who wanted to know, and Sigmund would be no more. The idea thrilled him.

I wonder, he thought, as he gazed up at the brightly-lit first-floor window, *if I could get in there from around the back and hear what they are saying*.

He looked at the street ahead of him, then twisted round in his seat to look behind. It was a long street, and he was feeling lazy.

Surveillance equipment, he thought to himself. *That's what I could do with*.

He was about to make a note to himself about looking into such things, when the mobile rang. Staring at it as though he wished it wasn't there, he let it ring six or seven times before he picked it up.

'Where are you?' asked the voice on the other end.

Because his mouth felt so incredibly dry, Vector licked his lips before he answered, and when he did, he lied.

'At my place. I've just pulled up.'

'Get your ass here. Now!'

'Sure. Right away.'

He slammed the phone back into its carrier.

'Yes sir. I'll be there right away sir, because I know that you're a right fucking bastard, sir!' He ranted to himself and with jealousy gnawing his groin, he glanced only one more time at the brightly-lit window before re-starting the engine and pulling away.

He should report everything – *everything* – he had seen to the man who had phoned him. But he wouldn't. He was grateful for his livelihood, but Abigail Corrigan aroused delicious sensations that lingered in his groin, set his prick to hardening, and his anus to tightening. And anyway, it was Stephen Sigmund alone that he was supposed to be watching.

As instructed, he handed his most recent taped surveillance of Stephen Sigmund to his editor, Squires, who frowned at it before putting it into a drawer. The drawer was then locked.

Vector turned to leave.

'Don't go. He wants to see you.'

He did not protest or say anything. He just nodded and closed the office door behind him.

The man Lance went to see existed on a higher plain than the editor. He was the owner, he was powerful, and also completely ruthless. He was the only man who truly made Lance feel nervous – even more so than his mother.

When Lance walked into the owner's top-floor penthouse suite, the man had his back to him and was staring out through the window at the London skyline. He did not bother to look round as he spoke. Lance was vaguely aware that he was not alone, that another man lurked in the shadows. The man blended well, except for his eyes. There was something unusual about them, something Lance preferred not to notice.

'You did a good job, Vector.' The voice of the man he had come to see was slow, his words precise – a bit like a pre-recorded tape.

'Thank you, sir.'

'However, Vector, this job is not yet finished. I require you to keep an eye on him. I want to know his movements. I want to know every moves he makes, every day, all day. I want to know details of how he intends to defend himself. I believe that Abigail Corrigan QC is defending him. I want you to catalogue their meetings, but stick to him more so than her. I don't want him to contact any other possible witness. This is one case that must be followed through to the bitter end; until he is ruined, humiliated, his status and his career destroyed. It is important that he is left with no credibility at all. Do you understand that?'

'Yes sir.'

'You will give the tapes to Mr Squires, your editor. He will ensure they get to me.'

'Yes sir.'

'I also have another job for you to do. No one of any consequence. Just small fry. A man named Carl Candel. I'll give you the details later.'

Lance continued to observe the back of the other man's neck. From where he was standing, 'the man' could have as easily been black as white. Like a silhouette, he told himself. A black shadow. That's all he was, all he ever had been. Not once had he ever seen the man's face.

The man made him feel uncomfortable. Always he had only seen the darkness of him against the lights of the city, and heard the sound of his voice.

As on other occasions, he wanted to be away, but this time for a secondary reason.

He achieved his objective and left before any questions could be asked about why some of the tapes he handed in were so much shorter than others. Awkward questions were something to be avoided. Whatever he had spliced from the originals he regarded as his private property.

As the scenic lift travelled slowly down the outside of the

building, Lance Vector surveyed the high towers of modern offices and lower yet somehow more imposing dome of St Paul's which was half-hidden behind one particular building. *A bit like the people I expose*, he said to himself. *Only a portion of their life is actually showing.*

Chapter 8

When Abby arrived at Stephen's apartment, he hugged her tightly against him. His tension was obvious.

'I'll get you out of this, Stephen,' she promised, her fingers stroking his neck and her words half-smothered by the closeness of his chest. 'I promise I'll get the charge dismissed.'

He shook his head emphatically. 'It's not enough for you to defend me. I need you to find out who set me up.'

Wincing at the pressure of his fingers on her arms, she looked up into his face. Dark circles emphasized the brown of his eyes, and his breath smelt of too much wine. Lines of worry had given him a permanent frown. 'I know I'm asking a lot of you, Abby.' His voice was anxious, but gentle.

She patted his arms, shook him a little as though he were being a silly little boy. Her face was serene, though her brows were furrowed. Never had she seen Stephen looking so helpless, so fragile. Her heart went out to him.

Now was the time for her professional capabilities to add dimension to her private life. This man had need of her entire attention. She took a deep breath before saying what had to be said.

'Listen. If I am to help you, you must listen. I will do all I can, but I do need to question the rent boy who said you bought his services. According to the police, he's adamant that you propositioned him.'

Stephen shook his head. 'He's my so-called witness. The one who's been asking me to meet him. I told you he asked me to meet him in some pretty dreadful places. He asked me to go to those lavatories. As I told you, he said he had some evidence that would be more than useful in the Swan and Swallow case, and you know how sorry I feel for old Rheingold. He refused to come to my office or my house. I was foolish to go. I know that now. But it is so important that I get to the bottom of this scandal. I know someone else is involved, Abby, someone very powerful. I just know it!'

'So what persuaded you?'

There was a swallowing motion in Stephen's throat as a look of shame came to his face. She had an urge to touch his throat, to follow the hardness of his Adam's apple just as she did the jerking of his penis when he got excited.

'I took your advice. I went in disguise.'

Suddenly, it was Abigail's turn to feel guilty.

'I saw the photograph. But into a gents' lavatory?'

'I thought I'd be OK. I used the same disguise as I used at the Red Devil Club on that night we first met.'

'Oh Stephen!'

He hung his head and guiltily she hung hers too. What could she have been thinking of in suggesting such a thing, casual as it may have been?

'What a fool I was.' He leaned his head against hers and the smell of him made her want to drink his skin and eat his body.

She settled for kissing his cheek. 'And what a fool I was for suggesting it in the first place.' She sighed. 'Never mind. It's happened. You've been accused of something you did not do, and we now have to do something about it.'

She took a deep breath, tilted her chin like she always did when the whiff of battle was in the air. Gently, she cupped his face in her hands. Inside she was crying. From the moment of their first meeting in the Red Devil Club, she had instinctively trusted him. She trusted him now. Like his approach to sex, Stephen's approach to his job and to justice was completely honest.

He sighed regretfully. 'If only he had agreed to meet me here.'

'If only.' Abigail measured her words carefully as she gave the matter serious thought. 'But why didn't he meet you here? You could have been as easily accused here as anywhere else. The tabloids would still have gloated over all the gory details. Obviously, that was not enough. They wanted a court case, an act of obscenity, lurid enough to spark public outcry. But they must also have wanted you out of *here*.' She eyed him coolly, but spoke quickly. 'Was anything planted while you were gone?'

Stephen stared. Although he had bedded her, the look on his face was incredulous, as though he had only just realized how intelligent she was. 'How did you know that?'

She smiled, felt it was weak, but hoped it wouldn't seem that way to him. 'It seemed elementary – to use a much abused and famous phrase. Get you out – get some in.'

He groaned and held his head in both hands.

'Later the investigators came in and took away some tapes

and some photographs, which I swear I've never seen before. I swear it!' He shook his head mournfully.

She reached for the wine he had poured her and studied him over the rim of her glass. Where was that confident character who oozed masculinity and had dominated their sex games?

Head still in his hands, he was now staring at the floor. From the sound of his voice and the fact that there was little wine left in the bottle, she could tell that his confidence was now swimming in a hazy mind. Because their bodies had fused, their minds and their emotions were fusing too. She could feel his anguish. She reached out and trailed her fingers through his hair.

Dark, frightened eyes in a flushed face glanced up at her. Then, almost as though he were melting, he sunk to his knees, folded his arms on her lap, and closed his eyes.

Touched by his aura of helplessness, Abigail sighed and ran her fingers through his hair again.

The back of his head reminded her of the last time they had been in such a position. She had been driving, and he had rolled up her skirt, pushed her legs apart, then kissed the thigh nearest to him before his mouth and tongue had kissed her pubic lips.

As she had changed up into top gear, she had climaxed, her hips jerking off the driving seat, her wet pussy saturating his mouth.

Despite his present forlorn demeanour she could not help but be aroused by the closeness of his body, the feel of his head in her lap, his arms against her thighs, his chest against her shins.

'Oh, Stephen. I feel for you. I'm so sorry.'

She saw his eyes close.

'Keep doing that,' he said. 'It's incredibly soothing. Marvellously pleasant.'

'Enjoy it and I'll keep doing it.'

She bent her head nearer to his.

Humming softly, she smoothed his hair away from his face and thought how vulnerable he looked.

'I'm going to ask a lot of you, Abby,' he murmured. 'I'm asking you to bare your body, your soul, to be nice – very nice – to licentious and cruel men in the hope of saving me and my career. This is just the beginning, you know.'

'I know. But I wouldn't be doing it just for you. I would also be doing it in the interests of justice.' She said it softly, sincerely. 'Where do I start? Who was this boy, and how did he get your telephone number?'

'He said he got it from a friend of mine – a parliamentary friend; Douglas Dermott-Embledon.'

'A would-be peer.'

Stephen moved his head. 'How do you know that?'

'Is the House of Commons leak-proof?'

He relaxed and let his head fall back into her lap. 'Is it hell!'

Abby congratulated herself on her natural ability for a quick response.

Douglas Dermott-Embledon was from a privileged family and held an equally privileged post in the Ministry of Defence.

He was also a member of the Red Devil Club. It had once been his great pleasure to take her from the club and drive with her down to where HMS *Belfast* was berthed.

How, she did not know, but he had a key to the old tub and seemed to know when security was at its most minimal.

Breasts swinging backwards and forwards over the chart table, she had moaned with pleasure as Douglas had licked her behind, then pushed his fair-sized member into her welcoming portal.

So far, Abigail – in her guise as Carmel and thus Jezebel Justice – had been very successful in discerning the better endowed men from the lesser. In Douglas, as with Stephen, she had not been disappointed. Neither had he been. Abby felt sure he would not be averse to a repeat encounter.

'Then I'll go to see him.'

As though he were a sad child, Abigail cradled Stephen's head to her breast, unbuttoned her blouse, and let him suck at her nipple. As he sucked, she crooned to him, stroking his hair, his face, and cradling him close with both arms. With her breast still firmly between his lips, she huddled over him, undid his trousers, and let her hand go down to his member. She kissed his face as his penis jumped in her fingers.

His eyes were closed, and as he sucked, his fingers pummelled at her breast.

'There, there,' she said softly. 'Relax. Leave it all to me, and I'll make it feel better.'

Her fingers curved around his hardening flesh.

She opened her legs so he could more easily fit between them and continue to find comfort in the feel and taste of her breast. His ribs pressed against her naked sex.

A sweet, wordless melody came from her throat as she rocked him in her arms and began to pull his erection to greater promise. Slowly, he hardened. Pulsating and hot, his erection grew.

Stephen did not want to open his eyes. Her breast was a comfort to him, a comfort he did not want to let go of. Behind the darkness of his eyelids, he could escape the world, but could not, and did not want to, escape what she was doing to him.

Her fingers were cool on his penis, her breast warm against his mouth.

The event reported in the newspaper had knocked him from where he had been, from being someone with status, a man of integrity, to being someone sordid, cheap, nasty.

He had his weaknesses. He was aware of them in himself, just as he was aware of them in others. In politics, in public, and in private, he was guilty of many things – but not of what he had been accused of – never of that!

Sex to him was the smell of female armpits, shaved, waxed, and perfumed with essence of roses, musk, sandalwood, or lemon. It was also the rise of a firm, female breast, it was a curving spine that swept from well-defined shoulder-blades to the pouting rise of a rounded behind. It was rich pink nipples that responded to the gentlest kisses, the tenderest touch; a narrow waist, flared hips. It was legs opening to reveal a pink slash of flesh between a forest or a feathering of blonde, russet, or black hair. And the scent of a woman; a smell that enticed, wafted and snared, drawing him closer until his nose was buried against a ruby-red clitoris, his tongue lapping, his throat swallowing her ambrosaic offering.

His penis was pulsing with a tempo that almost matched

the one she was humming. The sounds, like her touch, were calming his fears, comforting his scarred soul. Her hands stroked his head, his neck, his torso and hips, his penis.

When he came, his hips jerked in time with her dancing fingers. As his cream trickled over her fingers, he gripped her breast more tightly, clamped his lips, his teeth around the hardness of her nipple so she could not possibly escape him until the last, tense throb had left his stem and his body.

Vaguely, he was aware of her sighing above him. Her song, and her climax, were finished.

'Have I made you feel better?' she asked as she stroked his hair.

He sighed. 'Oh yes.' He looked up at her suddenly, got up on his elbow so his face was close to hers. 'But you know we have to be careful, don't you? You know we can't afford to go back to the way we were, to playing in the countryside, and taking a room at the Railway Hotel.'

Her smile was sad and her nod of assent was slow, regretful. 'What a shame. I truly came alive in that grim little room. I shall miss seeing your body outlined by that awful yellow streetlight outside the window. And then there's our tune – you know – the song the trains scream as they rattle along the rails.'

It made him smile. She was glad of that.

He kissed one arched eyebrow, then the other. 'So will I, and perhaps, until then, I shall never quite be the man I was. I shall depend on you for moments like these, moments when desire has to be coaxed rather than expected from my body.'

She understood, and understanding saddened her. It was even more imperative that she find out all she could about those who were so determined to ruin him.

They talked some more as they bathed together. Normally, Stephen would have chosen such a moment to instigate some sexual games, some scenario in which he would be the dominant one, and her his submissive slave. But as he had already said, sexual arousal in him was no longer an instant response.

As the warm suds soothed their worries, they considered what had to be done.

It was agreed that Abigail and Carmel could transcend both of Stephen's worlds, the professional and the sexual. That way, she could learn twice as much.

He told her about the police who had arrested him. One name was particularly familiar.

'I also remember passing other people. I remember a car driving away. A sleek car. Black with tinted windows. It seemed familiar.'

'Did you see its number plate or its make?'

He frowned thoughtfully and stared at the top halves of her breasts around which the white suds floated like blobs of soft meringue.

'I think it was personalized, though I could be wrong. I only caught a brief glimpse of it. There was a "G" I think, and only one number. One. It had to be a one.'

Abigail, her hair piled high upon her head, drew abstract lines in the bubbles that surrounded her. There was something on her mind that she had to say.

'Someone must have seen you dressed as a woman before. How else would they have recognized you?'

He stared. 'At the Red Devil Club!'

She nodded. 'Yes. That means I am going to have to hang

around there a lot more than I usually do. It might also be useful to find out what goes on upstairs. The membership list might be useful too.'

'What's the difference between what goes on upstairs and what goes on down? I mean, your dance is hot enough for me without anything else.'

Laughing, she flicked bubbles at him. 'You're biased.'

'Of course I am.'

Their eyes locked. Neither admitted what they were feeling, although both felt exactly the same way about each other.

'I'm going to have to do a lot of dangerous things. A lot of questionable things.'

'I know.'

She held her gaze steady. 'Do you? Do you really know what I'm trying to say?'

He blinked as realization sunk in. 'Yes,' he said softly. 'I think I do. No matter who you question, especially as Carmel, you are going to have to play along with everything they want you to do.'

She nodded very slowly. Her eyes held his. 'Can you live with that?'

Floating bubbles flurried and divided with the exhalation of his breath. 'I can live with it, but only on one condition. Okay?'

'A condition?' After despatching a frown, she tilted her chin and nodded vigorously. It was as if she were shaking any apprehension from her mind. 'Okay.'

'That whatever sexual exploits you get involved in, you tell me about them. At least then I can share them with you, as if I had been there with you.'

Perhaps it was the steam rising from the water, or perhaps it was purely her skin reflecting the warmth she was feeling inside, but she flushed. From her breasts, the flush crept up over her cheeks and shimmered beneath her scalp. It was not the flush of embarrassment, of guilt, or of shame. Excitement and hope were at the root of her sudden pinkness. Stephen's sexual audacity was not entirely dormant. By revealing the details of her enquiries, she would also be repeating her sexual adventures and, in repeating them, she would be helping him.

Across the piles of slowly deflating bubbles, he reached for her, water dropping from his fingers and his palm. She smiled and placed her hand in his.

'I'll tell you everything that happens. But first, I have other things to do, questions to ask.'

Her first task would be to talk to Carl Candel, the rent boy who had made arrangements to meet him, and the arresting officer who had – so say – witnessed the incident. That way, she should at least get some idea of what she was dealing with. It seemed a simple matter.

It did not, however, turn out quite the way she had expected.

'Filthy, unnatural beast. He does not deserve to represent the good people of this country. He should resign!'

Lance was listening to his mother, but not with quite the same attention he usually gave to her loud exclamations. Before lunchtime, he'd phoned the press office at Westminster to find out who was likely to be representing Stephen Sigmund. The answer had cut him to the bone. Abigail Corrigan. If he had been his normal self, he would have informed his editor of their liaison and provided him with the necessary evidence. In turn, his editor would have splashed the photograph and a suitable headline across the front page of the paper – something like LEGAL BEDFELLOWS or BYE BYE BI-SEXUAL. But Lance had not told them anything of the goings on between the politician and the barrister. Somehow, if he did that, he would be exposing himself as well as Abigail. He couldn't do that. In fact, he had a strong urge to protect her, to keep her relationship with Sigmund private. Not that he would be willingly protecting Sigmund. On the contrary, he would do all in his power to destroy him – as ordered. But Abigail; he still wished to protect her from all this. He would keep her apart from it, and when Sigmund was eventually destroyed, he would step forward, ask her out again, make a point of being where she was.

For the time being, he would give his newspaper all it wanted about Sigmund. Plenty of overtime would be booked in on that. Yet it would be Abigail Corrigan he was following, Abigail who was his prime objective.

Chapter 9

DARREN IS A WANKER, said the bright green graffiti. It was bigger than the rest of the scrawl that covered the grey, concrete walls in the block of flats where Carl Candel lived. It was also brighter and therefore probably fresher than the rest of the rude comments and exclamations about acquaintances and life in general.

Two small children who looked too young to be out gazed at the woman in the pin-striped suit, her silver blonde hair slicked back beneath a black fedora. She was carrying a leather briefcase and vaguely wondered if they were old enough to have learned the basic skills of mugging.

''Ello,' said one.

''Ello you old cow,' said the other, grinning as if her words were funny as well as taboo when directed at someone as other-worldly as her.

Abigail Corrigan raised her eyebrows, stared at them hard, but made no comment. She pressed the button that would bring the lift.

'It don't bloody work, you silly cow!'

Giggles echoed off the concrete walls and the grey metal of the grubby lift doors.

Abigail winced. The smallest child said this, a girl with tangled hair and wearing a bright pink track suit that looked several sizes too big for her.

Judging by the fact that the "lift coming" light didn't come on, and there was no sound of whirring machinery, Abigail took the budding young misfit at her word, and headed for the stairs.

The smell of urine, lighter fuel, and stale spew was strong. Luckily, Carl Candel lived on the fourth floor. If it had been the tenth, she might very well have thrown up before she reached it. Others had no doubt felt the same, judging by the amount of half-digested stomach contents already deposited at those angles where the stairs turned and changed direction.

Carl lived at number forty-three.

The open verandah that ran past ten blue doors much the same as his was empty, but then, it was only ten-thirty. Kids at school, adults at work (some), others, along with unemployed adolescents, still in bed or semi-comatose in front of a television set.

She reached to heave a rat-a-tat on the letter box since the door was devoid of a knocker. As her fingers touched the door, it creaked slowly open. Smoke and the smell of something burning came out into the air.

She shouted as loud as she could into the billowing smoke. 'Mr Candel?'

Nothing.

Pushing caution aside, she rushed in, and although she had never been in this place before, she instinctively found the kitchen where a pan of what might have been lentils, but were now reminiscent of black gravel, burned on the cooker.

Quickly finding a cloth, she grabbed the burning pan, carried it to the sink, and turned on the tap. A cloud of steam rose to dampen her hair and mist up the cold glass of the window.

She frowned. Lentils? For breakfast? She looked around at the wipe-clean cupboards, the uncluttered work surfaces. Nothing seemed to be out of place.

Next to a bowl of freshly-made salad, were two glasses and a half empty bottle of Moroccan wine – a brand recently recommended on television, she remembered – and slices of French stick, all buttered, all neatly arranged in a basket.

Did this guy entertain for breakfast? Salad? Wine?

The bread crusts were hard to the touch. Last night, they must have been laid out last night.

She called again, but knew in her heart of hearts that Carl Candel would not answer.

Another smell came to her nose that vaguely resembled burnt pork. There was nothing in the oven. Nothing on the top of the cooker or beneath the grill. Wrinkling her nose, she followed where the smell took her.

She found both the smell and Carl Candel in the bedroom.

The bedroom itself boasted a decor that was not exactly expected in a council flat of meagre proportions and uninteresting design.

Apparently a man with an eye for the dramatic, Carl Candel had taken it from the ordinary to the phenomenal.

The bed was low, and like the carpet and the curtains that formed a ceiling above it, the colours were warm, vibrant; a variety of rich reds, oranges, russets, and deep greens.

Everyone's favourite, thought Abigail. A Bedouin tent, all

set for a heroine awaiting her sheik and a fate worse than death. Only Carl was that heroine, and his fate was death.

Her throat felt like a gooseberry; as though tiny little hairs had sprouted all down it, and were preventing her from swallowing. But she eventually made the effort, cleared her throat, then reached for the telephone.

Her heart was thumping. So was her head. But she kept her cool, kept her voice level and precise.

She explained where she was, who she was, and what the circumstances were.

'He's naked, lying face down on the bed, and spread-eagled. His wrists and ankles are tied at each corner. There's a metal rod sticking out from his rectum. There's a wire running from it direct to a three pin plug. He's been electrocuted.'

There was a pause on the other end of the phone.

'You're joking.' The voice was incredulous, almost scared. The listener was not necessarily horrified, but more obviously fascinated.

Abby's voice remained steady. 'I'm not laughing. Neither's he.'

She put the phone down.

Before the police came, she wanted to have a look round. Despite the area he lived in, Carl Candel had a sense of style and displayed good taste. Watercolours in black frames hung on white walls in the living room. The carpet was white, the furniture black leather, chrome, and glass. A red light blinked above the CD button on the sound system. Wrapping a tissue round her finger, she flicked a switch, and the disk holder slid out. Leonard Cohen. Dark, she thought, sensual, like Carmel, her other half.

The blinds were still drawn. She thought about opening them, but stopped herself. After all, who had shut them in the first place? It might have been Carl, or it might have been the murderer. There might be prints on them.

She went again into the kitchen. Wine, salad, French bread. Dinner. Such things said dinner. So why had it taken so long for the lentils to boil dry, and what else was there to go with them? Surely something more palatable than a dish of sullen colour and dull taste?

Two uniformed men arrived before the Scene of Crimes Officer.

They muttered something about her staying around for questioning. They went into the scene of the crime, then came out again.

When the plainclothes bod got there, he introduced himself, although he didn't really need to. But of course, he didn't know that.

'Paul Bennet.'

'Abigail Corrigan QC. I came here to question Carl Candel about the Sigmund incident. I am acting for Mr Stephen Sigmund, MP.'

Up until then, his eyes had been cruising over her body as though he owned it – or would like to. He blinked before looking at her face.

'Then I might as well inform you that I shall be asking Mr Sigmund a few pertinent questions.'

'And he will be giving you a few pertinent answers, Inspector Bennet – like he was with me last night.'

Paul Bennet smirked. She could have easily slapped his face, hit the arrogance from it. It took a lot of self control not to.

'What makes you think this,' he paused, '*man* – was killed last night. You a pathologist?'

As though she were a school teacher, and he was the wayward pupil, she beckoned him with her finger. Her eyes glared without blinking once, and her mouth was serious.

'Come here,' she ordered and, begrudgingly, he obeyed.

In the kitchen, she pointed at the wine, the bread, the salad. 'Last night's proposed meal, but all untouched. Left just as it was, including the bottle of wine.'

'What about that?'

Just as she supposed he would, Bennet pointed at the burnt saucepan that was still smouldering in the sink.

Abigail turned a knob on the stove. It pinged – not unlike a sonar on a Second World War submarine.

'Timer. Someone used a timer.'

A mocking look and tone came to Bennet. 'Now why would that be, Miss Corrigan?'

'Because, Mr Bennet,' she emphasized the Mr almost as though it suited him better than inspector, 'whoever it was killed him wanted the circumstances of Candel's death noticed. The smoke was already filtering out along the passageway when I arrived, and the front door was open.'

Paul Bennet was almost laughing. 'Miss Corrigan, I should think it was noticeable enough. Him lying there with an iron bar up his ass, and two hundred and forty volts cooking his bowels to well done. Wouldn't you?'

Abby maintained her serious expression. 'Whoever killed him wanted maximum media coverage. He or she also wanted him discovered within a certain time period. Fire is lethal in these blocks of flats. People take notice if they see smoke coming out from under a door. Someone would notice. Someone would report it, and whoever killed him wanted it reported within a certain time scale.'

Bennet's smile disappeared as he got his notebook out from his pocket.

'So. What time did you arrive here?'

'Ten-thirty. As I said.'

Just as Bennet started to look serious, a guy from pathology intervened.

'Been dead a few hours, Paul. Last night sometime. I'll give you more details after I've given him a good seeing to back at the lab.'

'I think he's already had that!' Paul Bennet sneered as he put his notebook away.

Abby held her head high and folded her arms across her chest. She stared at Paul Bennet as if daring him to say what he had to say, willing him to ask her what her relationship was with Stephen – if she fucked him, if she sucked him. That's what he'd really like to be asking.

Bennet retreated, but the look was there, though the words were left unsaid.

'So,' he said flatly. 'What were you doing here exactly?'

Abigail looked at him defiantly.

'I came to ask him about his statement regarding the charge against my client. Unfortunately, someone got here before me. Now I'll have to depend on the statement he gave the police, and the statement of the arresting officer. Won't I, Mr Bennet.'

She looked at him accusingly. If he did notice it, he didn't comment.

'At your convenience, Miss Corrigan. At your convenience.' He smirked again as though he really had made an outstanding joke.

Jerk, she thought, and told him she'd call in at the police station. She left it at that.

Despite her cool exterior, she had a nauseous gripe in her stomach. *Imagine*, she thought, *just how the victim must have suffered as the ribbons of electricity had fried his insides.*

When she left, she could feel Paul Bennet's eyes upon her back. She shuddered. In the darkness of the Red Devil Club, many faces looked back at her. Not all had got to know her as Carmel. Not all had been fucked by her. Paul Bennet was one who had.

Lance Vector was in two minds whether to follow her. But the police were here, and having reported back to the office that Carl Candel was dead, and then to the man in the penthouse suite, he had been told to stay and find out what the police's conclusion was. He didn't want to be too long about it if he wanted to surprise his mother with the piece of salmon he'd purloined for her supper. He'd had no qualms about taking it. After all, Carl Candel wouldn't be wanting it, would he?

But it was hard not to follow Abigail, especially after watching his latest recording.

It had been a blue sky day when he had followed them. The air had been crisp with the first hint of winter, and crisp red and brown leaves were clinging to twigs and rustling as the breeze shook the branches.

These sounds of nature hid the sound of following feet. In a woodland spot where green moss clung to overhanging rocks, Stephen and Abigail had made love.

With the fierce intensity of like-minded souls, they had wrapped their arms around each other, their kisses hot and unending. Almost, he had thought, as though they'd been super-glued together.

Although the air was crisp, they had taken off their clothes; at least, eventually. At first, Sigmund had ordered Abigail to take hers off, his voice suddenly firmer than it usually was. She complied willingly, her breasts pimpling slightly in the coolness of the wind. Lance wished it had been him who had ordered her to take off her clothes, him who now ran his hands over her body.

Breathless with anticipation, he had watched and although that same jealousy towards Stephen Sigmund was still with him, he wanted him to take her, to make her do anything he wished her to do. As the spectator, the man who only watched but also felt what the lovers were doing, whatever Stephen wanted would be what he wanted too.

Stephen had told her to spread herself against the rocks. She had arched her back as her flesh had met the cold wetness of the moss-covered stone, had mewed that she didn't want to do it. But Stephen had insisted.

The sight of her naked and exposed against the khaki greenness, was in itself enough to give Lance an enormous erection. The fact that Sigmund was ordering her to do it made Lance even more eager to lose his virginity inside her gleaming body.

With the dexterity that only the most professional peeper could ever hope to master, Lance balanced his video recorder at the same time as patting his rising erection.

He would not, he told himself angrily, he simply would not wank himself off again. Before seeing Abigail Corrigan, he would have done so without a second thought. Now, it would no longer suffice.

Laid out now over a bed of autumn leaves, Abigail was mewing in sweet delight as Stephen guided his penis into her.

Hidden behind a rock, and lost in a forest of emotions, Lance bit his lip, aware that he wanted Abigail badly, that he wanted to take Stephen's place inside this intoxicating woman.

Again and again he had pressed the replay button on his video recorder last night. Again and again, on normal distance, and on close-up, he had viewed the pink, moist lips of Abigail's sex, the hanging balls and noticeable size of Stephen's penis. And again and again, he had watched as Stephen took his penis from her at the most important moment, and let a torrent of creamy whiteness splash uncontrolled over her breasts and belly.

He sighed as his recollection reached its conclusion and looked at the police cars, the block of flats, and the jump-suited boys from forensic.

It was only after closing the car door, that a certain realization came to Lance Vector. His instruction had been to find out what the police's conclusion was regarding this crime. At no point had they asked him what the crime was. It was, he thought to himself, as if they might already know.

The following day, the occasion and circumstances of Carl Candel's death were plastered in thick black headlines both in the tabloids and the broadsheets; after all, even the chattering classes have a love of the erotically macabre, though they'd never admit to it.

Beneath the thick, bold type, was the name of the freelancer who had got hold of the story first and had touted it to every editor in town. That name was Lance Vector.

Chapter 10

The lawyers acting for Medina Frassard stated their intention of taking the matter regarding Valeria's alleged slur to court. It was not unexpected. Abby phoned Val and told her about it.

'Cow! What now?'

'Await the court date – unless you've got any intention of settling out of court or changing your mind about the CRE.'

'Screw her!'

Abby raised her eyebrows. She was long past the state where she winced at Val's flow of expletives. Like the uniform, the strength and the single-mindedness, the swearing was all part of Val's make-up, or perhaps her defence.

'Okay. Then into battle we go. I'll let you know when I get a date for the hearing.'

'Thanks, Abby. You're a real pal. Anytime I can do anything for you . . .'

'. . . I'll ask. Never fear.'

Val sounded as if she'd have liked to continue talking, but Abby's thoughts had already moved on. She would be defending Val soon enough, and although Val might end up paying damages, she would still have her career and her

139

status. Stephen's case was more involved and a lot more than money was at stake. Today she was meeting someone who might be able to throw some light on his particular case.

Douglas Dermott-Embledon was pleased to receive Abigail's call, and even more pleased to meet her for lunch. She wanted to ask him why he had given Carl Candel Stephen's private telephone number.

The restaurant was French, its decor a creamy adaptation of Napoleonic decay. It was a place she had been to before where she could take clients and know nothing told in confidence could be overheard.

In the past, she had entered the place full of confidence, assured that no matter the crime of which her client was accused, the fact that she appeared in calm control would put them at their ease. Today, things were different. Someone she cared for was accused and in danger of being destroyed. Now it was her who was ill at ease.

Get a grip, she thought to herself. *You can't fall apart this soon in the case. Too much depends on it.* She assumed a bright smile for the man opposite her.

'I've seen you perform,' Douglas said.

In more ways than one, Abigail thought to herself, and smiled secretively. Her brain was alert. Her tongue wet and ready to lick this witness into shape.

'Your defence strategy was something to behold in the Theobald case,' Douglas went on. I am told that your summing up was sure-footed. Impeccable.'

Theobald was a man charged with having had an incestuous relationship with his daughter. The prosecution had omitted to mention that he had not known that she was

140

his daughter at the time of the incident. His wife had gone off with another man and taken the baby girl with her many years before and he had lost contact. The child had grown up to look like her mother when she was younger; blonde, leggy and blue-eyed, the looks he still preferred. It was a case she had won.

Abby took the hand that was offered her, noted the silky smoothness of his refined fingers, the polished perfection of his nails. 'My fame goes before me. I thank you kindly for your comments, sir.'

He seemed to appreciate her calling him sir. Despite his hair being silver, the eyes of Douglas Dermott-Embledon were sharply grey, their shade reflected by the subtle sheen of his tie. When young, thought Abby, he must have been irresistible and in no need of adornment. Now, older, his clothes were impeccable, his hair not too long, but flirting gently with the edge of his collar. She did not need to ask what his body was like beneath the silk shirt and well-cut suit. She knew that already, knew that from the night he'd taken her down onto the ship. Those cool eyes had watched as she brought her breasts out over the top of her dress, bent over, then cried out as her nipples brushed the cool glass of the chart table. He had moaned as she hoisted her dress up over her behind, her black suspenders tight and slightly restrictive against her creamy flesh.

But that was Carmel who had done that, a woman with red lips, black hair and black eyes.

This was a different woman, a woman he knew as Abigail Corrigan, QC, and he was showing her due respect.

Although he already knew why she was there, she

141

explained she was acting for Stephen Sigmund regarding the charge of intent to commit an indecent act in a public place. He nodded amiably and seemed not to be biased either way with regard to Stephen's guilt.

An understanding man, she thought. A man of similar tastes, similar fascinations. Despite his status in the public eye, Douglas, like Stephen, still yearned for female flesh and unhindered sex. No matter that the public itself and the journalists who pandered to it were outright hypocrites with their own skeletons in their beds as well as in their cupboards. Public figures were expected to be on the other side of perfection. Latter-day saints who needed to be made of stone and have no sexuality, no passions, no fantasies. Could it be that those once worshipped were then scorned because they mirrored the public's own image?

Douglas smiled at her. The same even smile had been on his face since the time he had taken her hand. 'So you want to ask me questions, my dear. You are at liberty to do so – after we have eaten.'

She ordered a light salad. He ordered the same for himself, though without butter for his bread, and without flesh from fowl or beast. He also ordered a light rosé, chilled to just the right temperature.

'I prefer claret with dinner,' he said in a matter-of-fact voice, 'but I tend towards something light for luncheon.'

Her reaction was suitably polite, suitably spoken. 'Heavy lunch equals heavy afternoon, and one's pile of work becomes a mountain. I heartily agree with your choice.'

'Please. Call me Douglas.' He clasped his hands in front of his face and beamed. Behind his respect for her, she

142

caught a look of lust that surged for a moment, but was quickly brought under control. *A Cheshire Cat*, she thought to herself. *A cat who likes to be preened.*

When lunch had been eaten and the wine drunk, she asked him about the rent boy and the telephone call.

His fixed smile lessened. 'I don't remember giving Stephen's number to that boy. I told Stephen that. If I did and I gave him his number, then I sincerely apologize. But somehow, I cannot believe that, old as I am, I have forgotten that someone asked me for a private telephone number of a man I respect.'

Abigail judged he was getting agitated.

'So how did you know Carl Candel?'

The wide smile constricted to pursed lips. A chillness turned his eyes a darker grey.

'He went to school with my son. Told me he was writing a thesis on financial sleaze within Government and could I refer him personally. I said I would have to speak to Stephen first, but being busy . . .'

'So, perhaps someone else gave him the number?'

'Perhaps.'

In that one moment, everything distinguished about the man now seemed decrepit, washed out. No matter that his dark blue suit was still sharp, his hair snowy white. His shoulders were suddenly hunched, and all his vigour seemed compressed; shrunk within his clothes.

Abby knew what he was going to say even before he said it.

'He's dead, isn't he? Candel, I mean.'

'Yes.'

'I don't read the popular press, but rumours have reached me that his ending was pretty terrible.'

'Yes.'

'Poor boy.'

'Perhaps you could enquire who *did* give him Stephen Sigmund's telephone number.'

He nodded.

'And Stephen. Could you testify for him?'

Douglas spread his hands. 'Anything I can say that might help, I will.'

'Could you testify truthfully that he was not known by you to be homosexual, that his preference was most definitely for women?'

He thought for a moment, then nodded. 'Yes. Yes, I think I could do that. Stephen likes women as much as I do.' He smiled and his eyes twinkled. 'I bet he's pleased at having someone as stunning as you to defend him.'

Abby did not reply. Instead, she got out her notebook and pen.

'Please could you give me any details concerning Stephen and his predilection for women? Any specific instances that you may recall.'

She felt no jealousy in her asking this question. There was only her desire that such happenings be well documented so she could judge how well they might stand up in court.

'In full detail, my dear?'

His eyes bored into hers. She met them without blinking.

'In full detail, sir. If you would.'

Douglas sighed, leaned back in his chair, then cleared his throat.

'I did not mean to be giving them undue attention, but it was at a country house weekend given by some high and mighty civil servant. I saw Stephen Sigmund talking to a young woman I knew as a parliamentary researcher. Pretty enough girl, warm brown hair, big blue eyes, the sort that Roedean mould and Paris fully fashions, if you know what I mean.'

Abby nodded and re-crossed her legs. Douglas licked his lips before he continued.

'She and Stephen seemed to be getting on like a house on fire. It was obvious they were going to end up having sex.'

'How do you know that?'

Douglas shook his head fitfully as though he were searching for the right words. 'Because it was obvious.'

'How obvious? *Did* they end up having sex together, and if so, did you see them in the act?'

The patrician jaw dropped like a lead-filled jam-jar. 'Do you mean . . . in detail? Everything?'

The pen made a snapping sound as she slammed it against the notebook.

'Sir. I cannot possibly provide evidence purely on hearsay, on your assumption that Mr Sigmund was really and truly heterosexual. I need an eyewitness account. Did you actually see them copulating, and if you did, I would much appreciate the details.'

Douglas cleared his throat as he viewed her with a more jaundiced expression than he had earlier adopted. 'I did, though I would have thought it ungentlemanly to say so.'

Abby took up her pen again and eyed him questioningly.

He sighed, and clasped his hands on the table before him.

'I did see them. They went to the stables.'

'At night?'

'Yes.'

'And you saw them clearly?'

'Yes.'

'Was there a light on in the stables?'

'No, but there was a beautiful moon. I remember it very well because it shone through a window and lit up their flesh. They were naked by then, and she was on top of him.'

'So her bottom was very white, very noticeable?'

His gaze seemed to drift away from her, yet around her. As if it had become liquid. She surmized it was not her he was thinking about, but the memory of Stephen and the naked young woman.

He used his hands as though he were feeling what he was seeing. 'Her bottom was very broad, but very shapely. Rather similar in looks to a pear, but, of course, it was not the colour of the fruit. On the contrary, it was silver. It shone like the moon itself as she bounced up and down on Stephen Sigmund's stem. I remember her groaning, then laughing and crying out with delight as she turned round to face me in my hiding place. Without once letting him slip out of her, she carefully turned – you know – like a lemon on a squeezer.'

He took a deep breath and licked his lips again. He trembled slightly.

His mouth, Abby thought, must by now be as dry as a desert.

As he recommenced, Abby continued to make notes.

'I remember her breasts were small. She was the original English pear all over. But they were pretty breasts, and had

146

big nipples that danced like roses in a breeze as she resumed her bouncing on his member. Her belly was round and curved down to a copious clutch of pubic hair. I remember thinking it looked like Devon thatch in the moonlight. I've walked around my Devon estate in the moonlight. I've seen the effect it has on thatched roofs, and,' he said with a glint in his eyes, 'on naked bottoms.'

Even your own, Abby thought, but only nodded.

Douglas continued. 'As she bounced, she cupped her breasts and threw back her head. I could see Stephen's hands gripping her hips, forcing the timing of her movement. Such a delicious sight, one I would like very much to see again.'

Abby stopped writing. 'How did you know it was Stephen? After all, you saw them leave together, but there was a gap between that and you seeing them naked in the straw, and Stephen, from your description, was lying beneath her.'

He stirred from his remembering.

'I could see his hands.'

'But could you see his face?'

'Yes. Later.' He looked stunned that she should ask, and that he could have been telling a young woman such a lurid tale.

'Tell me.'

Her voice demanded that he continue.

Douglas flicked his eyes over the other diners, sipped his drink, then went on. 'They changed places. She lay down in the straw, and he got on top of her. I saw his face. I saw him come. I know it was Stephen. I would know his face anywhere.'

'And the girl. Who was she?'

For a moment, she thought he wasn't going to answer her.

'Fiona Platter. Nice girl. Nice family.'

'Can you phone her address through to me?'

He nodded. 'Yes. Will you question her?'

'Of course.'

Chapter 11

Colours danced over Lance Vector's face as the images on the video screen altered position, varied movement, and throbbed with passion.

Stephen and Abigail had driven to the forest that day, and he had followed them.

Stephen Sigmund, his naked buttocks bunched with muscle, was making love to Abigail Corrigan against the green rocks, among the curled leaves, and she looked to be enjoying it. That fact alone made Lance more and more irritable.

'I've had enough of you!' As he shouted, he stabbed a well-scrubbed finger at the remote control.

She was enjoying that man. He didn't want her to do that, to show so well that she was relishing everything he was doing to her. *It shouldn't be Stephen*, he reasoned, *it should be me. It should always be me.*

His breath was audible and his dark eyebrows met heavily above the bridge of his nose. Pressing another switch on the remote brought the auxiliary machine into play. The other machine played a different story, though one character remained the same: Stephen Sigmund; a public lavatory, a place Lance had been ordered to attend, a film he'd been ordered to make.

The tape played, but despite it showing Stephen Sigmund in a more shameful light, Lance did not really see it.

Eyes staring, he tiptoed through his mind and thought of all the things he would like to do to the tall, slender young lawyer who spent so much time with Sigmund.

First, he would strip her naked. Then he would find for her one of those dog collars with steel studs set into it. He would fasten it around her neck, make her walk on all fours as he jerked the leash attached to it. He would set her food before her on the floor and force her to eat it from there.

In his mind she was a virgin when he had first seen her. Certain people at the Humphries gathering had called her the Snow Queen or the Ice Maiden. Such names were enough to persuade him that what he believed was indeed correct. To his mind, she had seemed unapproachable, unsullied, and he wished deeply that she still was.

But she had sinned by lying with Stephen before giving Lance the chance of lying with her. Such a sin had to be admitted to and purged from her system. It would take a long time to humble her and make her see the error of her ways. It would also involve his fantasies becoming reality. Even now he was still following her around, still getting used to her routine.

Tonight, she was with Stephen, the man he had been ordered to pursue with a view to exposure. He knew she would be there until morning.

Of course, he could report back to his editor that they had spent the night together. But he didn't want to do that. To do so would be admitting that the woman he wanted had been tainted by another's body. In his mind, that was not acceptable and anyway, Stephen would deny that they had slept together that night. He had a big house and invited many guests to stay. His denial would no doubt be accepted.

It didn't matter to Lance. He knew where she was in reality and where she was in his mind. Another scenario was taking form. Again she was naked in the basement and wearing the studded dog collar.

Sometimes, he decided as his anger boiled within, he would make her sit like a begging dog as he rebuked her for all her shortcomings. As he laid down the law to her, he would squeeze her breasts, and stare into her eyes, daring her to moan, daring her to say anything. In his company, he would force her to be silent. He would only have her talk in that prim and precise way of hers when he took her to tea with his mother.

Of course, his mother would not know that this young woman lived naked in the basement, a chain connecting her collar to the wall. In his mother's company Abigail would wear a dress of his choosing. It would be black and have a white collar and white cuffs. It would reach to the floor. His mother would like that. In his mother's presence, Abigail would also have to wear underwear. He would choose that too. It would be made of black satin and be tightly laced at the back. Black suspenders with sharp barbs would connect with the tops of equally black stockings. Buttocks and sex would be left uncovered. His mother would not know that. Only Abigail and he would know that particular secret.

The thoughts made him smile. It was only one scenario

that came to his mind as he watched his favourite tapes.

Not that he was taking in what was happening on the screen. He stared but did not see the public lavatory, the three men standing, whispering. If he had, he would have remembered that he had disobeyed orders, that he had arrived at the place half an hour before he was told to.

It suited him to shoot preliminary scenes before the main footage. That way he could be sure he was getting a natural shot. He had shots of Sigmund going into the lavatories, and a shot of him and the police team coming out. From that footage, he had lifted the photograph that had appeared in the paper. The rest of the stuff he kept "just in case". In case of what, was of no consequence. When he had first seen the footage, he had narrowed his eyes at the three men whispering before Stephen Sigmund had actually arrived. All were familiar, and one more so than the others.

Fiona Platter had a flat in town down a pretty little mews in the heart of Belgravia.

Money whispered with the easy opening of the door, the dark charm of the Spanish maid, and the smell of country flowers in the hallway and the chrome and grey lounge.

Fiona did not seem particularly pleased to see the tall, slender Corrigan. Her smile was as false as her fingernails.

'You're the barrister bitch, aren't you, darling?'

Her tone was sharp, but Abigail was ready for her.

'Yes. And you are Fiona Platter, darling, the high society bitch who was seen tumbling in the straw with Stephen Sigmund at a country house about two months ago. I want to ask you if it's true.'

Abby's directness caused the colour in Fiona's face to vanish in a minute. Her red lips pouted as she glared at her maid who was lingering for instructions by the door.

The maid did not wait to be dismissed.

Fiona continued to glare at the closing door, then at Abby who sat looking so efficient, so professional in her trim black suit, white collar, black stockings and patent loafers. She sniffed impatiently before she spoke.

'All right, darling, all right. I understand you are defending Stephen about this rent boy business. What has it got to do with me?'

'I want you to testify that Stephen is very much heterosexual.'

'I do not think I care to, darling.'

'Don't you care about his reputation, his career?'

'Not really. He was a cock passing in the night, and I was a safe harbour to berth in. That's all, darling.'

Abby eyed her quarry with something more than professional appraisal. She wanted to hit the smug deceit off her perfect lips, her perfect face. She imagined Stephen heaving his pelvis against that of this woman, his hands grappling for what there was of her breasts. Fiona Platter did indeed have small breasts and wide hips. The fact pleased her. *Was she jealous?* She pushed the thought from her mind.

She heard the rasp of silk stockings as Fiona arranged herself on a grey leather sofa, and crossed one silk-clad leg over the other.

Her dress was as grey as the sofa she lay on, yet silken with wide bands of blue and pink around the V-neck and the cuffs. It was designer, but not immediately recognizable.

Abby was in no mood to be intimidated by some spoilt little bitch who took advantage of a man's body but cared nothing for the rest of him. And especially when she herself cared so much for him. It was becoming ever clearer that she did, but at this moment in time, she dare not fully admit it – even to herself.

'I think you should consider this very carefully, darling,' Abby said, her smile as hard as her intent. 'You were seen rolling in the stable with him, your bottom all silver in the moonlight. You even managed to turn round on him without his cock falling out of you. Quite a sexual athlete, aren't you? What would your Sloane buddies think of you if they saw your backside spread across the front page of the tabloids?'

Fiona's big, blue eyes fluttered nervously. 'What a fucking bitch you are, darling.'

'Yes,' replied Abigail through gritted teeth, 'takes one to know one. But I should warn you, I can be much more of a fucking bitch, *darling*, if given the chance. Do you want to take that chance or testify?'

A slow smile came to Fiona's face and she leaned forward, her expression speculative. 'Are you having an affair with him?'

The question took Abby completely off guard. She could not help but hesitate before she answered.

'What's that got to do with it?'

Fiona's blue eyes glittered like chips of broken glass. With a wicked smile on her broad face, she lay back on the sofa and slowly, so slowly, she began to caress her breasts and her belly.

'Everything,' she said, the word drifting from her mouth. 'I can see the emotion in your eyes. You want to clear him. But it's more than that, isn't it? You care for him. You care a lot, Abigail Corrigan, you and your spotless reputation designed to make men think that you never sin, never love, and certainly never screw. But that isn't the whole picture, is it?' There's more to you than meets the eye, and you want Stephen Sigmund in the frame with you.'

Now it was Abigail's turn to blink. True, she was feeling these emotions. But were they that obvious? Was she wearing her heart in her eyes as opposed to on her sleeve? She pulled herself together.

'Will you testify?'

Fiona leaned forward again and stroked Abigail's black stockinged knee with her blue painted fingernails. 'Yes, darling. But only on condition that you do something in exchange for me.'

Bisexual, Abigail thought to herself with slight panic. *She's bisexual and wants me to go to bed with her.*

It came as something of a relief to find out that was not quite the case.

'I like watching too,' said Fiona excitedly as she leaned towards her and touched her hand, her eyes wide like a small child at Christmas. 'But only with men. I like to see a man putting it inside someone else. Do you like that too, darling?'

Relief must have shown in Abby's eyes. It certainly did in her voice. She even managed to laugh.

'I must admit, my experience in that particular field is sadly lacking.' It was true. Varied as her sex-life had been, she had never performed before an audience. She wondered

155

what Stephen would say; decided he would approve, and anyway, it was for his benefit.

Initially, Fiona was surprised at her lack of experience, then she was suddenly all brightness, all excitement. 'Then we must do something about it.'

She picked up a mobile phone and dialled a number.

'Send Julian,' she ordered. She glanced again at Abby and winked. 'Oh, and send Dominic as well. I've got a friend visiting and she's got quite an appetite.'

Abby was worldly-wise, but she still looked at Fiona a mite quizzically. 'Am I right in thinking you have just ordered two men?'

Fiona shrieked with laughter. 'You bet. One has to be so careful nowadays. The beautiful can so easily be tarnished. These studs are guaranteed. Clean and trim. And they're all yours – at first!'

She laughed again. Her laughter was infectious and Abby couldn't help feeling excited at the prospect of having two young men procured for her.

Fiona was as infectious as her loud laughter. It was easy to see why Stephen had gone with her. Her upper-crust exterior was as brittle as a sugar coating on a chocolate drop. Beneath her haughty veneer, she was sexually honest and open to suggestion.

While they were waiting, the two young women consumed half a bottle of wine and took most of their clothes off.

Fiona wore a white satin basque with half cups. Over the top her nipples peeked like two pink eyes. From between her legs, her pubic hair erupted like an April shower.

Stephen, Abigail decided, had very good taste. There was

nothing cheap or nasty about Fiona. She was all peaches and cream, English rose complexion and English pear shape. There was a friendliness about her that was hard to ignore once her Sloane Square exterior had been breached.

The two young women eyed each other like gladiators weighing up the strengths and weaknesses of their next opponent. Except they weren't opponents. They were two women of similar tastes and similar sexual appetite. Each had an outer persona that hid a different one beneath, and strangely enough, each knew it.

Abby wore only black stockings and matching suspender belt. Responding to how she was feeling, her nipples were hard and her breasts pert.

Fiona gazed at her with delight, her eyes dropping from her breasts, over her belly, and to the lips that smiled from between her thighs. Her eyes opened wide and her voice was full of amazement.

'My, my darling. I see you shave your pussy. May I touch it?'

She seemed genuinely enthralled.

Abby smiled and nodded her assent. She had decided to shave recently, knowing that her disguise as Carmel was better protected without the tell-tale signs of such silvery blondeness below. Fiona's long, white fingers reached and touched her. Tremors of pleasure erupted where her fingers gently stroked the silky flesh. There seemed to be no sexual intention, but a genuine curiosity to know exactly how shaved lips felt.

Fiona sighed. 'Your skin feels very soft. Is pleasure more intense without hair?'

Abby shook her head and suppressed her desire to press herself further onto Fiona's knowing fingers. The feeling passed as Fiona retreated.

'I wonder if I should shave mine off,' said Fiona thoughtfully as she ran her fingers through her abundant nest.

'Oh no. Don't do that.' Abby reached out and touched the long silky hair that hung a quarter of the way down Fiona's inner thighs. It feels like a real pussy,' she said wistfully. 'Like a Persian cat, luxuriant, intriguing.'

Their mutual admiration was based purely on friendship. Granted, sensations were aroused by their caresses, but such touches served only to ignite their desire, which was for men, not for each other.

Obviously, the Spanish maid was used to seeing her mistress lounging around half-naked. She was also used to answering the door to handsome young men and signing a delivery invoice even before they crossed the threshold.

Silently, she escorted the two young men into the room, then quickly left.

'Darlings!'

The two young men both embraced Fiona. She threw her arms around each of their necks, and stood on tiptoe so she might kiss their lips as well as their chins.

'Come. I have an assignment for you.'

For the first time since taking her clothes off, Abby felt suddenly vulnerable. Could she really go through with this for Stephen's sake? She decided she could.

Holding the hands of each, Fiona brought Julian and Dominic to her. They were smiling, and as their eyes travelled over her, she could see that they liked what they were seeing.

'This is Abby, and that,' she said, nodding towards a white door whose panels were etched in blue, 'is my bedroom. Come.'

The bedroom had white walls, white ceiling, white floor. On one wall a large, frameless painting hung, its abstract design a mix of various whites. Like a sudden rainbow, bottles of perfume and pots of cream sat before a gilt-framed mirror, and curtains of heavy muslin hid the questionable colours of the world outside.

'Make yourself at home, Abigail, darling.'

Fiona's voice was soft and kind as she led her to the bed.

Regardless of Fiona's kindness, Abby's heart was thumping and an odd sort of guilt was whirling in her mind. Sex was entering her professional world, and she could not stop it from doing so without forfeiting information that may prove useful in Stephen's defence.

'Lie down.'

Abby slipped her feet out of her shoes and slid onto the cool satin of the white bed.

Clouds of white mist seemed to swim before her eyes as she eyed the two young men who were pulling their shirts away from smooth, tanned chests, and sliding their trousers down muscular legs.

These, she decided, were men who liked their work, whose chosen career was a vocation more than a job.

Their eyes still smiled. One had dark brown eyes and blue-black hair caught in a leather tie at his neck. The other's eyes were hazel and his hair was predominantly dark brown, though streaks of sun-kissed blond ran from his forehead to his shoulders.

Old, familiar feelings were surging and whirling inside her. *I want them*, thought Abby to herself. *I want them and nothing will stop me from having them.*

Realization came quickly. No longer was she doing this just for Stephen. She was also doing it for herself.

Fiona stood at the foot of the bed as the two warm bodies stretched out on either side of her.

'Relax,' said Julian, the one with the dark eyes and dark hair.

'Leave it all to us, baby,' said the guy with blond streaks whose accent suggested Southern California.

Only once did she glance at Fiona who was still at the foot of the bed, her hands kneading her breasts and her fingers tweaking her nipples. Then she lay back, closed her eyes, and let her body take over.

Their palms were warm upon her breasts, their flesh hot against her. Against her hips, she felt the moist, hard heads of their erections. *Like battering rams*, she thought, *nudging against my defences, pushing them over before they rush through the gate.*

'Give me your mouth, baby. Kiss me.'

Dominic squeezed her cheeks as he forced her mouth to face him. She could have drowned in his smell, been consumed by the suction of his lips and the probing of his tongue.

Other lips kissed the hollow between her neck and her shoulder. Hands, then fingers manipulated her breasts, rolled her nipples, pulled them, squeezed them, and caused her back to arch and her legs to open.

Breathless beneath their lips, she raised her hips as if

inviting them to suck other lips, to probe a different mouth. She ached for them to do that, longed for their fingers to pull her lips apart, to slide along her flesh and burrow into her portal.

Just when she thought about wrenching herself from their grasp, pulling her lips from them and saying – no – demanding what she wanted, other lips kissed her shaven lips, and another, more gentle tongue slid over her most sensitive flesh.

The probing tongue, the gentle lips, retreated as male hands took her body as their own.

Men surrounded her, men were over her, and men would shortly be in her.

Lost in pleasure, she kept her eyes closed as the firmness of their hands and fingers explored her belly, dived between her legs, and separated one silken lip from another.

First one finger entered her, then two. Would they take her now? Would they force her to climax even before they had pushed their hard erections into her ever-willing hole?

Tightly closed, keep your eyes tightly closed. It seemed the best thing to do. Without seeing what was happening to her, she could at least surmise, even fantasize.

Fiona, she assumed, was again standing at the foot of the bed, her fingers now embedded in her own vagina, sliding along her own greasy lips rather than hers.

And these men. Their bodies, so hot, so hard against her. They were forcing her legs wider, cupping her buttocks, and at the same time, peeling back the leaves of her sex, invading her vagina as though it were no longer hers, as though she had given it to them of her own free will.

Even as they lifted her and one man slid beneath her, she did not open her eyes. To open them would spoil her own dream, her own fantasy. No matter that her fantasy was identical with what was happening to her, its power lay in her imagination, and her imagination was the switch that turned on her desire and her orgasm. Reality, the black and whiteness of life, was nowhere near as exciting.

The man beneath her gripped her breasts as his penis entered her.

She cried out as she took him in, then mewed as the sudden intrusion was soothed by the feel of the other man's hands running down her back, his fingers gently trailing down her spine.

Now the warmth of a body was behind her as well as beneath her.

Crisp pubic curls kissed her behind as another penis divided her buttocks, the moist head dripping with a slippery fluid that trickled over her anus and dampened her inner thighs.

Strong hands held her above one man. Strong hands also held her in place for the man behind to push his way into her body.

'Let me,' she heard a soft voice say, then felt cool fingers – female fingers – plaster her anus with slippery cold cream.

All this for Stephen. *All this for you, my love.*

Unfettered, the truth of what she was doing had escaped. Yes, she was enjoying it. Yes, she would do it again if she had the chance. But the truth was that she would never have got round to it in the first place if it hadn't been for Stephen, if she hadn't needed to do it for his sake.

The most sensitive part of her sex was pressed more firmly against the man beneath her as she was entered from behind.

Her cry was silenced by a kiss and was replaced by a low, squirming kind of sound that said perhaps she liked it, and perhaps she didn't.

Full of men, invaded by two ripe weapons, her breasts played with, pulled, pushed and pummelled; for Stephen, and for herself.

Pressure built up around her clitoris. In her body, there was friction in one channel which was replicated by friction in the other. Both moved in alternate time. As the front one thrust, the rear one withdrew. As the rear one thrust, the front one ceased to thrust, but because of the weight upon it, did not withdraw.

Beyond her control, the fires of climax flamed higher. Surrounded by men, invaded by men, and watched by a forgotten Fiona, her climax gathered like a storm in her loins, then as the men stiffened and climaxed within her, she yelped, yelled, and still without opening her eyes, let the ultimate sensation wash over her.

Later, she again asked Fiona if she would testify.

'Oh, yes,' she replied, an awestruck wickedness in her eyes, and her mouth wet with anticipation. 'But you will come and see me again, won't you? You will come and see your darling Fiona. Yes?'

'Yes, Fiona. Yes. I think I will.'

Chapter 12

Beneath the offices where barristers, solicitors, and articled clerks surveyed volumes of law and dictated their conclusions onto pocket-sized portable machines, were the dungeons. The dungeons were low and long and held the archives going back to the first time a learned counsel had ever crossed the threshold from the street above.

The dungeons were a private world, a secret vault where only those seeking past truths ever ventured.

At Abby's suggestion, it had been arranged that Stephen hot foot it over from the House of Commons just around the time everyone was leaving chambers. Once everyone had left they would be left undisturbed.

An army of cleaners descended on the offices at around five forty-five, their quick banter and heavy steps echoing along the narrow corridors where the floor was not quite level and the walls were not quite straight. Doors swayed open then slammed shut as they dusted and cleaned. Metal bins were banged on the floor in an effort to encourage discarded paperclips, spent pens, shredded affidavits and half-eaten sandwiches to leave their sticky bottoms and relocate into a black plastic bin liner.

The cleaning women, most of whom were black and from Hackney, stuck rigidly to the upper floors. They never ventured into the dungeons. They had no need to. The paper there was sacrosanct. Indeed, not all of it was typed. The very oldest were in long, feathery handwriting, the words copious, the deeds purposely extended to cover several pages. These had been written in the days when lawyers were paid per folio.

By the time Stephen arrived, the women had already dusted and cleaned around Abby. Heavy footsteps sounded from the floor above.

'Their feet are like thunder, and they blow through this place like a hurricane,' said Abby with a glance at the ceiling which throbed beneath their onslaught.

It was good to nestle in his arms a while, sweet to push her nose and her lips against the warm comfort of Stephen's neck.

His lips kissed her ear. He tensed. 'What have you found out?'

She took his hand. 'Follow me, and I'll tell you.'

A square bolt, once shiny brass, now black with time, was slid back across the door. Just inside, Abby's long fingers felt and found a bank of light switches. She only switched on one.

Shadows fell from high shelves, dusty boxes, files, and green steel cabinets. Beyond the circle of light, the room cast its personal shadow.

Abby locked the door behind her and leant her back against it to make doubly sure it was properly closed.

She reached up to Stephen, touched his cheek, which felt as only a man's cheek could: a mix of soft and bristle. Her thumb caressed the corner of his mouth. In immediate response, his lips parted. She willed both her mouth and her eyes to smile at him.

'I'm so glad to see you.'

He hesitated to say anything. Trepidation silenced all the things he was feeling, all the things he wanted to say. Not for himself was he fearing to hear what she had found out, but for her. Would it hurt her to tell him the very intimate things she had undergone for his sake? Stephen was not by nature a jealous man. He didn't want her to feel shame on his behalf. He gloried in knowing that other men coveted her, that other men would die with envy if they knew the things they did together. He would also enjoy imagining what she did in the arms of another man, and what he would do to her.

She started by telling him about Fiona.

'I hear,' she said with a quirky grin on her lips, 'that you rolled with her in the hay at some country gathering. Douglas told me about it. He watched you. Did you know that?'

This, Stephen decided, was his chance to put her at her ease, to ensure that she would tell him of her adventures without withholding a single detail.

He cupped her cheek, let his fingers take in the silky softness of her skin; relished the effect it had on him.

'Yes,' he said and held her close, his hands spreading across her back, feeling her firmness, her softness, the running contour of her spine. 'I had Fiona in the stable, and I knew that Douglas was watching. So did Fiona.'

Abby had not asked Fiona if she had felt she was being watched. The thought that they had aroused her. The image of straw crackling and rustling beneath the passion of naked bodies sent hot currents through her. Her fingers traced

167

fragile lines over the nape of Stephen's neck as she looked up into his eyes. Her eyes, she knew, must be sparkling, so hot was the desire that rushed through her.

'Tell me about it.' There was a low, swishing sound to her words as though they were impatient to be off her tongue. 'Tell me.'

'I'm going to,' he said, for he knew he had to; for her, and for him.

'Even before we left the house, Fiona was begging me to do it to her. We'd been stood talking beside a white marble mantelpiece. In between lascivious talking, we sipped our drinks, eyed each other, and sent obvious signals with our eyes, our lips.

'Her body was close to mine. I could feel the smooth hardness of her thigh against my leg. She wore a very short skirt. It was white and floaty. Her jacket had jagged patterns all over it in purple and red. She held her drink in her left hand. The back of her right hand rested against my crotch. Every so often, she moved her fingers. My cock moved with them. I wanted to moan. She knew what she was doing to me, but would not move from where we were until I had promised to screw her in the stable. Douglas, she told me, would be watching. He would like watching, she said. Douglas always liked watching.

'So, as you know, I went with her to the stables.' He paused, kissed her. His touch, his smell made her feel warm all over. He began unbuttoning her blouse. She slid out of it and groaned as he took her bare breasts in his hands. His lips lingered around her cheek. As he resumed his story, each word he spoke, each breath he took tantalized.

'Once in the stable we took off our clothes. I played with her breasts, pinched her nipples, and then I kissed her.'

As he spoke, he enacted everything he said. Abby moaned, then squealed before his lips silenced her.

'I sucked on her nipples,' he went on, then bent his head and did the same to her.

'Ohhh, don't stop!'

He did stop, but only to resume his tale and allow his hands to wander.

'I ran my hands down her back and over her behind – like this.'

Abby sighed with pleasure, closed her eyes and gripped his arms. Pleasure was burning her, singeing her pubic hair, setting her inner organs dancing, hardening her nipples so much she thought they would explode.

Stephen relished the feel of her bottom wriggling against his hands. He enjoyed the firmness of her flesh, the luscious shape of each separate orb, the tensing of her muscles each time his fingers ran between them.

Supposedly, he was recounting his sexual encounter with Fiona, and yet she was only a slide rule. She was certainly not the true measure of the woman in his mind and in his hands.

'Then I pulled her skirt up,' he went on, his fingers moving vigorously over the blackness of Abby's skirt until he held it somewhere around her waist. Because Abby never wore knickers, there was only nakedness from stocking tops to waist.

The blackness of suspenders running across her white flesh to her stockings made her appear more wanton, more exposed than if she had been stark-naked.

There was a sound of footsteps in the passage outside. This was followed by a dull thud. Then more footsteps walking away.

The two lovers took no notice. They had far more important things on their minds then nosey cleaners.

He undid her skirt, and once it was removed, he enjoyed the silky softness of her exposed flesh. As his fingers explored her naked behind, her hips – gently at first – began to grind against him. There was now nothing between him and her except her stockings and garter belt.

'I liked her behind.' His hands pressed her buttocks so that she ground more tightly against him. 'It was big, fleshy and bounced when she rode me.'

'She rode you? Tell me about it.'

There was no real need for him to tell her all about it. She already knew the details from Douglas. All the same, she wanted to hear it from him.

'Yes.'

She sighed as he slid his hand between her legs and his fingers pleasured her inner lips. Beneath his finger, her close-hid bud hardened and responded. 'I got on her,' he continued in a hushed voice, 'and she got on me.'

He kissed her again. She ran her hand down to the front of his trousers and undid his zip.

'I came on her, and she came on me.' By the time he said this, his penis was already in Abby's hand, hot, hard, and desperate for attention.

'Tell me more.' Her demand was almost lost on the quickness of her breath. Her breasts, her belly were pressed tight against him.

His thumb stroked her chin as he sought her lips. She wanted to drown in the exquisite sensuality of him; wanted to forget about the law, about the trouble he was in, and never wanted to go back to the Red Devil Club ever again.

When his lips left her, his eyes did not. He shook his head slowly and smiled.

'No, my darling. Now it is your turn. Tell me what happened today.'

Surprisingly, she had no hesitation in talking about what had gone on at Fiona's place. With almost fastidious attention to detail, she told him of the two young men Fiona was in the habit of hiring. She told him of how first one, then the other had pleasured her. She told him of how both of them had taken her at the same time, of the size of their weapons, the hardness of their bodies, and the sweet smell of masculinity they left hanging like a shroud over her skin. She had died for them, loved them, submitted to them, and had done everything they wanted her to do.

'Do it to me,' he gasped, his fingers tangling in her hair and pressing demandingly against the back of her head. 'Please. Do it to me.'

Once his eyes were closed and he was moaning at the thought of what she had done, she dropped to her knees, and almost naked before him, she took his penis in her mouth, licked it, sucked it and stroked it. And then, when he was crying out with the utmost pleasure, she took his balls tightly in one hand, and sucked his penis into her throat.

In the barrel-roofed vaults where the legal history of a nation was stored, Stephen cried out as his semen spurted free and gushed into Abby's throat.

171

Afterwards, they talked about what other questions needed to be asked, and who else would step forward and categorically state that Stephen's desire for the opposite sex was so obvious that he could only have been there to interview a witness. They needed the testimonies of other women with whom he had enjoyed brief liaisons, to put his sexual preferences beyond question.

Of course there was Valeria, but as Val Spendle, the only black, female police commissioner in the country, she would definitely be wary of participating in this kiss-and-tell exercise.

But somehow, they did need to find other women who would bear witness to his heterosexual nature and so doing, place doubt upon the likelihood of him propositioning a rent boy. Even then, they would still be floundering without definite evidence of who was really behind the slur campaign being waged against him, and quite probably, the Swan and Swallow fraud too. It was a daunting task.

'I need to speak to the journalist who wrote the original article, and the one who took the photograph.'

Stephen nuzzled against her hair. 'The little bastard. I could wring his neck for what he's done.'

'Hopefully, you'd be wringing his neck for the murder of Carl Candel, but somehow I don't think so. All we have against him is the fact that he was the first to report on the incident.'

'I'd still like to wring his neck.'

She didn't answer. She understood completely.

They dressed and continued to talk about Stephen's case, ready to make their way back to Abby's office. She reached out and turned the handle of the door she had earlier closed to ensure their privacy. It wouldn't budge.

'Oh no!'

'Is it locked? Let me try.'

Stephen tried. It did no good.

Abby began to beat her fists on the door and shout. It was a hopeless task. An idea occurred to her. 'Have you got your mobile?'

'Yes.'

'Great! We can telephone the caretaker, the police, anyone, and get out.'

He shook his head. 'No. I brought it with me, but it's in my briefcase which, unfortunately, I've left in your office.'

Both experienced declining spirits.

Abby shivered.

'Come on. Let's walk,' said Stephen, and put his arm around her.

Cuddled together like some slow starters in a three-legged race, they walked up and down the aisles between the high shelves of old files and the chipped and scratched metal cabinets.

Exasperated that they might very well have to spend the night there, Abby sighed as she huddled close. After a while, her neck began to ache, so she threw her head back and let her gaze sweep the ceiling and the top shelves of buff folders.

Names printed in faded ink on the backs of files slid dreamily past. Coloured files from more recent times replaced the buff. To keep her mind off being cold, Abby recalled the significance of those colours. Yellow, disputes; pink for divorce; blue for libel. Every so often, a passing file title would catch her eye, then disappear. Most titles she saw but did not take in. After all, her main concern was getting out of here and getting Stephen off the hook. It wasn't about perusing litigation from the past.

'I suppose we'd better think about snuggling down somewhere for the night.' Stephen hugged her closer as he said it.

'I could think of better places.'

'I could think of worse.'

They were just feet from the door when they heard the bolt being slid across.

As it started to open, Stephen pulled at it and Christopher Probert practically fell in.

'Christopher!'

'Good grief! What the devil are you doing here?'

Christopher Probert looked more horrified than surprised.

With smooth efficiency, Abby immediately manufactured and delivered a suitable excuse.

'I was inclined to think there was an old case down here that was relevant to my client's defence. Unfortunately, one of the cleaners, in her most conscientious intent, decided the unbolted door was a security risk. Voila! That is why we are here.'

'Oh!' Probert managed a nervous laugh. 'Just as well I'm here, then.'

'Just as well.'

Followed by Stephen, Abby eased herself past the slick lawyer. Time for a quick getaway. She wanted no awkward questions from him tonight.

It was only as they were walking to the car park that

Stephen asked Abby why she was so thoughtful.

She took a deep breath of night air before replying. 'It might be nothing. Perhaps I'm getting paranoid.'

'Explain yourself, woman.'

He was smiling. He noticed she was not. Her brow was still puckered in thought.

'Christopher never questioned whether I had found what I was looking for. Besides that, he didn't bother to explain why he had come back to the office and down to the dungeons. Probert's usually like a greyhound out of a trap when it comes to getting away from the office. He never hangs around there till early evening, let alone late at night.'

As they walked the ramps to the fourth floor of the car park Stephen frowned, then looked over his shoulder.

Abby caught him looking.

'Is something wrong?'

He shrugged. 'No. I think I'm just tired. I thought I saw something.'

Abby looked to where he had been looking. There were only cars. Not even shadows. The stark brightness of the fluorescents saw to that.

She touched his arm. 'Get some sleep.'

They kissed before parting. Silently, both got in their separate cars. Perhaps later, secretly, they might again come together.

Lance Vector made a note in his diary. This was one meeting he would report to his superiors.

Chapter 13

Despite his determination to continue his investigation into the Swan and Swallow affair, Stephen was becoming uneasy. In his dreams, unseen things came and went, half-formed notions, flitting suspicions. Even in broad daylight, he experienced paranoia. With every corner, he walked round, each car journey he took across London, he fully expected a barrage of reporters to leap out of a shop doorway or cab window.

Sometimes the journalists and photographers were laughably visible. Those were the ones he didn't worry about. No. It was the feeling that other eyes were watching him, eyes in a head and on a body he could not see, didn't want to see, in fact. But that person, he persuaded himself, wanted to see him. He phoned Abby and told her of his fears.

'Are you sure you're not being paranoid?'

'If I am, you can get me committed.'

'Oh, I don't think I need do that. Your madness is self-inflicted for the most part, and none of your sins are illegal between consenting heterosexual adults, even bondage, even games. I don't think you're really paranoid. Crazy maybe, but then, so am I. Crazy for you, my darling, my love.'

He laughed. Her words had had the desired effect. That was good. Anything she could say or do to lift his spirits was worth the effort. Now she had to turn him to the matter in question.

'I want you to come into the office.'

He stopped laughing. Her tone was serious.

'Have you made any progress?'

'I'll tell you when you get here.'

By the time he did get there, the last secretaries were leaving and the contract cleaners were arriving.

'I'm sorry,' he said breathlessly as he rushed into her office. 'I got delayed There's been an accident on Westminster Bridge and I had a devil of a job getting through it.'

'It doesn't matter.'

No. It didn't matter. Abby's spirits soared. He was here on business, serious, legal business, and yet somehow she knew that things would go beyond that.

Ruffled hair and a pinkness in his cheeks gave him an innocent boyish look. Given the chance, she would snatch that innocence and turn him back into what he really was; one hell of a nice guy and a good lay.

But this was business, so after he had kissed her, she bid him sit down.

'This man who's following you, do you think he's from the press?'

He nodded. 'Yes. In fact, I'm almost positive I've seen him before.' A smile came to his lips. It was alluring and warmed his face. Abby had to stop herself rushing around her desk and kissing him right there and then. 'In fact,' Stephen went on. 'I saw him at the same place I picked you up.'

Abby eyed him quizzically. 'The Red Devil Club? You've seen him there?'

'No, no.' He shook his head. 'No. The second place. When I saw you as you really are, as a barrister, not an erotic dancer.'

'Exotic,' she said.

'Pardon?'

'Exotic. You mean exotic.'

He smiled. 'Erotic, Abby darling. I know what I mean.'

A need for truth replaced their momentary lapse into humour.

'So,' Abby began, clasping her hands in front of her and trying her best to keep her eyes above the level of Stephen's waist. 'You saw him at the Humphries celebration.'

'Yes. I saw you speaking to him. He was with your colleague who burst in on us the other night.'

They said his name simultaneously. 'Vector.'

'That's right,' said Stephen. 'His name was Lance Vector and I didn't like him.'

Perplexed, Abby leaned back in her chair. 'Him! About twenty-six or so, though I wouldn't swear to it. Types like him with tousled hair and pink cheeks always look younger than they really are. And this one's a real snake. He's the nasty piece of dirt who broke the news of your "indiscretion", the one I've been trying to question.'

'I could call him worse than that.'

'No doubt. I've been trying to contact him. He's being elusive. Almost as elusive as our friend Oliver Hardiman. I will have to make the effort to question Archie Ringer about him – as Carmel of course. If Vector is going out of his way to follow you, I will have to find out who he is connected with.'

'Do you think he follows you all the time?'

'No. No, I don't think so. In fact, I'm pretty certain he's following me only when I'm with you.'

She stared. Was she really that insensitive? Was there nothing in her intuition to warn her when this creepy character was near? She shivered as she spoke.

'We'll have to be very careful in future.'

'We've been careful.'

Suddenly, he was looking at her and his eyes were sparkling like they used to. He smiled. 'Has anyone fixed that bolt yet?'

Abby was ready for him. All the while he'd been speaking, her sexual yearnings had been surging just below the surface of her outward calm. All the while she had thirsted for his lips to be on hers, hungered for his body to be on her and in her. She was as hot for him as he was for her. 'No. No one's fixed the bolt,' she said slowly as she closed the file before her. 'But there again, the cleaners are already gone. Come with me. I have to put this away. My clerk would do it usually, but he's already flown the coop. Leave your coat on the chair. You won't be needing it.'

Both knew that the other was burning with desire. Both held it in check so they could relish the full effect of it once they were down in the dungeon. Yet neither touched the other as they walked along the passageway which was well carpeted and warm.

As before, Abby produced a key at this point, unlocked a

door, and the carpet gave way to shiny brown linoleum. Stephen followed, his eyes studying her from behind, the curve of her spine, the slim waist, the well-formed buttocks.

He glanced over his shoulder.

Was there anyone behind him?

There was nothing. The door they had come through had already slammed shut.

Lights with china shades threw dubious shadows over row upon row of bundled documents.

Abigail walked a little way along. Something was nagging at her. Vector was being elusive and she needed to question him. But now was not the time or place to think on such things. Stephen was with her. They were alone among a hoard of old documents, the building empty and creaking as it settled down for the night.

As she hooked up her skirt and felt the coldness of the wall against her bare behind, and the heat of Stephen's penis nudging at her pubic lips, she resolved to ensure she got to Vector the following day, or if not him, she'd get to Archie and she'd ask him a few questions.

Chapter 14

It was two days before she saw Douglas Dermott-Embledon again, but this time, he did not see her, or at least, he did not see Abigail Corrigan. He only saw Jezebel Justice, and she was dancing naked on the stage.

Her body shone in the light of well-placed spotlights and made it seem as though her skin was only a fragile suit that could be flayed away from her flesh, leaving the real woman bare to the lustful eyes that watched her.

Tonight, the silvery hair that grew between her thighs was cleanly shaven. Tonight, she was truly naked, the lips of her sex exaggerated by the application of powdered rouge. Like a smiling mouth, she thought, when she had studied her reflection before taking the stage.

That night, once her act was over, she avoided going into the bar. She knew Douglas would be there, waiting to proposition the dark-haired, dark-eyed, and most alluring Carmel. Again, he would ask her to inspect his ship – the battleship on the water and the one between his legs.

From the shadows that hid her, she watched him. He was tall, so his eyes were always above the milling crowd. He was looking for her. She could see that much.

What she saw next was unexpected.

Douglas smiled broadly when Archie approached. Their heads closed together until it almost seemed as if one had eaten the other whole – like twin turnips that had grown into one.

Another man joined them.

Abigail – who was now Carmel – recognized Oliver Hardiman, the man who had wanted to be introduced to her on the night she had met Stephen. The man who fixed overseas investments.

Stephen would want to know about this. But first, she needed to ask a few questions. Smiling, she made her way over to the threesome whom she would, under ordinary circumstances, much prefer to avoid.

'Carmel! Darling!' Archie kissed both of her cheeks. Douglas took her hand, kissed both the back of it and her palm. His eyes betrayed what he was thinking.

Hardiman greeted her too. 'Nice to see you again – without your friend.'

Abby smiled. Valeria had learned nothing much from him. Could *she* learn more?

Instinctively, she knew that if she was too alluring, too obviously offering him the chance he had missed on their previous meeting, he would back off.

Be as you were, a small voice said inside her head. *Be as off-hand with him as you were on that first occasion.*

'Do I know you?' She held her chin high as she said it, her head slightly to one side.

His smile was slow. At first it didn't look as though he would bother to explain the details of their last meeting.

Mixed responses seemed to flicker in his eyes and around his mouth. At last he gave in.

'I asked to meet you. If you remember rightly, you introduced me to your friend and went off with another woman. A tall blonde in a grey trouser suit. Do you remember now?'

'I might do.' Her dark eyes gazed at him very steadily. Her expression betrayed nothing.

'Are you available for supper?'

'I might be.'

Although she would have liked to talk to both Archie and Douglas, Oliver Hardiman was a bigger fish to land. Somehow she had to know more about him, more about his part in the Swan and Swallow affair and the death of Carl Candel. She began to play up to him, provocative, teasing, until he suggested they find a little privacy. So, like Valeria before her, she went with him to his room at the Ritz.

Once the door to his room was closed a slight nervousness gathered in her stomach. If this had been the Railway Hotel and Stephen with her, that nervousness would quickly have turned to excitement. Instead, she only felt apprehension. Sex was a possibility; even so, she had to keep her mind clear, had to be ready to learn anything she could about this man.

It surprised her that he did not immediately kiss her, clasp her to him, or rip off her clothes. But he did none of those things. Calmly and purposefully, he walked to the bedside table and took out a large black leather bag.

She heard the sound of a zip being undone, then saw him glance over his shoulder at her before taking out the bag's contents and laying them out on the bed.

He turned to her, his hand undoing his tie, his blue eyes

flickering and seeming to concentrate on her navel rather than her face.

'I want to wear these.' His voice was almost apologetic.

Abby stared. There it all was laid out, neat, tidy and sordid on the bed. Leather bits and pieces that would restrain rather than cover anything.

You've never done anything like this, she said to herself. *You've never got involved in inflicting pain on anyone, and yet this man is going to ask you to do it. Can you do it?*

She thought of Stephen and immediately told herself that she could. That she had to. This man knew things, things that could save Stephen's reputation and throw some light on the people behind his disgrace. So she smiled and asked him what he wanted her to do.

He was a hairy man, so she was glad that he didn't hug her or try to kiss her. He was also not the most generously endowed of men, and what he had hung, listless and unimpressive, between his lean thighs.

'Tie me up first,' he ordered, 'then tell me you are going to beat me until I do what you want and say what you want me to say.'

Good grief! She was surprised. Act one, scene one, and she was in with a good chance of having him tell her exactly what she wanted to know. Of course, she would have to be subtle and form her questions in a casual manner, so that he didn't realize what she was up to.

As directed by him, she slid a pillow beneath his bottom and tied his wrists to the headboard and his ankles to the foot of the bed.

'It's in the drawer.'

Even as he said it, she could see the tip of what she definitely knew to be a whip poking out above the rim of the drawer. It was only about eighteen inches long and had nodules of spiky rubber all along its length.

As she held it before her eyes, she ran her finger down it and felt the hardness of the nodules and the sharpness of their points. She smiled and narrowed her eyes. Her thoughts about how to proceed were slowly falling into place. It was almost as though she were in court and about to cross-examine a particularly difficult witness and one she didn't like.

'I'm going to enjoy this.'

Immediately, she knew she had said the right words.

'Oh please, mistress. Please don't beat me.'

'Quiet!' The whip sang through the air and landed with a sharp whack on his bare behind. 'Speak only when you have something useful to say, slave. Dirt. Pig! Is that clear?'

'Yes.'

She lifted the whip again, beat him again, and watched with interest as the hair on his behind shivered and curled into the crack between his buttocks.

'Mistress,' she said. 'Call me mistress!'

The redness of his behind intensified as her whip landed again. He cried out, so she hit him again. His cry reduced to a whimper.

'Do we now understand? Will you now speak only when you have something to say?'

'Yes, mistress.'

'That's better. Now. Where shall we begin?'

As she spoke, and even when she had stopped speaking, she trailed the end of the whip over the pinkness of his

187

behind. His flesh quivered and it pleased her.

Now for the set piece. Now for finding out.

'Do you consider yourself a powerful man, Oliver?'

'Yes. I suppose so.'

She hit him again. 'Yes or no.'

He whimpered a bit more convincingly than before. 'Yes.'

'Are you also a wealthy man?'

'Yes.'

'What do you do to make yourself so wealthy, Oliver? Is it something wicked? Something evil?'

'I don't—'

His voice broke off as the whip again landed on his buttocks, the fine end of it licking like a small flame between his thighs.

'Aaaagh!'

Now his cry really meant something.

'Are you a cheat, Oliver? Have you ever taken something that wasn't yours?'

'No.'

This time he screamed as the whip bit into his flesh even though there was only a light redness there. Abby guessed he was losing himself in the part he was playing. Good. Soon he would be so lost in his pleasure, he wouldn't really know the significance of her questions and his answers.

'Tell me all about it, Oliver. Tell me now!'

Once more the whip laced across his naked backside. Once more he yelled out then whimpered before he began to tell her things about the cheating he had done; recent cheating, cheating that could only relate to the Swan and Swallow affair.

A coldness spread throughout Abby's mind. She knew she was breathing heavily, but not with passion. Anger simmered inside her. She would have liked to have beaten his backside black and blue, but it was imperative she played a cleverer card than that. She had to be subtle if she was to find out anything at all.

Her face remained impassive as she formed the most important question.

'Who told you to do this?'

From his shoulders to his bare behind, muscles tensed and his body hair stood erect.

'I can't tell you. They're too powerful.'

Three times more the whip rose and fell. He cried out. 'No! I can't tell you. Please! I can't! I can't!'

'Tell me. Tell me at least what sort of people they are.'

This time she made sure the fragile head of the whip again licked onto his most tender flesh; the soft velvet sack that nestled so secretively between his legs.

'A media man. And a judge.'

It was tempting to ask what their names were, but she couldn't risk doing that. Lost in his own sexual perversion, Oliver was in full flow. There was just one more question.

'Would you kill to get what you want, Oliver?'

'No, mistress. I'm not a violent man, mistress.'

He sounded as though he really were telling the truth.

'No,' she said softly. 'No. You're not the type to do it to others. You much prefer it being done to you.'

Hopefully she would never see Oliver Hardiman again, but as an act of confirmation that she did not wish to ever have to do this again, she did the same as Carl Candel's killer had done. The difference was that the whip she pushed into his rectum was not connected to the electricity. Nonetheless, he cried out, his buttocks clenching against the rigid intruder.

He murmured long, low and in a voice full of pleasure.

Abby made for the door.

'Don't wait for me, Mr Hardiman. And don't ever try to proposition me again. Okay?'

'What!' He raised his head from the pillow. She could hear the surprise, even the fear in his voice.

She was leaving him there for the chambermaid to find.

'You can't leave me here like this!'

'Don't worry. They're used to all sorts in this place.'

With that, she left him. Smiling, she made for the lift, the foyer, and the world outside. Oliver and his sort were something she wanted to leave far behind.

She glanced at her watch. Tonight she had things to do. A taxi first to the house where she lived as Carmel. The usual quick change, the usual secret route until she got to where she had left her car.

Once in it she phoned Stephen to let him know she was coming. He sounded forlorn, tired. After putting down the telephone, she made an instant decision. She also phoned Valeria.

Valeria was the only person in the world – besides Stephen – who knew she had two sides to her life. But then, so did Valeria.

'He needs cheering up,' she told her, 'and you did say for me to call if you could do something for me.'

'What do you want me to do?'

'Us, darling. It's something we've done before. Remember

that morning when we talked about leading double lives?'

'That morning when we had this guy between us and he was wrecked because we'd had him and he'd had us in every permutation we could think of?'

'You've got it.'

'I'll see you there.'

When Abby got to Stephen's apartment, the lights were already low and sweet music was playing.

'Oh, Abby.'

The moment she was through the door, he clasped her to him. He felt good against her. He smelt good too. The feel and warmth of his body turned her on like it always did. A hard bulge pressed into her belly. His lips were warm and tasted slightly salty. There and then she could have drowned in his kiss, submitted to anything his body and his mind might want her to do.

Now, she said to herself. *I have to tell him right away about Douglas and the others.* He already knew what had happened to Carl. Paul Bennet, the police inspector, had seen to that.

He frowned when she told him the rest. 'This thing seems more complicated than I'd thought.' He looked at her hard. 'More dangerous too. You do realize that?'

She nodded and felt a warm glow that he cared for her safety. 'I know.'

She described Hardiman to him, mentioned his name.

He shook his head. 'I feel I should know that name, know the description, and yet it doesn't spring easily to mind.'

Unwilling to let him go, to turn from her and fall into despondency, she cupped his face in her hands. Held him tight.

'My darling, you are so tense. You need cheering up.'

He smiled and she felt his face muscles relax beneath her touch.

'You're not kidding.'

'I'm going to do something about it. I'm going to take away your tension – all your stiffness.'

He raised his eyebrows which somehow seemed to lighten his features. He almost managed to smile. 'Like what?'

She kissed him, put all her affection into that kiss. 'You're going to experience man's greatest fantasy. And you're going to enjoy it. I promise.'

If it was possible to melt in her eyes, that was the way Stephen was feeling.

All day, despite going about his parliamentary business in as carefree a manner as possible, it was almost impossible to escape seeing raised hands, and hearing the rasp of secretive whispers. Eyes glanced at him, then flitted away, as though they did not wish to become tinged with the unspeakable, the ultimate horror – the horror of being caught out!

The look of her, the feel of her made him less fractious, though the ultimate worry was still there. Abigail got him out of his clothes and into the bedroom.

He kissed her, his proud erection tapping against her belly as she hugged him to her. She resisted the urge to touch it, to feel its velvet softness in her hand. A surprise was in store, and he would need all his strength, all his hardness to cope with that surprise.

'For a while,' she promised. 'I will make you forget everything except this pleasure I have prepared for you.'

She helped him slide between the cool cotton of the

bedclothes. Then she went to answer the doorbell.

Stephen watched his penis sway gently beneath the sheet. A small gob of liquid christened the stark whiteness. He stared, longing for her to come back, dive down onto it, lick that juice from off his very tip.

Instead he looked up as he heard a familiar voice. Smiling, Abigail came back holding the hand of an equally smiling Valeria.

'Darling,' said Valeria in a husky tone. 'Abby told me you need some cheering up.'

Stephen could not prevent his mouth from dropping open. Suddenly, the cares of recent days didn't seem so important – at least not at this moment in time.

They stood there – both of them – at the foot of the bed, and slowly, oh so slowly, they began to peel their business clothes away from their bodies.

Valeria had pale brown skin that shone as though she dabbed it with shiny stuff or rubbed it with baby oil. She wore a black bra from which her breasts spilled. Dark nipples stared like eyes from over the trimming of lace.

Stephen lay transfixed. This was a dream turned reality; a pre-waking vision he had sometimes had, one that usually left him with an immense hard-on that only the frantic caress of his hand could hope to get rid of. Hesitantly, he squeezed the very tip of his cock until he cried out, until he was sure that this was no dream, that two very beautiful women stood at the foot of his bed.

One, Valeria, was dark haired, lean as an athlete, and highly desirable.

She was naked now, the brownness of her body tight on

her bones, her nipples a purplish-black, her pubic hair black and curling tightly to her body.

Valeria was sight enough to send his blood racing to harden his member. But to have two women, and for the other to be Abby, was double the pleasure.

Abby was running her hands over her body, lifting her breasts, offering them to him as though they were plump fruit, and only he had the right price to pay for them. Never could he tire of gazing on her creamy flesh, the curve of her belly where it swooped between her thighs.

She opened them slightly. 'All for you,' she whispered, and pulled her pubic lips apart so he could see for himself the treasures they covered.

Valeria did the same.

'I think I must be dreaming,' he said. His breath rushed from his mouth as though there was no longer any room for it in his body – what with his blood racing like it was.

'Please,' he said, and held out his arms.

They lay on the bed and their warmth pressed against him, a soothing pressure that made him feel secure, that made him forget. He kissed each of them, then closed his eyes and enjoyed the sensations their closeness was generating.

Their breasts cushioned his chest, their bellies were warm against his hips. Each girl kissed his neck, bent one knee, and lay that leg across his. At the top of his thighs, he could feel the furry crispness of their pubic hair, the slick warmth of their exposed labia.

'Just lie there,' said Abigail, her breath hot against his ear. 'Close your eyes, lie there, and let us do this to you.'

For one moment he considered he might not wish to do

that; his blood was racing, he wanted to fuck them, fuck them both, but all at one and the same time. It was only to be expected. After all, it was not often a man was lying in bed with two beautiful women who wanted nothing but to comfort him. But their reasoning came to him. If he closed his eyes the sight of their bodies would be hidden from him. He would have nothing to rely on except hearing, taste, and touch.

'Please,' said Abigail softly, and kissed his eyelids.

On closing them, he suddenly knew he had done the right thing.

Their hands ran over him, evoking sensations, and taking those sensations all over his body. He groaned as they pulled the sheet away from him, felt their hands – one encircling his length, and one fondling his balls.

'Relax,' he heard her say, and he did relax.

'Open your legs,' she said, so he did that too.

Their hands continued to caress him and elicit the most delicious responses. But their mouths had moved on.

One luscious mouth was clamped over the head of his penis. The other was sucking at his scrotum so his loose sac lurched into her mouth like a portion of crumpled silk.

As Stephen groaned softly beneath their expert hands and the power of their mouths, he thought of how often he had wanted this to happen, but more often, he thought purely of Abigail, of Carmel, and of the naked dancer who exposed her body at the Red Devil Club.

As her lips found and pleasured his most sensitive spots, Abigail was thinking of him. There was no way she was going to let him be crucified by a vicious and biased press. No matter what it took, she would infiltrate where necessary whether as Carmel, Jezebel, or Abigail Corrigan QC. The end justified the means, and she meant the end to be a dismissal of the charge levelled against him.

As she suckled his balls, the soft skin that enclosed them folded over her nose, so soft that she could almost have sneezed into it. Scents of fresh sweat, masculine deodorant, and manly pheromones gently wafted over her face, entered her nose, and entered her mouth.

Adjacent to her, Valeria's plum-coloured lips moved swiftly up and down Stephen's stem and left a glistening coating in their wake.

Beneath her, she felt Stephen's muscles tensing, his pelvis moving gently up and down on the bed. Abigail left off what she was doing, her lips kissing his flesh all the way from his scrotum to his lips.

'Are you enjoying this?' she asked him.

He opened his eyes, but not widely.

'Oh, yes.' He sounded like someone who has just been wakened from a very deep sleep.

Her heart melted, and her smile reflected just how loving, how protective her feelings were for him.

Silently, between kissing his chin, his lips, and the very tip of his nose, she studied the colour of his eyes, the dark lashes that surrounded them like tall grasses around highly reflective water.

He closed his eyes when she kissed them, opened them again when her lips travelled on to kiss his cheeks and follow the firm line of his jaw. Delicately, like a hummingbird feeding on a blossoming hibiscus, she dipped her tongue into the dimple in his chin.

'This is all for you,' she said between kisses. 'I have done this for you, and I will do much more yet.'

He could not help but moan. She had left his face and was nibbling his nipples and tangling her fingers in the hairs that grew on his chest.

If his throat had not been so overcome with sounds of pleasure, he would have told her that he understood, that he knew that there would be this, and there would be much more. As in sex, they were kindred spirits.

She had Valeria get up on her hands and knees for him, and even held her friend's pubic lips open so he could see the plummy richness of her inner flesh, the ragged petals of her inner lips. Then, as he came to her, she held his rod, kissed its tip, then guided it in, one hand holding him, the fingers of the other hand still holding apart the lips of her friend.

His fingers denting Valeria's flesh, he thrust into her, then held her tightly against him until his member had plunged the deepest it could go. Valeria whimpered with pleasure, her eyes closed, oblivious and uncaring that Abigail's mouth was kissing that of the man fucking her. By virtue of her position, she knew she was just an appendage to their pleasure, and the knowledge did not disgust her.

Beneath the touch of her hands, Abigail felt Stephen's back muscles shiver, then tense as he thrust into Valeria that much harder.

Her hands swept further, her fingers following the line of his spine. Eventually, accompanied by a groan of satisfaction, her palms caressed his tight, hard buttocks, and her fingers poked precociously into the deep cleft between them. At first, startled by her intrusion, his anus was hard to

197

penetrate, but once her other hand was massaging his swinging balls, all resistance ceased, and her finger plunged in.

Their tongues entwined as his body jerked forward. His murmurs of ecstasy were lost in her mouth as she sucked in the rapacious wetness of his desire.

With each forward pulse of his pelvis, she squeezed his scrotal sac, released it on the backward stroke, then squeezed it again.

'Are you enjoying this?' Her voice was no more than a rush of breath against his ear; like the sighing of the wind, the soft closing of a door.

'Oh, yes . . .'

His answer was drawn out, long and seemingly endless until her lips again sucked on his.

His concern had lessened, jerked out of him by the motion of his pelvis thudding against the rounded buttocks of the dark-skinned Valeria. Worry was dead, drowned in the flock of sensations that centred on his weapon and browsed through his scrotum and in his anus.

And her body was against him, soft-skinned, yet firm. Sexual, lustful, but caring what he wanted, and what became of him.

It was after she had plunged her finger in up to the knuckle, that he came.

With one almighty motion, his pelvis rammed against Valeria, his seed leaving him like fire leaving the hot barrel of a flame thrower.

His eyes stayed closed when he came, his lips hungrily seeking those of the woman who was his other half, his lawyer, his playmate. As they kissed and as he came, she twisted the finger that was in him, squeezed his balls, and pressed them tightly against his body.

The evening did not end there.

She told him it wouldn't.

'Make the most of it,' she said, and as she straddled his limbs, his penis rose up to meet her descending vagina.

Valeria caught hold of her wrists, took them behind her back, and tied them with a stocking.

Then, as Abigail bounced up and down on Stephen's erection, Valeria herself mounted across his belly, her back towards Abigail.

As Valeria leaned forward Abigail did not need to know that Stephen was playing with her friend's dark boobs, his fingers twisting her tight little nipples that were already as hard as hazel nuts. Valeria dipped further forward so that one nipple could not help but go into Stephen's mouth. She took the other in her hand and rubbed it against his cheek.

With fingers outstretched, Stephen's hands came over her shoulders.

Abigail, her own hands tied behind her back, leaned forward so that both his hands were filled with her ripe breasts.

As Valeria groaned with the pleasure of him sucking her, Abigail groaned because he was squeezing and pinching her teats just as he had been Valeria's.

All the time, as this went on, Abigail bounced up and down on Stephen's groin, his penis held tightly by her muscles, her vagina just as firmly parted by his cock.

Many other positions were tried.

Both girls bent over the bed, bottoms high, and both girls got six of the best. Not slaps, or canings, but six deep thrusts from his stiff tool; first one girl, then the other. As he went into one, the other girl masturbated her friend until the six thrusts were up. They went on like that until the first girl came, then the second.

After that, it was his turn. Each girl knelt before him, and alternating, counting to sixty as they did it, each girl sucked on his cock whilst the other played with his balls. Once sixty seconds had passed they would swop places until the time came when Stephen could take no more and his seed spurted into the mouth of whoever held him.

'Like Russian Roulette,' Abigail whispered to him later.

'Or the cat getting the cream,' he countered.

So that night, Stephen Sigmund forgot his troubles, forgot that someone was out to ruin his reputation and implicate him in a public scandal and a murder enquiry. That night, he had fulfilled a lot of men's fantasies. That night had been his, and like a barrier, a defensive wall, it held back tomorrow until it could be held back no more.

Lance Vector waited ages before he spotted Abigail Corrigan. He followed her car and parked behind it outside Stephen Sigmund's home.

Another woman came that night. She had brown skin, black hair, and a very expensive taste in clothes. Her legs looked endless.

Although he did not recognize her as being anyone in the public eye, he took her picture for future reference and made a mental note to ask around about her. Perhaps that creep

Archie who managed the Red Devil Club might know her. He could ask him the next time he was there. He wasn't quite sure when that would be. In future, his presence as a reporter would not be tolerated. That jerk Archie Ringer had told him so. He'd been very annoyed with Lance for publishing his article voicing his disapproval of people in public declaring their sexual preferences. Originally, Lance had told Archie that he would simply run his eye over it and tell him where his writing might have gone astray. He hadn't said he would publish it, but he had. Lance knew that he had to use anyone and anything available to expose those who needed exposing. All the same, he didn't really like upsetting his contacts.

Through a light drizzle that softened the glare of the street lights and the headlights of passing cars, Lance had followed the Mercedes to Stephen Sigmund's place. And now he waited, thinking of having his body unite with Abigail's, and thinking even more about how he would shame her before he did so.

A light went on upstairs. He stared at it, knew it was merely a table lamp, and imagined its soft light shining on their bodies – naked bodies.

Of course, their visit could have been innocent. They might merely have dropped in for a chat, a drink. He wanted to think that, wanted to believe that Abigail Corrigan was mending her ways and that somehow her virginity would re-establish itself.

His experience of the world told him otherwise however. He was a purveyor of sin, a sniffer-dog of vice. Abigail was falling, he told himself. She was falling from grace and flouting the law.

He didn't question the fact that there was no law to govern sexual interludes in private. Lance was geared to reporting people's sex-lives as though they were the only ones that did it, and the only ones who shouldn't be doing it.

As he sat there thinking about her rolling around with Sigmund, visions of her chastisement came to his mind. He would beat her. Yes. He would beat her. But first, he would have her naked, her arms fastened high above her head so that her breasts bunched together. Not that bunching together would make them less vulnerable. The dog collar would again be around her neck. Yes. He liked the thought of that. And because he was always concerned about his mother's well-being as well as her good opinion of him, he would gag Abigail's mouth so her shouts would disturb no one.

Then he would pick up his camcorder, get her on film so that each time she was tempted to stray from him and from the path of righteousness, he would run the tape through the machine so that she would tremble and be in awe of him. Once she admitted her guilt, he would kiss her all over, and like he had seen others do, he would have her kiss his lips and kiss his penis before she begged him to take her, to lay her down, spread her legs, and push himself into her.

Hidden by the dark shadows of the city street, he touched the front of his trousers, rubbed his fingers up and down a few times, then groaned as his semen gushed into his well-scrubbed, well-pressed jeans.

Chapter 15

The morning newspapers were full of speculation about Carl Candel's death, and Stephen Sigmund's part in it. Most of it was spread over the front page, but taking up two thirds of page two was an article entitled "OUT WITH IT".

Abigail stared at the photograph of a smiling Carl Candel that was obviously taken some time before his death and not too long after he had left school or college. The photograph of Stephen was more recent. Although it showed him with his head high, there was a hunted look in his eyes. Outwardly, she groaned with the weight of his pain, and inside, she had an irresistible desire to hold him to her, to stroke his hair and whisper soothing words into his ear.

After reading the first paragraph, the author's name caught her eye. Archibald Newton Ringer. Having never taken an interest in Archie's life, she had been unaware that he held such strong views on men in public life not declaring their sexual preferences. The article in itself she could easily have dismissed, but he was citing in print that he himself had seen Stephen dressed as a woman. He would swear to it.

Although Abigail knew the precise reason why Stephen had been dressed that way, the public, because of the manner in which the media presented it, would take the view that where there was smoke there was fire.

Regardless, also, of transvestism not being evidence of homosexuality, Archie was catering to the public's ingrained conception that the two did go hand in hand. Anger made her cheeks burn, her chest heave. She raised her hand, bunched her fingers. 'Archie! Why have you done this?' It was hard not to hit her desk top with her clenched fist. Her concern was too great to ignore.

Once her heartbeat and her breathing were under control, she picked up the phone. She had to speak to Stephen, if only to try her best to soothe his hurt pride, his jagged nerves.

His voice was soft as though recent events had taken something from it.

'Are the press still hanging about?' she asked him.

'Yes, and they're doing their best to make more out of it than there is. I'm only glad you were with me when Candel got killed. Otherwise, they'd be saying I killed him.'

'I'm glad I was with you too.' Her voice faltered. 'Did you also see that Archie Ringer said he saw you dressed in women's clothes?'

'Yes, but I notice he doesn't mention me going off with a dancer by the name of Carmel, does he?'

'No. I wonder why?'

She wanted to say more, much more; about how she wanted to be with him, to lie naked beside him and enjoy the feel of his hands swooping up and down her body, the look of his eyes as he hung over her, his member deeply embedded in her flesh, the rough hardness of his thighs against the softness of hers.

There seemed to be enough in the words they did say, as though everything else she wanted, he wanted, was automatically transmitted by telepathic means.

'You know how I feel about you,' she said at last. 'And because I feel that way, I have to go. I have to ask questions. I feel obligated. It was my idea that you go in disguise.'

He told her he knew how she was feeling, told her that he appreciated all she was doing for him, all she had done. She knew he meant her realizing his favourite fantasy and providing a willing accomplice. She was glad she knew Valeria.

'Will you participate in another fantasy for me?'

'Anything. Anything at all that will help lift your spirits.'

She heard his grateful sigh. 'Put your hand on your breast. Pretend it's my hand. Will you do that?'

'Yes.' Her answer was immediate, though the way she said the word was long and slow.

Just like her answer, she moved her hand slowly, cupped her palm over her blouse. It was as though she were feeling the shape of her breast for the very first time.

Her breathing altered. She gasped at her own touch, then closed her eyes.

'That's it,' he said in response to her gasp. 'Imagine it's my hand.'

She undid one button, then two, let her fingers into the gap and touched the warm smoothness of her breast.

'How does it feel?' His voice was low, husky.

She sighed, caught her breath before answering. 'Delicious. My fingertips are cold. My breast is warm.'

'And soft? Tell me it's soft. Please . . . Please . . .' His words rolled with his hushed breath over the telephone.

Abigail swallowed and because her breast was responding to her touch, her legs responded also and gradually parted.

'My breast feels soft, but firm. My skin is like satin. I am sliding my fingers across it, tracing its shape. Now I am running them around my nipple . . . Oh!' She said it suddenly, plaintively, wantonly. Hard as a plum stone, her nipple grew beneath the lilting touch of her fingers.

Stephen spoke again. 'Is your nipple very hard now?'

'Yes. Yes, it is!'

'Put down the receiver. Put your telephone on speaker.'

She did as he said, flicked the "speak" switch, and leaned closer to it so that she could keep her voice low and hear his better.

'Now what, Stephen? What do you want me to do now?'

Her body was quaking for the need to hear his voice, for his directions as to how she should pleasure herself, and at a distance, give him pleasure too.

'Are you wearing stockings?'

'Of course.' She always wore stockings. That way, the naked-ness of her sex seemed to extend halfway down her thighs.

'Are they black?'

'They are always black.' Of course they were. Black stockings accentuated the white nakedness of her flesh.

'I want you to pinch your nipples, to pull on, play with as I do.'

'I will. Yes. Yes. I will.' She said it breathlessly, almost as if the words and the moan that escaped from her throat were one and the same.

She heard him groan too, heard him sigh, then take a deep

breath. With that sigh, that breath, she could imagine the hardness of his cock, his own hand working on it as hers would have done if she had been with him.

'Put your other hand under your skirt. Run it up over your stocking. Stroke your inner thighs with your fingers – but lightly – very lightly.'

Murmuring sweet mews of delight, she followed his instructions. As her hand moved upwards, so did the hem of her skirt. Cool air touched her flesh, and a soft throb began in her sex. Mounting desire urged her to quicken her movements, to bypass her thighs and get straight to her sex and tease the ache that hung so heavy between her legs. But she would not do that. She would obey him. At this moment in time, her hands were his hands, and his pleasure was her pleasure.

'Take your fingers higher, but keep your other hand on your breast. Feel the soft crease where your leg meets your body. Trail your fingers across, then slide one – just one – downwards until it meets the very tip of your divide. Are you doing that for me?'

Her hand and her fingers followed his instructions. Her breath rasped from her throat, but she managed to speak. 'Yes, Stephen! Yes!'

A loud sigh tumbled like surf on the beach, then reformed as the sweet sensations of arousal soared and dived around the movement of both hands; the one on her sex, and the one on her breast.

'Hmmmm,' he moaned long and low. It was wordless, and yet that sound told her all he was doing, all he was feeling. On the other end of the telephone, his eyes too would be closed, his hands too would be exploring and giving him pleasure.

'Push your finger further. What do you feel?'

Flesh slippery with sexual juices divided as she obeyed him. She gasped before she spoke. 'I feel the touch of my flesh, and the touch of my finger. Both are feeling, both are giving and receiving pleasure. My flesh is warm and wet, and clings to my finger. My finger is hard, yet gentle as it travels onwards. My petals divide, I feel – it feels – I . . . !'

Her words were lost on a tide of sensation. Her finger had found her clitoris, her clitoris was responding to the touch of her finger.

'Have you found it?'

'Yes . . . !'

'Travel on,' he gasped, his voice demanding, his breathing laboured with the heat of his own desire. 'Travel on. Slide over your flesh, dip your finger into your body. Do it!'

Regretfully, for she had enjoyed the touch of her finger on her bud, the touch of her clitoris on her finger, she did as he said.

As her finger entered her vagina, she cried out.

'How does it feel?' he asked.

'Ohhhh . . . Good!'

'Push it in, out. In, out. In, out!'

'I am. I am!'

There was urgency now in her voice, demand in his.

Climax was coming to both of them. Of course she could not see the expression on his face as his semen travelled up his shaft, but she knew instinctively that he was feeling as she was. She just knew it.

'Press your thumb upon your clitoris. Tap it gently, firmly, then gently again. Tease it, please it, and when you feel it coming, when you feel it release its tension, plunge your finger into yourself more fiercely, more quickly. Will you do that?'

'Yes!' she cried. 'Yes. Yes. Yes!'

She was coming. In one, spring-loaded spiral of sensation, her climax was coming, twisting, spinning like a fast-turning top that whirrs and whirrs until gravity grasps it, slows it and sends it soaring out of control, shooting off in all directions until the spin slows, topples, and eventually falls over.

Silence followed. She heard him breathing. No doubt he could also hear her.

'Was it good?' she asked him. Basically, she knew it must have been, but were his spirits any improved? Under the circumstances, it was a lot to expect.

'Oh, yes. It was good all right. It was almost as good as you being with me. Did you enjoy it?'

'Yes.'

'Are you still wet?'

She touched herself before she replied. Residual sensations made her hips jerk away from her hand.

'Very,' she said, smiled, and hoped her smile was reflected in her words. 'You have made me very wet, my love. Very wet indeed.'

He did not answer. Not for almost a minute. When he did, his question took her unawares.

'Is that what I am? Your love?'

A vision of him came to her head. The darkness of his hair, the velvet brown of his eyes. That lopsided smile that made her melt, made her laugh. Denial was impossible.

'My love.' She said it softly, sincerely. And that, she said to herself, is why I am laying myself open to the advances of other men and to danger – for the sake of my love.

She told him again that she had to go, that she had to make more enquiries. He understood, wished her luck, told her to be careful.

Paul Bennet was the first person she wanted to talk to. She had intended going to the police station to see him. As it happened, he got to her first. He telephoned, and that was something she was glad about. She didn't have to see him, and he didn't have to see her.

He confirmed that he had been keeping a watch on those toilets that night. It was the usual pitch – there was nothing much else going on, and the right time to catch some sleaze balls.

'But did you see Stephen Sigmund actually committing the act you are charging him with?'

Bennet paused. 'He was in there, and the deceased – Carl Candel – was in there.'

'But did you actually see them committing the act, Inspector?'

'Not exactly, but . . .'

'Did you go into the toilets?'

'Yes.'

'So where were Mr Sigmund and Mr Candel?'

'In the gentlemen's toilets, and Mr Sigmund was dressed as a woman. I recognized him at once. Mr Candel confirmed what they were there for.'

Her confidence took a nose-dive, but she quickly

recovered. 'So you, yourself, did not see an act take place?'

'No, but then I didn't need to. Candel admitted what they'd been doing.'

'Mr Sigmund denies this. He said it was to do with other things – with a financial scandal. He states that Mr Candel informed him he had evidence to the effect that the wrong man is being tried.'

'That's his story. There's always some fantastic excuse with the likes of him. All bum bangers are the same.'

Abigail's face reddened. 'Regardless of your vulgar comments, Inspector, you still have a case to prove. My client is not denying he was there, but he refutes that any homosexual act took place. He was there because Candel claimed that he had vital information regarding corruption in high places.'

Bennet sniggered on the other end of the phone. 'That isn't what Candel said.'

'Then Candel was lying.'

'How do you know that, Miss Corrigan? Unless of course you yourself are otherwise intimately aware of Mr Sigmund's likes and dislikes.'

Abigail swallowed what she truly wanted to say. So far, Bennet had not recognized her as Carmel, and she had no intention of aiding the recollection.

'Well, I certainly won't be able to question Candel, will I, Inspector?'

Bennet sniggered. 'Not after the last bum bang he had, Miss Corrigan. Let's face it, the last bum bang he had literally blew his mind!'

Abigail slammed down the phone.

Contrary to her usual physical state after making enquiries, she was seething. Paul Bennet was an arrogant pig. But it wasn't just his arrogance that was troubling her.

As Carmel, she had picked him up at the club – or rather, he had nagged her into accepting his company. His good looks coupled with a hint of danger drew her to him. Against her better judgement, she had gone with him. Archie, she remembered, had helped her make her decision. "As a favour to me," he'd said, and she'd gone along with it.

Handsome as he was, she suspected Paul Bennet might also be violent, but like a magnet, such an assumption only heightened his attractiveness. Like many women before her, she thought she could counteract such a character trait.

Sensing this fact though, she was alert to any signs of violence from him. She simply could not afford to be bruised or injured by him, so she had gone along with everything he had wanted her to do. Even now, she could remember the tightness of the rope around her wrists and her ankles, the creeping fear as he had gagged her mouth and covered her eyes. Only by a superb effort of self-control had she endured all that happened next.

Without a doubt, she had heard the clicking of a camera as she had lain there trussed up like a game fowl. Obviously, Paul Bennet liked to keep pictures of his sex sessions. But it had not stopped merely at taking pictures.

He had caned her behind and oiled her anus. Then, as he pushed his fingers into her rear portal, she had heard the clicking of a camera.

He put other objects inside her, taking one item out, and putting another in.

For the first time since tuning into her 'other' life, she had felt defiled.

After he had pushed himself into her oiled passage, and sent his river of semen into her hallowed depths, he untied her, asked her to stay the night, and asked also whether he could see her again.

Fear had gripped her, yet she congratulated herself on her self-control. 'No,' she had said. 'I don't make a habit of second dates.'

His fist had clenched, and she had stepped back before it could connect with her face.

Luckily, he had drunk too much to be as quick on his feet as she was.

She left.

On the next occasion she saw him at the club, he made a bee-line for her, threatened to make a scene if she didn't go with him. She had refused, and when he had starting shouting and lunged at her, she had brought her foot up into his crotch, and with mute delight, had smiled as the softness of his scrotum and the sleek confidence of his face had crumpled under the violence of her kick.

Archie's 'boys' had taken over from then on. He was instantly banned, though Archie did take him into the office first.

For what, she didn't know for sure, but could guess. Paul Bennet was a policeman. No matter what his status, no matter that those of higher office than him frequented the place, it was wise to keep him sweet. Keeping him sweet meant payola. A hundred pounds? Possibly. Perhaps more.

She wanted to ask Archie Ringer about Paul Bennet, and also about Douglas Dermott-Embledon. She would also refer to the article in the papers.

It was a Tuesday night, and although it was not her night to dance, she went along to the Red Devil Club, her black wig neatly framing her face. Her blue eyes, camouflaged by black contact lenses, were alert, aware of every lewd glance, every hot look. No one could have guessed her true identity, and no one would have wanted to. She was all black and red, a stunning contrast to her white skin. She was beautiful, and appreciated as she was.

'Hiya, doll!'

Carmel, the dark-eyed beauty who glided rather than walked through the darkness of the club, the tables, the seated and standing customers, ignored them, but took note of who they were.

A tall American was eyeing her up and down and licking his lips like some old hound about to get dinner. She laid her hand flat on his chest, pushed him gently to one side, but used him as an excuse to wend her way to a door marked private that opened into a marble-floored passageway. Turning immediately right, she walked to the end, and entered Archie's office without bothering to knock.

Archie was sitting behind his desk, head back, eyes closed, and moaning as though he were having the most beautiful dream. He must have heard her enter because suddenly his eyes flicked open. They had a wild, glazed look about them as if he wasn't really seeing her. Abigail glanced round the room, half-expecting to see that he was watching some horny video or had some lean youth in there naked and twirling on the spot so he could see everything he had to offer.

There was no one and nothing.

Archie himself glanced down into his lap and gulped before looking up at her.

'What . . . um . . . do you want, Carmel?'

The long, lithe woman, who he could half-fancy if she had been a boy, closed the door firmly behind her.

Much as she loathed him, she put on her warmest voice. 'I'm sorry to disturb you, Archie, but as our agreement is up for renewal shortly, I thought it prudent that I come along and smooth over any problems that might have occurred in the last few months.'

'Problems?'

His eyes were as wide and vacant as his voice.

'Yes. Like that bit of trouble with Paul Bennet. It's just that I remembered I never thanked you and the boys for rescuing me from him a while back. I owe you for that.'

At first, Archie looked as though he wished she weren't there at all, let alone apologizing for something he'd already forgotten.

His soft lips stretched into a smile. 'Do not trouble yourself, pretty lady. The matter was taken care of and forgotten. Our agreement will be renewed, I can assure you. One appearance, once a month. Same as before.'

'Thank you for that, but you understand, I could not help being concerned. I believe he was a policeman.'

'Yes. He was.'

'An inspector?'

'Yes.'

Archie was blinking and seemed suddenly sparing with his words. It was out of character.

Abigail – Carmel – persisted. 'I hope I didn't make any

215

trouble for you. It's not entirely diplomatic to ban someone like him, is it?'

'No. No. Not really. Not really.'

He seemed to be gasping suddenly, his breath coming in short, swift rushes mixed with a low groaning noise. If both be-ringed hands hadn't been resting before him on his desk she would have been sure he was masturbating.

Apart from raising her eyebrows slightly, her expression did not betray her thoughts.

The groaning stopped and Archie cleared his throat.

He sighed. 'My dear Carmel. Do not trouble yourself about the gentleman concerned.'

He made as if to get up from his desk, then stopped. His hands disappeared into his lap. There was the unmistakable sound of a zip being fastened before he got to his feet. Abigail – Carmel – eyed him speculatively.

Her need to help Stephen overwhelmed her curiosity. 'I'm sorry if it caused any trouble. I presume you gave our policeman friend some incentive to prevent his naturally inquisitive nose from sniffing any deeper?'

Archie took hold of her arm and laughed as he guided her towards his office door.

'Indeed I did, young lady. Indeed I did!'

'Did he cost you very much?'

She knew she might appear over inquisitive herself, but she just had to know exactly what bribes someone like Bennet was likely to accept.

Archie hesitated before he answered. There was a speculative look in his eyes, and he had sucked his bottom lip into his mouth.

His hesitation disappeared just before he smiled.

'I suppose I could tell you. In fact, seeing as you have been with me a while now, I think I can safely take you into my confidence and initiate you into the inner circle of enlightened individuals who partake of my services. I have asked you to go upstairs with them before, but you know my policy. The decision is yours. No one here is forced into entertaining my more important acquaintances.'

What am I doing? she asked herself. But it was too late. She had asked, and Archie had answered, and with his answer had come an invitation, an invitation she did not necessarily require.

If it were not for Stephen and his plight she would have clung onto her independence, her aloofness to whatever other people in the club got up to in the upstairs rooms. For Stephen, she would sacrifice her principles and her body, if necessary.

She smiled at Archie, nodded in the affirmative, and whispered a long yes.

'In half an hour, I will take you upstairs. For membership of this inner club, Bennet was willing to stomach being banned from the main club. Like some of our other members, those who wish to preserve their privacy, he enters from the back staircase.'

And Hardiman too, she thought to herself, unless the predicament she had left him in at the Ritz had encouraged him to mend his ways. She doubted it, and knew she had to do her best to avoid the man. Next time she saw him it might be revenge he was wanting rather than sex.

So slow had been their progress to the door, and so even-toned had been Archie's voice, that she was hardly conscious of being back in the marble-floored passageway before the door closed behind her.

Being of a naturally inquisitive nature – a bit like Bennet to some extent – (perhaps that had been where the attraction lay that had made her accept his invitation?) she walked down the passageway, lifting the spikes of her black high heels so that she made as little sound as possible.

Taking a deep breath, she slid her fingers around a bright, brass knob, and turned it. The door opened, and she peered in. There was nothing to see. The room was in darkness, and she dare not switch the light on.

She became suddenly aware that Archie's door was about to open, and not wishing to be considered nosy and perhaps lose her part-time vocation – at least, not until she had helped Stephen – she stepped quickly in behind the open door.

The knob in her hand, and the door almost closed, she heard Archie's voice, and she heard someone else too.

With the door open no more than an inch, she peered out. Realization of what Archie had been doing hit her like a bag of set cement.

When she had entered his office, he had seemed to be in ecstasy, and accordingly, she had looked all around for some instrument of arousal. She had seen none. She also remembered his hands travelling to his lap and the sound of a zip being fastened. For one moment, she had thought that perhaps she had caught Archie having a swift hand-job whilst leering at some naked youth.

The truth now hit her as she watched the naked dwarf stalk

out of Archie's office, his penis reaching almost to his fat little knees.

She gulped. What was this? Her impression of the world of dark nights and brightly-lit clubs had always been in direct contrast with her other world of lengthy tomes and shuffling judges in red gowns and white wigs.

Alluring it might have been, seedy even, sordid. But it was also real, tangible, and fulfilled that half of her nature the law could not provide for.

The appearance of the naked dwarf and the realization of what he'd been doing below Archie's desk made her pinch herself. It made her wonder afresh at her acceptance of Archie's offer to go upstairs.

Never having been there before, she had only guessed at what might go on up there. It had occurred to her that those with sexual hang-ups went up there to thrash around wildly with some raging nympho in private, but the appearance of the dwarf made her wonder.

Like an escapee from some adult fairy tale, he had come out of Archie's office and marched off towards the door at the very far end of the passageway, and hence – she supposed – to the rooms upstairs.

What, she wondered, awaited her up there?

Because more hefty questions were still in her mind, she had not considered the personal consequences of a trip upstairs. But someone was intent on damaging Stephen's reputation and she was certain the perpetrator was one of those who frequented the rooms above. It was no longer enough that Stephen be proved innocent. Whoever had orchestrated such a thing and paid Carl Candel for his part in

it, now had to be brought to book. It could also be assumed
that whoever had arranged the meeting between Stephen and
Carl, had also arranged for Carl to be murdered.

A memory of Carl came to her. Carl Candel lying face
down on the bed, the metal rod sticking out from between his
buttocks, the redness, the blackness of the marks on his skin,
and the terrible smell of half-cooked flesh.

The shudder that came to her had to be endured. So too
did the going upstairs.

Archie Ringer breathed a huge sigh once Wee Willy had
closed the office door behind him.

He had needed those fleshy lips around his penis, had
needed to close his eyes and ride a swell of pleasure in order
to forget he had ever met Lance Vector, the tabloid leech.

'You had no business publishing that under my name. I did
not, Mr Vector, give you permission to reproduce that article,
and I did not specifically say that it was I who noticed that
Stephen Sigmund was dressed as a woman.'

No matter how much he had shouted, Vector had sneered
and tossed what looked to be about a hundred pounds on his
desk.

'Your cut, old chum. Spend it on your vices – or your
boys.'

'You had no business . . .'

Vector had looked at him in disgust, then turned his back
and opened the office door. He had paused before going.

'Nice little business you got here, Archie. Take care now.
You know the only reason you're not front-page news, is
because your clientele own the paper. But, as you no doubt

also know, they do tire of things. One club this year, another one next year. And then, Archie old chum, beware! Beware, old chum, because old Lance will come to get you!'

Archie had told him to get out. He had only wanted the journalist's opinion of his writing. If *he* had published the article, it would have been in a gay magazine and he would not have divulged names. But Lance had told him he needed to put in the name of the person concerned in order to stress the point he was making. Lance Vector had lied and had published without his permission, and Archie felt guilty about the way things had gone.

Vector himself had been unsettling enough. But he was a mere shrimp in the big scheme of things and didn't even know it. But Archie knew it. There were bigger fish than him, cruel, monstrous ones with cold eyes and teeth that could bite.

The other man came to see him. He wasn't the man himself, the man who owned the club as well as a newspaper and employed Archie to run it. But he was one of his minions – one of his more forceful minions.

He was smooth to look at, this other man, his skin nut brown, his hair black, tied at the nape of his neck, and hanging in a tangle of curls down his back. His eyes were like hot coals – a scalding yellow bordering on orange. An unusual man. A dangerous man. All the same, Archie could quite easily have fancied him. But you didn't make sexual overtures to that sort. You waited for them to make sexual overtures to you, and however they wanted it, you complied.

Charwallah was dangerous to know and even more deadly if you happened to be the subject of his latest mission. Not for the sleek Anglo-Indian the crude obviousness of the gun or the knife. Archie had it on good authority that Charwallah made a study of ways to kill, ways to have men tormented before they died. Apparently he was a bit of a history buff with a specific interest in the more gruesome killings of the past. Charwallah's recent visit had been the last straw. In a threatening tone, he'd asked Archie about the night he'd spotted that damned MP in that female get-up. Takes one to know one as they say. Charwallah had asked who the bloke had been talking to, what he'd had to drink, who he'd gone off with.

He'd told him that Sigmund had come in with Valeria, a ripe black tart with looks that most men would die for. He'd also told him that Sigmund, with blonde wig flying, had gone off with his exotic dancer, Jezebel Justice, whose real name was Carmel. He described her black hair, her long legs, and the disdainful look in her ebony eyes. Charwallah looked keen to know her better.

'Where can I find this woman?'

At the time he was asking the question, Archie had no option but to speak in a very high voice on account that Charwallah was crushing his balls. Charwallah's fingernails, which felt as if the natural ones had been replaced with ones made from steel, were digging into his soft flesh.

He'd given him the address. He'd had no option.

The event had completely unsettled him. Wee Willy had helped him to forget – up to a point. Carmel had entered the room and, on seeing her, Archie's nervousness returned. He did his best to appear calm, even friendly. Anything she asked him he would answer regardless. For once, she seemed quite keen to see what went on upstairs, and he would show her that too. But, poor girl, he couldn't possibly tell her that something nasty was on her trail.

Chapter 16

'This way, my dear.'

Archie Ringer's voice was as hushed as their footfalls on the thickly-carpeted stairs that led from the club below to the more private establishment above.

Abby followed. She would do anything he wanted until she judged the time right to ask him about the article he had written. For now, although alert, she allowed herself to enjoy the opulence around her.

Rich oak panelling lined a wide landing, and brass picture lights emphasized bob-tailed horses in eighteenth-century paintings. Mahogany doors with brass handles and brass numbers ran down a warmly-lit passageway.

'Good evening, Mr Ringer, Miss Carmel.'

The sudden voice came from a silver tray that passed her at waist level and held an ice bucket with champagne and two glasses. Its appearance startled her. Where had the voice come from? As it continued along the passage, she could see the short, stocky legs and body of the dwarf she had seen earlier.

'That's Wee Willy,' said Archie, with a grin.

'Really?' Abby raised an amused eyebrow. 'There's not

many who'll admit to that, now is there?'

It was easy to laugh. Laughter hid the apprehension she was feeling. Here she was, upstairs in some sort of inner sanctum where only the most revered of Archie's clients ever went. *What did they get up to up here? Was she entirely sure she wanted to find out?*

Aware that she was keeping a very obvious gap between her and Archie, she was also telling herself to relax. *Go with the flow*, she told herself. *Think of Stephen. Think of his body, naked, his penis erect and waiting for you.* Coolness born of determination and affection took over. Suddenly, Archie didn't seem so bad.

'In here.' Archie's wide smile exposed a mouthful of bright, white teeth, outdone only by the flash of gold fillings. He stooped slightly and unlocked a door marked private. He reached in. A light came on.

'In here,' he said again, his teeth gleaming like a light beckoning ships onto rocks. Odd, she thought, that she'd never seen him smile like that before. More sincere, somehow. Archie was a strange man, his face a mask he assumed for the public who frequented the bar below. Tonight, that mask had slipped a little. There was an odd liquidity in his eyes, a wetness around his mouth that made his lips look as if they were made of saturated clay. He looked jittery, as though something had upset or even frightened him.

His palm was clammy against her back as he guided her through the door and along a narrow passageway of blue and beige, a cool, modern atmosphere as opposed to the richness of the more public landing.

The pictures that adorned these walls were soft, contemporary watercolours that depicted shapes rather than recognizable things.

He paused before the first one, an odd concoction of tangerine cubes overlaid with swirling circles of white and blue. 'Do you like it?' There was mischief in his eyes, but she knew she had to answer.

'There's a certain quality about it. I would say it was calming, peaceful.'

His smile yawned across his face. 'It's a façade,' he said. 'It is a mere mask to what lies beneath the surface – just like people – just like us.' A sheen of sweat seemed to tremble on his forehead.

His arm shook and his hand wavered as he took hold of the picture frame. Amazed, Abigail watched as the picture opened up away from the wall. It was a trick of sorts, not really a picture frame at all. The whole thing was a small door. Behind the door was a pane of glass, and beyond the glass was a room.

'This,' said Archie, waving his hands in a flamboyant fashion, but biting his lip, 'is where my most valued clients act out their fantasies.'

For a moment, Abigail froze, her eyes bright as she stared at the glass and the room beyond where two figures were absorbed in an act of domination and submission. Obviously, the window was a mirror to those within the room.

Ever alert to useful information, she heard what Archie had said, but more importantly, she understood the implications. Men, she judged, were at their most vulnerable when indulging their most depraved desires. With careful teasing, a man could be made to divulge his most important secrets without being aware that he had done so.

'Fairy tales turned to fact.' Her eyes met Archie's. She spoke slowly. 'Fact can be stranger than fiction – but very arousing.'

'Then look,' he said as she drew near the glass. 'Look and see if you can imagine what he's feeling – what she's feeling.'

Even though she didn't particularly like being near Archie, she put up with it for the sake of seeing the room on the other side of the glass.

Coolly, calmly, she watched what was going on.

Archie pressed a button just beneath the edge of the glass. The silent tableau suddenly became vocal.

'You are a dog, aren't you? Nothing but a dirty little dog.'

The voice was female, the woman it came from almost six feet tall, her body bound in strips of studded leather that left certain squares of flesh unfettered and open to view. Her hair was golden brown and tied into a high ponytail that reached almost to her waist.

False, Abigail decided.

Cringing on all fours at the woman's feet was a man wearing nothing but a thick dog collar. A chromium chain ran from the studded collar he wore around his neck to her hand. His head was hanging down, face unseen, and he was wailing.

'Please. Please.' It was a pitiful sound, a sound begging for more rather than for less. He got what he asked for, yelping like a beaten dog as a black-booted foot connected with his ribs.

'Damn dog! You are a disgrace, you mangy whelp. Think

you would like to be more than you are, don't you? Think you would like to be a dirty little dog, don't you?'

'Please . . .'

The word was lost on a wail as the woman who held the chain leash shoved the toe of her boot between his thighs and pressed his drooping sac against his body.

'I know your sort,' went on the voice. 'I know you'd like me to get on my hands and knees and for you to bump up and down on me. But you're not going to, because I'm not going to give you pleasure. You're going to pleasure me!'

Spellbound by the scene before her, Abigail watched as the woman took the length of chain down over the man's back.

'Put your hands behind your back,' the woman ordered. 'Get up onto your knees.'

Abigail gasped. Before her eyes, his face bathed in ecstasy, was Douglas Dermott-Embledon. *What price now Government departments?*, she thought.

She saw him flinch as the woman brought the chain through his legs and looped it around his stiff member before taking it back through his legs and fastening it at the back.

The eyes of the would-be peer rolled in his head, and a low groan grated from his throat.

'Now,' said the woman, smiling with satisfaction as she leant back in a leather Chesterfield chair and viewed him through the valley formed by her naked breasts. 'Now you will pleasure me.'

With that, she opened her legs. Obviously, her costume of criss-crossed strips of leather was designed with such an occurrence in mind. From within a bush of black hair, the pink lips of her sex shone with sexual moisture.

On his knees, Douglas walked forward, his penis throbbing and his eyes fixed on the yawning divide.

'Get to it!'

The voice was as sharp as the sound her leather whip made as she laced it across his shoulders.

'Yes, mistress. Yes.'

Douglas bent his head. His tongue licked delicately at her flesh before she grabbed the back of his head and pushed him onto her.

'That's better,' she cried, and laughed as she jerked her hips up and down on the chair, and laid the whip, with increasing ferocity, across his back.

Could he breathe? Abby asked herself. Was he likely to drown in the nectar that poured from the woman's fully-bloomed flower?

'Enough!' The woman's order made her wince.

The man in the room huddled over like a frightened hedgehog. It was, Abby supposed, a stance he was expected to take, and had probably assumed many times before.

'I think this one's almost finished. We'll stay and watch, shall we?'

Abigail only nodded. She had almost forgotten that Archie was even there.

Through the glass, she saw the woman stand up, spread her legs and brace herself. Douglas was still trussed up, and still on his knees.

'Get on it!'

Vicious fingers with black-painted nails dug into Douglas's silver-grey hair. His face creased up and showed his age. Forcefully, his head was pushed once more onto her sex. She was tall, though not tall enough for Douglas to accommodate her entirely. He had to bend his head back, and as he bent his head, he groaned. The chain that wound around and around his stem and his balls, pulled more tightly.

The woman's hips tilted backwards and forwards. Her head was thrown back, and short gasps of delight raced from her mouth.

'Keep going, you little dog. Keep going!'

Douglas did keep going. If he tried to slow, she beat him with the strip of leather and pushed her pussy into his mouth with grim determination. Tight restraint obviously agreed with Douglas. Having someone who was restrained mouthing her pussy, obviously agreed with the woman. Their need to come superseded anything else. It was etched on their faces, breathless in their voices.

Abigail changed stance. No one, she told herself, could watch something like this and not be affected by it.

Although she was not with them, she knew at what stage they were, knew that his sperm would be swimming up a pulsating canal, that the woman's clitoris would be hard, though the rest of her sex would be as soggy as wet dough.

Smooth, debonair Douglas liked to be disciplined. What a turn up. But what about Bennet? The thought of what sort of things he got up to made her shiver. She remembered how degraded he'd made her feel in her disguise as Carmel. She also recalled how repugnant she had found his comments regarding Stephen.

'Bennet accepted club membership very gratefully,' Archie snorted.

'More so than money? I find that hard to believe.'

She stared determinedly into Archie's eyes. In that one moment, she thought she saw some expression there that was secretive and a little frightening, but Archie quickly turned his eyes back to the scene beyond the glass. Douglas was climaxing into the earth of a potted plant that had been conveniently placed there by the woman.

'That's it,' she was saying. 'My plant needs your milk on a regular basis. Come on. Cough it up!' She gripped him and shook the last droplets from his member.

Abby stared at the scene, heard what the woman said, but was also listening to Archie.

'Bennet knows a good deal when he sees one. Anyway, he's like a lot of other men with responsible jobs. He needs a little light relief now and again. Not that I like the man mind you, but then, darling lady, there are few people I like, and I've found no one yet who does not indulge in their own private fantasies when the moment occurs.'

Archie pressed the button that turned off the sound, then placed the picture back across the glass. He made an attempt to appear jovial, but she sensed some underlying worry, some niggling doubt.

'You look worried. What's the problem?'

He started, pursed his lips and suddenly avoided looking at her.

'Oh. Nothing really.'

She touched his arm, wondered about the thickness of his coat sleeve and the thinness of the arm beneath it. The fact that he was trembling was obvious.

'You can tell me, Archie darling. Come on. What is it?'

He looked, looked away, then back again.

Then he patted her hand.

'Nothing for you to worry about, my dear. I'm just a little annoyed this evening. Something went astray. Something important.'

'Oh really?' This was too good to be true. He was telling her what she wanted to hear without her having to ask a question. 'I'm surprised such a fastidious man as yourself, Archie, could be so careless. What have you lost?'

He sniggered, patted her hand again.

'Something I wrote, and something I said. Never, my dear girl, never, ever trust the press. They're all charlatans, all snakes. But keep away from a journalist called Lance Vector. He's a muckraker. And a thief! He stole an article I wrote and changed it about to suit himself and that sordid paper he writes for.' He clicked his lips as he shook his head. 'Never trust a journalist or a lawyer!'

Abby winced but didn't bite. For the first time, it occurred to her that Archie was as much a victim as Stephen was. All the same, she was still angry that he had given Stephen's secret away. His dress that night had been worn purely as a dare. It was more than annoying that his charade had ended up with such a lot of bad publicity. But now she had to try her hand at discovering the root of it all without letting on that she was Stephen Sigmund's barrister and lover, and that her black hair hid her natural colouring, as did her contact lenses. The fact that she applied make-up as Carmel and completely altered the look of her face, was also something she preferred to keep to herself.

However, as regards the case in hand, her legal training

called for clarification. She jumped straight in at the deep
end.

'Do you mean the piece in the paper? About the guy who
was dressed as a woman – the one with Valeria?'

'Yes.' He sounded relieved. 'The one you went off with
that night.' There was an instant quizzical look on his face.
'Did you know he wasn't a woman?'

Shiny as satin, her red lips smiled then curled as she
purred her response and gave him a look that would leave
him in no doubt of whether she knew or not.

Archie laughed.

Smiling still, Abigail tossed her dark hair so that it swung
in a smoky cloud from side to side. 'He was most definitely
a man. Most definitely!'

Chapter 17

She took a taxi when she left the club and got the driver to drop her at the two-bedroomed brick-built terrace where Carmel – the exotic dancer – lived alone and in absolute privacy.

Few of the neighbours had seen her in daylight, and those that had, only glanced her way and never spoke. She was just a trim figure in a very short skirt walking quickly from the taxi to the front door with nothing but the half-hearted glow from a streetlight to glance on her features.

Under cover of darkness, a slim young man left the house from the rear, his collar high around his face, a broad-brimmed hat pulled low over his eyes. Without looking to right or left, the lithe figure walked swiftly along the alleyway and out onto the road which ran between both rows of brick terraces.

As the figure exited the alley, a sleek car, black as a panther, went slowly past and turned into that part of the street where the house was situated.

Pulling collar nearer to chin, the figure turned in the opposite direction to that of the car. Home beckoned, and the night was getting damp.

* * *

Lance Vector yawned and rubbed his eyes before looking at his watch. It was two forty-five and Abigail Corrigan's Mercedes was still in the car park.

Earlier, he had driven in and around the car park, checking that there was only one entrance in and one out for a car. There was, and besides the doors to the staircase, there were only two other doors and both were marked private. Both, he assumed, were for the use of the security men and the maintenance crew.

From where he was parked, he could not only see where Abigail Corrigan's car was, but, by using a pair of powerful binoculars to eye the front entrance to her apartment block, he could check on who went in and who went out. He'd seen nothing of her. Her car had remained parked all night.

Disappointed, he eyed some gaunt youth who was sauntering to the car park steps, pausing in the corner as if relieving himself.

Lance sighed impatiently. 'Like tonight,' he muttered to himself. 'Nothing but a bucket of pee.'

Tonight had certainly not been successful. His editor would press for more lurid exposés, more innuendos to cast in Stephen Sigmund's direction, but unfortunately he had none to give. Of course, he could still blab that Sigmund was involved with his barrister, but Lance didn't want to do that. For the first time in his life, he wanted to protect someone rather than destroy them. Besides that he was tired, and his patience was at an end.

'Oh fuck it!'

He sighed bravely once he'd made up his mind, switched

on the engine, and slipped as quietly as possible away from the kerb.

As he pulled away, another car, black as midnight, slid into the gap he had left. Silently, a window was wound down and a soft burr of redness waxed and waned behind a dense cloud of cigarette smoke.

Inside the car park, the lean youth with the turned-up collar and wide brimmed hat glanced swiftly over his shoulder before pulling a small key from a shallow pocket.

A stray wisp of light-coloured hair fluttered from beneath the blackness of the hat. Eyes of Wedgewood blue glanced once more over the solemn grey of concrete walls and sleeping cars.

The first door marked private was blue. The second was pale green and used only by those living in the adjacent apartments.

Through the door; across the service road at the back; then another key; a wooden door in a red-brick wall: a courtyard garden. Another key, another door, and at last, the hat was removed, and Abigail Corrigan shook her hair free. She was home, and as far as she knew, no one was any the wiser that she had ever been out.

From the very first, she had surmised that buying this place was a good idea. The ground floor and the private entrance into the courtyard gave her privacy. She saw little of her neighbours, and did nothing to encourage their friendship. To those living in the same block, she was a workaholic who stayed late at her desk and alone.

No one could possibly know that she had two lives, that she was Abigail, but she was also Carmel who some knew as

Jezebel Justice. And anyway, it was dark in the alley that passed the wooden door to her courtyard. She was convinced her secret was safe.

Without switching on any lights, she made her way through the kitchen and out into the hallway. Her step was free and easy. Each room, even in darkness, was blatantly familiar to her. Only when she saw the strip of light that filtered out from beneath her bedroom door did she stop in her tracks. Normally, she left the study light on. But tonight, it was off and she was positive she had left it on.

With quickening heartbeat, she stepped softly across the black and white tiles; one foot in a white square, then one in a black.

The door handle was within reach. Her hand opened, her fingers uncurled. Then she hesitated, tilted her head as though that would help her hear better. There was little except a rustling noise – like the sound of moving bedclothes.

Her heart beat quickened. *Someone's in there. Now what?*

Movies came to mind. *Pretend you've got a gun. No,* another voice said, *this is stupid. It isn't,* said its opposite reaction. *Be positive. Yes. Be positive.*

She took a deep breath. One hand went back into her pocket, one finger pushed forwards into the soft silk lining.

Again she reached for the door handle, turned it slowly, and just as slowly, pushed open the door.

The blue silk shade of the table lamp cast a cool light on Stephen's sleeping face. He murmured something in his sleep, turned over, and threw out his arm.

It gave her a warm feeling to see his fingers curling and

uncurling over the pillow where her head should be. Even in his sleep, Stephen was reaching for her.

At last, she relaxed.

Although the urge to wake him was strong, she resisted it. Stephen needed his sleep as much as he needed her. At this moment in time, perhaps more.

But she also needed him, needed to feel that no matter what she did, she aroused him still.

Asleep he might be, but she undressed as though he was awake.

Bare shoulders gleamed in the soft light as she let her coat fall to the floor. She was naked to the waist. Her nipples were hard and her breasts cold from the effect of the night air that had caressed them. Still pretending to herself that he might be watching, she threw a kiss in his direction. Then she stretched and cupped her breasts as though she were offering them to him. She bent her knees slightly and swayed her hips from side to side.

Slowly, she ran her hands down over her belly to the waistband of her trousers, tucked her fingers into them, and pushed them down over her moving hips and from there down over her thighs. When they reached her knees, she turned, bent over, and wiggled her backside towards him.

If he was awake, she thought to herself, he would see my sex winking at him and then he would grab my hips and lunge straight into me.

The charade continued. She pulled off her trousers and her boots, and running her hands down over her body, she moved to the bed. It was then that she saw him grin, saw one eyelash flutter as his grin became a smile.

'That was very nice, Abby darling. Now what will you do for the main performance?'

He threw back the bedclothes and they laughed as they fell together.

But the laughter was short-lived. Passion erupted as flesh met flesh and lips met lips.

Hot with desire, she closed her eyes and wished. The wish could not possibly come true. There was no turning back the clock, no pretending this was the first time, the Railway Hotel and the trains rattling on the curving line outside the window. Yet still she pretended and ran her hands over his body, felt the hardness of his shoulders, his arms, the vague hairiness of his chest. Flesh rose and fell in delicious contours beneath her travelling fingers. His stomach tightened beneath her touch, his navel retreated as she trailed one finger around it and pushed gently into it.

Its skin soft as a velvet glove, his penis tapped a steady tempo against her belly as if begging her for immediate attention.

His body still moved, but his lips left her. 'I want you.' His voice and his breath were hot against her ear.

Pretending receded. First time, second, hundredth. What did it matter? He was here and nothing had really changed between them. Not sexually. Their appetite for each other was as strong as ever.

She opened her eyes, saw his and told herself she always wanted to see his.

'Then take me.' Her words came slow, but his action was swift.

The hardness of his loins pressed against her. The round

hardness of his knees went between hers and pushed her legs apart. Thick veins stood proud on his biceps as he held his arms rigid, his chest hovering above her. There was a deep intensity in his eyes that made her feel vulnerable, weak as a kitten. It was as though he were trying to read her, trying to ascertain why this woman affected him as she did. Why he wanted her, why he had to have her, on any terms she demanded.

Abby, tantalized that he could be so close, and yet not in her body, mewed like an injured kitten.

Cupping her breasts, she murmured what she wanted him to do to her.

'Take me.' Her voice was reminiscent of a breeze running through sand dunes; soft, hushed.

A wave of dark hair fell over his forehead. His eyes sparkled with the same intensity as before.

She knew he was keeping her in suspense, knew instinctively what he wanted her to say.

'I want you to put your body into mine. I want you to play with my breasts, to use them as you please; to pull them, pinch them, tantalize them until I scream for mercy. I want you to push your cock into me.'

A look of satisfaction came to his eyes. 'Say it as I want you to say it. Say it as a man likes it to be said, not as a woman likes it.'

At this moment in time she would have done anything he wanted her to do. Her body was screaming for him, raging with a fierce heat that only the immersion of his stiff rod could dissipate.

The words he wanted to hear formed in her brain. Because

her body was so hot, her throat and tongue were extremely dry. But her need was great. She just had to say what he wanted.

'Fuck me,' she whispered. 'Please. Fuck me!'

His face softened as his eyes filled with emotion and his body hardened with passion.

Abby groaned as she felt his erection slide like a burrowing animal between her thighs.

'Slowly?' he teased.

'Slowly,' she replied, knowing that he wanted to do it slowly, and what he wanted, she would want too.

Hot and tipped with the first hint of semen, the head of his member nudged against her pubic lips.

She groaned, raised her hips from the bed and opened her legs that little bit wider. How hot his penis was, how hard his body against hers, and how cold she felt, how needy for his flesh to fuse with her own.

'Give me more,' she gasped.

'Perhaps,' he responded. 'Just a little.'

With slow precision, he eased extra length into her. At first, her body yielded. Once he was inside, supposedly secure that he was the one in control, she sprang her trap. Clinging like a sucking mouth, the muscles of her vagina closed tightly around him. She wanted to eat him, to digest him until there was nothing left. That was the way she felt. She wanted him whole, his body always to be slamming against her, always to be in her; man and woman combined.

'Give me more,' she cried again. Demand caused her to curl her fingers and dig her nails into the hardness of his buttocks. He cried in pain, but could not stop thrusting his full length into her welcoming chamber. No longer was he controlling his own strokes, his own body. He was riding her, and yet, it was she who was controlling him, digging into his flesh so that he had to ram himself into her, had to press his weight onto her body and flatten her against the mattress.

'Come now,' he heard her say into his ear. 'Come now. With me . . . with me . . .'

The woman beneath him tensed, and despite his weight, arched her back so her belly rose and clung to his. Shudders ran over her and touched his own flesh, his own sensations. As his fingers dug then squeezed her pliant breasts, he thrust one more time, more mightily, more fiercely than he had ever done before.

Now it was her turn to cry out, but not for long. He covered her mouth with his own. His throat swallowed her cry as her womb swallowed his climax.

Afterwards, she told him about Archie and about Lance Vector. They discussed Oliver Hardiman's confession and guessed at who the culprits might be, but not with any conviction. But first, she told him about the scene behind the glass.

Although her recounting of events did have a very satisfactory effect on his penis, his eyes opened wide when she told him the identity of the man who liked being treated like a dog.

'Douglas! I would never have believed it!'

'Believe it. I was there. I saw it.'

Stephen looked suddenly thoughtful. 'I wouldn't like you to do that to me; in fact, I don't think I'd like to do it to you.'

It was Abby's turn to be thoughtful. Things were changing

between them. Her need to dice with the more perverse members of society was gradually melting away. Yet tomorrow she was booked to dance again at the Red Devil Club.

As she snuggled up to the man she loved and his hand closed over her breast, she made an immediate decision.

'I'm not going to be Carmel or Jezebel any more.'

She felt him tense, felt his fingers grip more fiercely on her upper arm. Just as suddenly as they had stiffened, they relaxed. His lips brushed the top of her head.

'I'm glad of that. I didn't think I would be, but I am. When do you intend telling Archie?'

That question was a little more difficult to answer. She didn't need the money Archie paid her. On top of that, she no longer needed the buzz the club gave her either. She hadn't really needed it since Stephen had appeared on the scene, though, of course, she had taken her time admitting it to herself.

'First, I have to find out all I can from Archie about the man who wants to ruin you. Once I've done that, the job is finished. You've a charge and a trial to face. You not only have to win that trial, you also have to point the finger at the person or persons behind it all.'

Stephen Sigmund had not been born without advantages, though he hadn't exactly had them thrust upon him either. Always in his life there had been an element of advantage in that his parents had encouraged him in everything he chose to do. Because his family was not exactly flush with money, some things had to be worked for and worked for hard. Even his very first bicycle had been bought with the help of odd jobs and the austere discipline that only an early-morning paper round can bestow. Now, he told himself, he was looking at another advantage, one he had only lately come across.

Abigail Corrigan was not only a kindred spirit to himself, she was a lifeline that fate had chosen to throw him. He was very glad it had.

He took her chin between finger and thumb and kissed her lips.

'I don't know what I'd do without you, Abby.'

Abigail had been spouting Legalese about using the media itself to point a finger in the direction it should be pointing. The look on Stephen's face and the tone in his voice made her halt in mid sentence.

With a cool look in her eyes, and a rose-bud pinkness on her lips, she said something he dearly wanted to hear.

'Then don't ever be without me, Stephen Sigmund. Make sure of never being without me.'

Charwallah to his friends, Charles Ahmed Wallis to his parents, picked up his mobile telephone and pressed the number that would take him straight to the top of the heap.

He was just about to press the "send" button, when a thought came to his mind. He smiled wryly to himself, then put the mobile back into its cradle.

His smile continued. His almond eyes, as yellow as those of a slinking cat, narrowed as he thought out his intentions. No matter that the man at the top would like to know about Abigail Corrigan's little secret, he would keep it to himself for the present time.

Tomorrow, he would pay a visit to the Red Devil Club. Before disposing of her, he would have some fun with the long-legged dancer who Archie knew as Carmel when she was at the bar, and Jezebel when she was up swinging her fanny on the stage. But Charwallah knew her little secret, and the knowledge made him smile. It also made him very hard. He was sure it was the best erection he had ever had, but then why shouldn't it be? He'd never fucked the law before. Well, not in the way he intended.

Chapter 18

The next night, she was back at the Red Devil Club.

Through the slits in her pale mauve mask, she regarded her audience. Half-hidden in darkness, they were gathered around small tables. Their glazed eyes, furrowed flesh, and wet, slack mouths were made all the more exaggerated, all the more monstrous by virtue of the meagre glow of small lamps set in the middle of each table. Blue smoke curled from cigars and cigarettes and red embers waxed and waned like flitting fireflies in the darkness.

Behind those eyes that watched her were minds surmising what she might do for them, and what they might do for and to her.

Wet tongues snaked over flaccid lips. Hard eyes, weak eyes, brown eyes and blue eyes, peered at her, lusted after her. Some squinted, some were wide, some blinked with amazement, and others never blinked at all, but just stared and stared as she swayed and danced across the stage.

Behind the anonymity of her mask, she could see those eyes. Some she recognized, others she did not. Her gaze did not linger. All eyes, no matter what their colour, were full of her body, and all eyes were unexceptional. All were easily readable.

Suddenly, she saw a different pair of eyes. She skirted over them, frowned, wondered if her imagination was playing tricks. Had some predatory cat got in by mistake, or was that really a pair of slanting gold eyes glowing in the darkness?

As her hips moved in time with the music, her gaze went back to those pools of yellow. *Tiger's eyes*, she thought, *frightening as well as alluring*. She was drawn to them. They were hypnotic. They reminded her of Stephen and their first night at the Railway Hotel when the gilded glow of a street light had touched a mean room with gold. It seemed an age ago now. So much had happened since then, and so much about her had changed. She did not feel the same way about the club and the world it represented. In the past, this place had meant excitement and she had thrilled to its erotic rhythm, its dark excesses. In the past, she had wanted to be here. Now she was here for Stephen's sake, because she had to be here. *Please God*, she prayed, *let this be the last time*.

Unknown to her, the man with the yellow eyes was toying with the idea that it might be just that. *But first*, he thought to himself, *I will have you. I will lay you down, strip your clothes from your body, and invade your sex with my own*.

Applause rang to the ceiling as Jezebel Justice, the woman known as Carmel, the lawyer known as Abigail, faded into the shadows.

In the privacy of her shower, Abby closed her eyes and let the warm water drift over her, white spumes of soap running unchecked over her breasts to fall in pearl like droplets from her nipples.

For a brief moment a hint of concern entered her mind. Just this once, she had forgotten to bolt the door.

Give it no mind, she told herself, and recalled Archie's assurances that his "boys" would deal with any unwanted attention from stage door johnnies. Such thoughts reassured her – until she felt a chill draught waft in beneath the bathroom door. She shivered. *Just a draught*, she told herself. Even if someone had opened the outer door, at least the bathroom door was locked. She adjusted the heat control on the shower.

The doorknob rattled. Her eyes opened wide. She reached for the thermostat and turned off the shower so she could hear that much better; just in case she was mistaken. Hardly daring to breathe, she gently pulled back the shower curtain and stepped out onto the bright blue tumbletwist mat. She stood perfectly still and stared at the doorknob which was made of brass and was now misted with steam. It did not move or make a sound. Had she been mistaken?

All was silent. Too silent. Too tense. Small creaks and groans from pipework and the other odd noises buildings make, seemed louder than usual. Even the water gurgling down the plughole seemed too noisy.

Slowly, the doorknob began to turn.

What do I do? She bit her lip. A variety of choices came to her mind. The first was to shout, so she did. 'Go away. This room is private and I wish to be left alone.' Loud as it was, her voice was still authoritative, not terrified.

The doorknob rattled again. The bolt held.

'Let me in, Miss Jezebel.'

She did not recognize the voice.

'I will do no such thing!' She should scream. She told herself she should scream, but her pride plugged her throat.

249

The doorknob rattled again. The door itself shook. *Could he get in? And what would she do if he did?*

She looked for something she could use as a weapon. Attack, she decided, was the best form of defence. There was little to choose from as regards a defensive weapon. A stool? A toilet brush? God, but she was getting desperate. The long black rod that she used in her act was on the other side of the bathroom door, propped tidily against a marble-topped washstand that doubled as a dressing table.

She reached for a towel. Her eyes stayed firmly fixed on the doorknob. It turned one way, then the other.

'Let me in, Miss Carmel.'

She shivered. What a voice. Like ice. She swallowed her fear and put as much professional authority as she could muster into her voice.

'I said go away. I don't let anyone in here! Now get lost!'

The door rattled again.

She screamed as loudly as she could. Someone must be around. Where were Archie's precious "boys"?

The cold voice laughed. His laugh, like his voice, was as cold as ice. It reminded her of icicles, long, thin as the blade of a razor-sharp stiletto knife.

'Let me in, Miss Jezebel. Miss Carmel. *Miss Abigail Corrigan.*' The last name was stressed.

Now those icicles stabbed into her heart. She froze. He knew her name. The creep knew her real name!

'Who are you?' Her voice was hushed.

'Someone who knows your secret, Miss Corrigan. Someone who wants to know you better. Now why don't you let me in?'

'No! No chance! Get lost!'

Now the whole door seemed to bend and buckle as whoever it was slammed his body against it. Abby wrapped her arms around herself and shivered inside the thickness of the towel. She leaned against the wall as though she were trying to melt into it. But of course she couldn't. Cold tiles, wet with condensation, were solid against her back. Adventure on the wild side of life was now decidedly unattractive. She thought of Stephen, longed for him, for his bed, his arms, for a more ordered structure to her life. These thoughts flew through her mind in a matter of seconds. They gave extra strength to the long-drawn-out scream that followed.

There were suddenly muffled shouts on the other side of the door. Someone had heard!

Scuffling and the sound of blows were followed by a cry of anguish, a thud; more voices, running feet. Then there was the thud of footsteps and Archie calling, 'Carmel? Are you all right?'

Breasts heaved against the towel that she still clasped to her body as she fought to get her breath. Thankfully she leaned her head back against the wall and closed her eyes. 'Yes,' she said at last. 'Yes.'

When she was quite sure her appearance was good enough to still be Carmel – black hair, black eyes, red lips – she opened the door. Archie looked worried and in that moment, her attitude towards him became less loathing.

'Are you sure you're all right?'

She nodded and took a deep breath. 'Who was it?'

Reminiscent of a pantomime dame, Archie flapped his

hands about. 'I don't know. One of the boys was passing. He heard you scream. Oh my word! My word!' he exclaimed, his long fingers scouring across his forehead and pulling his flesh into worried folds. 'What a mess! What a bloody mess!'

There were other people beyond Archie. One of the 'boys' lay out on the floor. A dark pool of red was seeping into the carpet around him.

'Is he dead?'

Archie nodded. 'I've called the police.' His eyes met hers and she knew immediately that the police officer most likely to arrive would be Paul Bennet. Archie confirmed it. 'I've called Paul Bennet,' he corrected. 'I need someone to clean this up. We have to be discreet about things like this. A death on the premises would ruin the club, if news got out.'

Staring at Archie through her coal-black lenses, a new truth entered Abby's mind. If that had been her lying on the floor, his policy would have been the same. Bennet would be along to tidy things up. The killer would not be hunted by the police, because no one would know anyone had died. The shivers that ran through her body stopped. The coldness remained and covered her like a translucent skin.

She was dressed by the time Bennet arrived, though her body was still cold. *Who was it who had plunged in the knife?* A more frightening question troubled her greatly. *How come he had known her true name?*

Paul Bennet looked her up and down, smirked, then asked his first question. 'Any idea who did it?'

Hugging herself, she kept her gaze fixed on his shoes. They were shiny bright, but, she guessed, smelly on the inside. Like him.

'No. I was in the shower. He was on the other side of the door.'

Hands shoved casually in pockets, Bennet pushed his toe into the man's well-padded side as he spoke to her. 'How come you left the door open? Were you hopeful?'

She jerked her gaze away from her hands and glared at him. 'Say what you mean, Inspector.'

He sniffed; grinned. 'You know, darling, were you hoping I might come calling and give you a great big one in the . . .' he paused. 'Shower?'

She flushed – with anger more so than embarrassment. Bennet was a pig of the first order. 'No Inspector. The only time my thoughts turn to you is when I see a heap of effluent or spew go down the plughole!'

Bennet's jaw clenched and a small nerve flickered at the side of one eye before he raised his arm and hit her.

She caught her breath and covered the warmth of her cheek with the palm of her hand. 'That's police brutality!'

Archie looked concerned. Bennet only smirked. 'It would be if this business was official.'

Abby's worst fears were finally realized as Bennet began giving orders to those gathered there.

'Grab those towels and pack them around him to soak up the blood.'

Dev and Ray the barmen did as ordered.

Smoking copiously and coughing vigorously, Bennet sat himself down and watched what they were doing. Just once he turned and ran his eyes down over her. In turn, she glared at him and truly hoped his bad habits would kill him.

'Right,' he said once the boys looked to be finished. 'Now

move this furniture and wrap the carpet up round him. Use tights, belts, anything like that to tie the carpet up, then put him in the car.'

'You'd better give him your keys.' Archie's voice sounded weak, almost as if he were half-asleep. He winced and awoke when Bennet shouted at him.

'Not my bloody keys. Your keys, Sonny Jim. It's your place, your mess, so he's going in your bloody car!'

Archie seemed to shrink into himself – a bit like a punctured ball. Apologetically, and with flickering eyes, he handed over the keys. His hand was trembling.

All through this, Abby, in her guise as Carmel, kept very quiet, but she took in all that was going on. It didn't take an Einstein to know that the body in the carpet would be dumped in the river or in half-set concrete at some distant building site. She shivered. It could have been her.

Sick to her stomach, she got to her feet. Bennet's hand caught her wrist. His grip was like iron, as hard as his eyes. 'Where do you think you're going, baby?'

She held her head high, looked at him squarely. 'Home. Tonight's performance is finished.' She glanced at the body, then at Archie. He looked away as though he was ashamed of what might happen next.

Bennet adopted that baleful grin of his. 'The night is young, baby. You've got nothing to worry about. Bennet of the force is here, and he's done a damn good job tonight. Besides that, my mouth's dry, my prick's hard, and I need a woman.'

'Not this one!' She spat the words. 'I've performed enough for one night. Let me go.'

She moved a leg. Remembering her cricket box kick from before, Bennet stepped back but still held her tightly. He turned suddenly to Archie. 'Is the main club closed?' There was violence in his voice and in his expression.

'Under the circumstances . . .' Archie began. Bennet did not let him finish.

'Fine. We'll go upstairs.' The coldness of his lips came close to Abby's ear. She made a great effort to hide her shiver, but it wasn't easy. 'Lots of things happen upstairs, you know,' he said to her. 'All the big dicks get up there – you know, people in the limelight who like to take their kicks in private. Archie takes pictures of them, you know. Just in case they're needed at any time.'

'Pictures? What are they needed for?' Abby's curiosity was aroused. Of course she didn't want to go upstairs with Bennet. Of course she didn't want to have any sexual dealings with him. But she remembered her first impression of the upstairs club. She had told herself then how vulnerable people could be in such circumstances. Now it appeared that someone was making full use of that fact.

Bennet's face came close to hers. His eyes looked cruel. Cruel, she decided, was definitely the right word. Not naughty or wicked, words that hinted at a giggle-filled coquetry. Cruel sounded what it was; without pity, and yet enjoyed by the perpetrator.

There was a chance that she could struggle and free herself, yet something told her to hold fast. Upstairs was beckoning. Perhaps the secret behind the identity of Stephen's accuser was up there.

'Come on, baby. Let me see how grateful you can be.'

Bennet jerked her out of the door and dragged her through the main floor of the club. Chairs were already piled on tables. They reminded her of skeletons, and skeletons made her wonder where the body in the carpet was at this moment.

The room he took her into was a pervert's dream. Her heart sank. *Please, not this!* There were manacles set into the wall at various heights, a thing that looked like a spit, fashioned and big enough for a human. There were metal contraptions that were chairs, but not chairs, with cruel spikes all over the seat and metal bands around the arms and the back. There were whips, batons, leather masks, and various harnesses hanging from the cold stone walls. To all intents and purposes, the room was a torture chamber.

The room sickened and frightened her. She did not want to be here with this man, did not want to do the things she feared he wanted her to do. But somehow, she knew she had to linger, knew she needed to spend some time here. If she was clever, she could convince Bennet that she would be willing to submit to his treatment without him tying her up. She needed that freedom to move, to search. But first, she thought to herself, make him want you, make him trust you. Well she certainly looked the part. Tonight, she wore a short black dress that had a square neckline and a pleated skirt. It was vaguely reminiscent of a gym slip and matched the black stockings whose tops peeped demurely from beneath its hem. The sight of her dressed like that had put a gleam in Bennet's eye.

Archie, she noticed, had followed them. He was standing in the doorway. He looked pale and his mouth hung slightly open. Bennet noticed him too. 'Get lost, poof.' The door slammed shut.

Bennet dragged Abby into the centre of the room. 'Little bitch!' He slapped her face like he had before. It made her slightly dizzy.

Think of Stephen, she told herself. *Think of helping Stephen.* Doing that helped the sickness in her belly dissipate a little. All the same, she knew this ordeal would be horrendous if she didn't keep her head. She swallowed, willed fear to enter her eyes, and looked determinedly up at him.

His eyes glittered. Spittle glistened at the corners of his mouth. 'Well, babe, my dolly little schoolgirl. Are you going to tell me what a naughty girl you've been? Are you going to scream when I beat your delectable little backside? Hmmm? Are you?'

Because his fingers were squeezing her lips, she couldn't answer. In her mind she was telling herself to stay cool. At the same time, she needed to pretend that she was so terrified, she would do anything to please him. 'Please! Don't hurt me.' Her words were as mutated as her mouth, but understandable.

He sneered. One nostril flared more widely than the other. 'Hurt you? Of course I'm going to hurt you, you stupid little cow!'

With his knee between her legs, his fingers tight around her wrists, he pushed her in the direction of the human spit. She played her part to the full, struggled and screamed. Each time she screamed, he shook her so hard, she thought her brains might be in danger of falling out.

From somewhere deep inside she summoned all the strength she could muster. *I need to find those tapes*, she told herself. *I need to know what's on them. I need to know who is being blackmailed*. She did not question who the blackmailer was. She assumed Archie was the villain of the piece. It was his club, wasn't it? His premises?

Soon, those thoughts were wildly dispersed as the door swung open. Archie, brandishing what looked like the black rod Jezebel used in her act, leapt across the room.

Bennet did not have time to turn and face him. There was a sickening crunch as the hard wood of the rod met the fragile bone of Bennet's skull. His eyes opened wide before going up into his head. A wet tongue trailed from a wide mouth as he slid to the floor.

Abby regarded Archie Ringer in a new light. In that one moment, he had turned from a homosexual nightclub owner into a knight rescuing a damsel in distress.

'Come on, Carmel. Let's get you out of this.'

'He'll kill you for this, Archie,' she said as she stepped over the inert body.

'It's likely, but if I put some miles between me and him, it won't be so likely, and that, my darling girl, is what I intend doing. I'm off!'

It wasn't really the time to go into detail, but she asked him the most pertinent question. 'What about the club?'

'Not my problem. The owner can deal with that.'

'Owner? I thought you were the owner.'

'No,' he shook his head as he eased her towards the door. 'I'm not, and at this moment in time, I don't really want to inform them that I'm giving in my notice. My absence will be enough to declare my intention.'

The door was left open. Archie's feet were moving as quickly as his flitting eyes. 'Come on! Come on!'

Abby stopped dead in her tracks. 'I can't. Not yet.' She grabbed Archie's arm. 'If you're not the owner, Archie, then you're not the blackmailer.'

'Blackmailer? Of course not. Not really. I only manage the place. Someone comes in and attends to the tape room. I have nothing to do with that side of the business at all.' He looked slightly offended. *Cute*, she thought.

'So who is the owner?'

He stared at her. A fine film of sweat erupted all over his face. He shook his head very vigorously. 'I can't tell you that. You see, I lied about the man who tried to get into your room. I know who he is. Know how dangerous he is.' Archie might be sweating, but his face was white.

Abby reached out, held his arm, and let her fingers dig through the expensive material and into his meagre flesh. 'Where is the tape room?'

For a moment, she was afraid he would not answer. His eyes moved first. He jerked his head in the same direction as his eyes were looking. 'There,' he said hoarsely. 'Third room on the left.'

'Is there a key?'

He hesitated, stared at her as though he was considering his reply in the greatest detail. Finally, he reached into his pocket and with a very shaky hand, passed her a thick, shiny key. 'I'm not supposed to have a copy. The man who takes care of the room lost it one day. I took advantage of the situation – just in case.' Suddenly, his bottom lip began to tremble. 'No one knows I have a copy. My life would be worth nothing if it were found out. The man who looks after the tapes is the same one who kills.' He bit his bottom lip. His upper one trembled.

She didn't have time to sympathize. Dangerous as it might be, she had to probe further. 'Well, I won't be telling anyone, Archie.' Brushing past him, she headed straight for the door of the indicated room. Perhaps in there she could learn a lot of what was going on. Perhaps in there was the face of the man behind the Swan and Swallow investment scam. In just a moment she might know enough to clear Stephen's name and to get Rheingold released from jail.

Archie turned to go, then thought better of it. 'Will you be all right, Carmel love?'

Now it was her turn to pause. This man's intervention with Bennet was much appreciated. She nodded. 'Yes, Archie. I'm fine. I'm grateful for you saving me from Paul the Perv. Thanks a lot.'

He looked sheepish. She sensed he had something more to say. 'Be careful, Carmel, darling. I don't know whether you know it, but you're being watched. I know his name, but I refuse to go into too much detail. We've already seen what he did to one of my best boys. If I could I'd kill him myself. But I'm not that brave, and anyway, he's in the pay of the owner and he's very dangerous.'

Abby felt suddenly cold. Key in hand, she hesitated before the door Archie had indicated. 'Did he also kill Carl Candel?'

Archie shrugged. 'I don't know for sure. It's more than likely considering the circumstances.'

'Circumstances?' Abby frowned.

'Yes. The circumstances of Candel's death. The killer's a bit of a history buff. Likes to update old practices. Wasn't there a king that was killed by having a red hot poker shoved up his Manchester?'

Even without the hint of rhyming slang, Abby would still have known what he was referring to. She'd found the body, after all.

'Do you know what he looks like?'

He nodded. 'Oh, yes. I know that all right. As I told you, he's the man who used to look after that room. He's got yellow eyes, and I hate him.'

She remembered the eyes in the audience, remembered Stephen had said he thought he was being followed. She had accepted that as a natural occurrence in view of the crime with which he had been charged and the media's obsession with such things. But it hadn't occurred to her that she was being followed too. If the man who had tried the handle to her bathroom hadn't mentioned her real name, she would have assumed he was only a stage door Johnnie – a nut, but still only a stage door Johnnie. According to what Archie had just said, he was anything but, just like Paul Bennet was more than a policeman. Were they all working for the "owner"? And who was the "owner"?

Archie waved and was gone. She stared after him for barely a moment, then turned and pushed the key into the lock.

Blue and grey shadows fell across surveillance screens and two computer terminals. Along one wall were a series of shelves containing tape after tape.

'Good grief!' She said it softly, then closing the door behind her, went straight to the shelves and ran her finger across the plastic spines of the tapes.

Each was numbered. Each was labelled. Somewhere, she decided, there had to be a book which would list the numbers. Against each number she would hope to see a name, perhaps even a one-word description of what they were up to on the tape.

After perusing the tapes and finding nothing that she could recognize as having any bearing on Stephen's problems, she turned her attention to the desks on which the computers sat. She rifled through the first desk, but when she came to the other one, she discovered that the main drawer was firmly locked. It had to be locked for a reason.

'Damn!' She said the word only softly, and yet it still seemed loud as it echoed off the cold grey walls, the plastic and glass screens, and the no-nonsense metal desks.

She needed a tool to open it, and there was nothing in this room that looked usable. Kicking off her high-heeled shoes, she raced on bare feet back along the corridor to the room where Paul Bennet still lay on the floor. She heard him groan, and hoped he wouldn't be coming round just yet, but to ensure he didn't, she retrieved the black rod she used for her act and gave him another clout.

The black rod did the trick, and Bennet slumped into silence once more, but it would be of no help in opening the locked drawer.

Quickly, she scanned the room. At the end of the spit was a locking pin secured by a thin chain. A bolt and a wing nut held it onto the main frame. In a matter of minutes she had wrenched it free.

She was about to leave the room when she heard Bennet groan again. Obviously the force of her blow was not as great as Archie's had been. So that she could continue what she was doing in peace, he had to be restrained. A wicked smile spread over her features.

With all the strength she possessed, she dragged Bennet to the spit on which he had been so keen to tie her. It had a ratchet affair at each end so it could be lowered right to the floor. Once that was done, it wasn't too hard to heave Bennet into the metal cradle. Before closing the upper lid over him, she undid his zipper and pulled his trousers down to his knees. Once the grid of metal bars was over him, she re-wound the ratchets so he was raised to the level of her waist.

His penis lay crumpled against his pubic hair. If she'd wanted to, she could have shaved it all off, smeared him with something nasty, or painted weird patterns along his shaft, but she didn't have the time. Instead, she turned him over so that his penis hung down through the bars. In the other part of the spit cradle, a square had been cut in the bars so that his bare bottom stuck through, white, flaccid and extremely vulnerable.

She smiled triumphantly. His purpose had been to have her bottom poking through that hole. Once at his mercy, he would have criss-crossed her flesh with a series of pink stripes. But first, he would have humiliated her by shoving first one implement up her backside after another. He would then have taken photographs – just as he had before. Well, now it was his turn.

One of the whips that lined the wall had a fairly thick handle. Feeling revulsion, but also the thrill of revenge, she eyed his ugly behind, then, after parting one cheek from another, she pushed the handle of the whip into his anus – just as she had done to Hardiman.

As his buttocks tightened, he groaned, but did not regain consciousness.

She clapped her hands together as she surveyed her handiwork. Ideally, she would have liked to have photographed him and sent the snap to his superior officers, but there wasn't time. Perhaps there was another way, she thought, as she eyed the surveillance camera that blinked its red light in the corner of the room.

She went back along the corridor to the grey room with its monitors and recording equipment. First, she forced open the drawer and found what she wanted, a small notebook. Then, she fathomed out how to record what the surveillance monitors were seeing.

Whirr went the tape, then click went the eject switch once she'd taped what she wanted.

She retrieved her shoes, left the room and went down the stairs. The main bar was in semi-darkness and empty. Two of Archie's boys had gone to dispose of the body in the carpet. Archie himself had flown the coop, and only a barman was still there. He was hanging onto the bar he usually tended, a half tumbler full of spirit clenched in one hand. Before him was a half-drunk bottle. He was talking to himself and didn't notice her.

She followed her normal procedure. At the small red terrace house, she went in as Carmel and just as dawn was breaking, came out as a young man.

Before leaving the house, she had phoned Stephen and told him what she had. She also told him that, in her opinion, whoever owned the club had not only recognized him on that first night he had been dressed as a woman, but had orchestrated the supposed act of lewd behaviour. The owner, whoever he might be, was also not prejudiced against murder.

'I'll be with you right away,' she told him.

'Be careful,' he replied.

Because of the events she had so far experienced, she was more cautious than usual as she left the lane at the back of the house.

With a quick glance, she saw the black car, and at the sight of it, slunk back into the scrubby damp bushes that poked out through cracks in the wall. Through the shifting leaves of the evergreen, she studied the car and attempted to ascertain who the driver was. The car's windows were tinted. The task of seeing the features of the driver was hopeless.

Remembering what Stephen had said about a car having driven away on the fateful night of his arrest, she dropped her gaze to the number plate. There was a "G" and there was a "1". It was definitely a personalized job. It had to be the car used that night.

Now it was no longer necessary to see the features of the man who was driving. She knew instinctively that he would have yellow eyes. Danger threatened. She had to get to Stephen, yet she knew that this man was waiting for her. Even now he was getting out of his car. Would he come her way, or would he go around to the front door? Either way, she knew if he saw her, she was dead. Regardless of her disguise, he would know it was her.

Just when she thought she would have to make a run for it, a taxi came by. Immediately, she was out from cover, waving her arms and shouting like fury.

The driver stopped. 'Okay, Okay. I saw ya', mate. Where d'ya wanna go?'

She gave him Stephen's address. 'Don't spare the horses. There's an extra tenner in it for you if you can lose that car behind us.'

The driver was immediately all wide-eyed enthusiasm. 'Phew! I've never been asked that before. *Hill Street Blues* here I come!'

Deep brown eyes glanced quickly into the rear view mirror in time for the driver to see Charwallah racing back to his car. 'I clock the guy,' he cried excitedly.

Breathless, Abby glanced back too. 'Good. Now lose him!'

'You bet!'

The driver, whose career in driving had not always been strictly legal and had always been somewhat reckless, pushed the pedal to the floor. The car lurched as they took the bends, whizzed down the small streets between rows of parked cars, skidded round tight corners, and pelted out onto the North Circular.

Cars gave way and blew fiercely on their horns as the taxi driver cut them up, swerved from one lane to the other in order to get an advantage and put a big gap between them and their pursuer.

'What you done, mate?' he asked, his eyes and voice bright with excitement.

'Nothing,' she replied, her fingers gripping her seat as the driver threw the car from one traffic lane to another. 'It's what that guy in the big black car wants to do to me that's the problem.'

'Oh really? What do he wanna do to you then, mate?'

'Kill me. He wants to kill me.'

She said it in an even voice, and instantly knew that it was true.

Chapter 19

Lance Vector had been watching Abigail Corrigan's place all
night. Nothing had happened and he was feeling gloomy
about it.

For most of the night, he had gazed transfixed up at her
window, had dozed occasionally. When dozing, he imagined
her, her breasts spilling out of a bra that was obviously two
sizes too small. He liked to picture her like that, liked to
think that her flesh would be bursting against its forced
constraint. It excited him and made him come in his hand all
the more quickly.

Sighing, he tucked his member back inside his trousers
and wiped away the stickiness from his right hand. Another
tissue was tossed out of his open window. His crisp, white
handkerchief that his mother spent so much time washing
and ironing was still in his breast pocket. She never
commented that it appeared hardly used each time he put it
in the wash. He also ensured that he bought his own box of
tissues. That way he didn't get asked awkward questions.

Guilt made him angry. Not guilt about his masturbation,
but guilt that he had dozed whilst watching Abigail's
apartment block. Normally, he was a light sleeper, but

because lately he had spent so much time watching and following Abigail Corrigan, weariness was catching up with him. How did he know for sure that she hadn't already left and, right beneath his nose, had gone over to stay the night with Stephen Sigmund?

The question niggled and made him shift in his seat. He frowned and caught a glimpse of himself in the wing mirror. He wiggled his eyebrows up and down, assessed his looks on a scale of one to ten, and decided on six. All in all, he decided, he wasn't bad looking.

The niggle remained. What if she had left her flat without him knowing?

He made a snap decision, turned on the engine, and pulled away from the kerb. Stephen Sigmund's place was only half an hour away, but it was hard not to make the journey pass more quickly, to push the pedal more firmly to the floor. He needed to know where she was. He needed to hold a diary of her day within his mind. Somehow, it gave him good feelings, almost as if he were directing her day rather than just fitting in with it.

A taxi pulled in ahead of him before the white pillars that fronted the house where Stephen Sigmund lived. A young man stepped out of it and seemed to reel off a stream of ten-pound notes to the grinning black driver.

Lance frowned so fiercely, his eyebrows met in the middle of his nose. A stray wisp of fair hair had escaped from beneath the young man's hat. It was removed and a shock of white waves fell to well beyond shoulder level. The coat collar was pulled up, the coat itself was unbuttoned. But he saw the blue eyes he loved look fleetingly at him and the street beyond. His heart beat against his ribs. He knew it was her and knew she had seen him. She looked unconcerned about his presence and seemed more interested in looking beyond him to the end of the street where red buses and a host of cars were already pushing their way into the city centre.

As she disappeared into Sigmund's house, he leaned forward and rested his chin on the steering wheel. There was no doubt that she had recognized him, and yet it did not seem to worry her. The fleeting, wary looks were reserved for something beyond the street he was parked in. They were also, it seemed, reserved for someone or thing far more dangerous than a lurking journalist.

Something had happened. Lance was convinced of it. Perhaps she had found out more about the case of Stephen Sigmund. Perhaps she had found out who had set it up and for what reason. It did enter his head that he might go bounding up to Sigmund's door. *But what*, he asked himself, *would you do when you get there? Tell them that the lewd act Sigmund was accused of was all a set-up? Tell them he was told to be there at a certain time and had disobeyed? And what*, he asked himself, *would he get for his trouble? Nothing. Bloody nothing! She was Sigmund's. It was him feeling her breasts, licking her belly, and probing the lips of her sex with his tongue, not him. Never him!*

Such thoughts upset him and he would have dwelt on them if he hadn't noticed the shiny black car turning into the road and slinking along it like a predatory cat. Automatically, he sunk down in his seat. He had seen the man driving it before. He had seen him one day when he had been summoned to go up to the penthouse suite to see the man who owned the newspaper he worked for. He had seen his eyes, told his mother about them, and she had said he had seen the devil. He had believed her, but had soon got over the incident. After all, it wasn't very likely that he would see more than one devil in his lifetime. But here the devil was again, and he was stopping outside Stephen Sigmund's place.

Suddenly, Lance had a strong urge to protect Abigail from this man. She wasn't meant for devils, not Abigail. She was meant for him and he would protect her from evil.

Fearing the worst from this wicked man, he slid further into his seat and watched through the gaps in the steering wheel as the man picked his place. Rather than parking outside Sigmund's, he tucked the shiny black car in behind a red BMW. From there he could view everyone who came and went from the house with the white pillars and tiled portico.

Slowly, Lance sat up straight. No matter what, he would not allow this man to have Abigail Corrigan before he had the chance to have her. So what if he did work for the baron in the penthouse suite, the same man Lance worked for? The man with the yellow eyes was not a journalist. Lance knew that much. He was dangerous and used by the big man for doing other jobs, secret jobs that no one else was party to.

Lance didn't like to think of Abigail falling into his clutches, and he would do everything in his power to stop that happening. If he lost his job, then so be it. He'd find another. Didn't his mother always say that the Lord provides? Saving Abigail for himself was the first act of selfishness he had ever performed since commencing his journalistic career. The paper would either have to forgive or forget him.

Inside the house, Stephen hugged and kissed Abigail before either of them spoke.

'Here it is,' she said, and waved the book in her hand. 'This lists the names of everyone recorded doing their favourite thing. It also lists what their favourite pastimes are.'

Stephen was staring into her eyes as she said it, his hand tracing delicious lines through her hair. He didn't seem to be listening, but as she liked the look he was giving her, she was not unduly concerned.

'I've missed you.' He said it sincerely as he hugged her ever more tightly against his body. She let the book fall from her hands, returned his hot kisses, and felt the hardness of his bare shoulder muscles beneath her searching fingertips.

'I'm glad to hear it. I've been out all night on your behalf. I only hope you're worth it. Do you know Lance Vector is sitting outside in his car?'

'And you didn't question him?'

She shook her head. 'I don't need to now I've got this.'

Their lips met again. His hand gently stroked the nape of her neck. His voice was just as gentle. 'You must be tired. Are you hungry?'

She nodded, then rested her head against his shoulder and sniffed male flesh. Her lips brushed his body as she spoke. 'I haven't got time to sleep. I need a shower, some coffee, and some toast. That'll keep me going for the rest of the day.'

He watched her walk to the bathroom before he went to the kitchen, turned on the coffee machine and put two slices of wholemeal into the toaster.

While the toast and coffee were doing, he stared out of the window and thought about the man he had been before Abby had come along. Dare he tell her how he was truly feeling? That his emotions encompassed more than sexual hunger? Even now, he could not just stand in the kitchen and wait for her return. He had to go to her, had to see her naked in the shower, the water cascading over her curves and running into the deep crevice between her legs.

There was an etched glass screen between them. Behind it, Stephen could see her creaminess turning slightly pink in the warmth of the water. Like a shadow dancer on a Japanese paper screen, she twisted and turned, her limbs reaching out, her body undulating as if moving to a tune only she could hear.

Stephen stepped out of the pants he was wearing. It seemed inappropriate to stand there half-clothed when she was completely naked behind the glass screen. Briefly, he stroked the length of his hardening penis. It jumped slightly and pulsated along its whole length.

The rhythm of her movement entered his mind. His stomach muscles tightened as his cock grew in supplication to her actions and appearance.

Slowly, he raised his arm, spread his fingers and gently touched the screen. The glass was unexpectedly warm beneath his touch. As if he were truly running his hand down her back, he ran his hand over the shape her body made.

He saw her pause in her cleansing as she became aware of his presence. She turned full frontal to him and pressed her body against the screen. Her breasts were squashed flat against it. They looked very white and her nipples looked very pink. Even her navel was obvious and pressed into a smiling shape.

As his fingers trailed across the detail in the glass, she wavered and moved against it like grass in the wind. He slid his hand down over the smoothness of the partition to the pale triangle of hair. She wriggled her hips, pressed her mons against the steam-stained glass so that the lips of her sex divided and sucked against it.

With a certain amount of self-control, he could have gone on a little longer. But it wasn't easy to stop himself from joining her beneath the shower of warm water. But he would not impose unless he was sure she wanted him. Much as he wanted her, he guessed how tired she was feeling.

Eventually, almost as if she were reading his mind, a long arm came out from behind the screen. A crooked finger beckoned.

'Come in,' she said in a low, husky voice. 'The water's fine.'

Her body was wet and warm against him. Her nipples were hard. Water from the shower spout ran over their heads and trickled in long droplets through their hair, over their faces and their lips. As they kissed, it ran into their mouths and lubricated their circling tongues. Along with the water, their hands ran up and down each others' bodies, tensing, pressing against certain areas, and merely caressing others.

There was no need for words. Language was constrained to that spoken purely by their bodies. Instinct replaced the need to communicate. Touch triggered the right reactions.

Their wet bellies clung together. Water raced over her curves, his muscles. It dropped like clear pearl drops from her nipples, soaked his pubic hair.

As his hard member pushed at her, the water ran along its

length. From its very tip, it dripped and trickled over her pubic lips. She moaned as his hands gripped her breasts, his fingers pulled at her nipples. Such moans were swallowed by his kisses.

He gripped her upper legs and pushed her back against the tiled wall. She gasped as he raised those legs and held them to his hips. Only his hands and the pressure of the tiled wall kept her from slipping down his legs and onto the floor.

His fingers dug into the cheeks of her behind. His penis tapped at her clitoris, then slid along her labia to its ultimate goal.

Fingernails digging into his shoulders, she closed her eyes and let herself drown in the things she was feeling. There was no doubt that her experiences back in the club had aroused her. Danger and excitement had increased her desire. And now, this man was quenching her thirst, his penis invading her flesh, his pelvis thudding against her trapped body.

There was sweet delight in cupping his buttocks and feeling the muscles tense and relax as he pushed himself into her. Each stroke consisted of the same movement yet varied in intensity and thus so did her response.

Tingles of pleasure intensified until they became an ache that needed curing. Her lips sucked at his shoulder, his neck and his mouth as their climax came nearer.

'Are you enjoying this?' His eyes spoke volumes as he asked her the question.

There were no words to express the delight she was feeling. She vigorously nodded her head. Her breath rushed from her mouth in quick, short bursts. Ecstasy was not easy to control.

He smiled and she sensed mischief. She purred like a cat as he ran his hands down her legs and took her heels in the palms of his hands. Pressing her ever more tightly against the tiled wall, and without his penis leaving her body, he pushed her legs back towards her. Leaning back as far as he could without coming out of her, he straightened her legs so that her feet rested on his shoulders. Now, his hands cupped her buttocks, and as he thrust into her, his fingers divided her firm cheeks and played havoc with her anus.

Sex, Abby decided then, was like surfing. She was balancing on a knife-edge of delight. Thrills of pleasure ran through her body, and just as if she were surfing, she did not want to fall into the water. She wanted the experience to go on and on, and yet, falling in could be the greatest pleasure of all.

Amid the circling steam, Stephen thrust himself into her. *I don't want this to end*, he thought to himself. *I want to go on fucking her forever*.

Again and again, he pushed himself and her against the tiled walls. Her body, his body, were soaking wet. There was an odd sucking sound on the up-stroke as his belly left hers. He kissed her, he sucked at her lips and her nipples. Her pelvis leapt towards him as he pushed his finger between her buttocks.

Now, it was coming. He could feel it rising inside him, flowing like molten metal along his shaft. Mindlessly, lovingly, yet driven on by the power of orgasm, he thrust against her, grasped her with one hand whilst a finger from the other hand pushed hard into her anus.

Their cries of ecstasy mingled with the steam and the

water, their hips ramming one against the other until the last ebb of orgasm had trickled away with the running water and the dissipating steam.

Abby was silent as they went into the living room and tangled together on the blue leather couch. So far, she had not told him the details of how she had managed to get hold of the book. She had also not mentioned the incident at the club when the blood on the rug could so easily have been hers.

'So how easy was it to get this?' He flicked the pages as he said it.

She sighed, nuzzled his chest and stared for a minute at his nipples before she answered. She sensed rather than saw his frown. 'Go on,' he said. 'Tell me.'

She did just that. 'Dangerous. Very dangerous.'

She felt him tense.

He laid his hand gently on her head. 'Tell me.' So she did.

He hugged her tighter after that. He didn't even laugh when she told him about how she had left Paul Bennet trapped and exposed in his favourite room.

'Do you think this book is the answer?'

Obviously, Stephen's mind was running along the same tracks as her own. She frowned.

'Not necessarily. But we could use it as a lever to ask a few questions. There are bound to be some very interesting people in that book.'

'With some very interesting hobbies,' Stephen added.

Abby nodded as she flicked over the pages. Then she frowned. Some names were marked with a red asterisk. She flicked a few more pages.

'Look.' She pointed at each red asterisk and the name beside it.

'Carol Anne Flowers. Nigel Porter. Stephanie Grockling and Amanda Ticklow. Peter Grimshaw and Maureen Pierce.'

Their eyes met. Those names were significant.

'All exposed in the tabloid rag lately.' Stephen's voice now sounded grim. His face looked grimmer.

Abby added to his statement. 'And all reported by Lance Vector.' After untangling herself from Stephen's limbs, she rose quickly to her feet.

'Where are you going?' Stephen asked.

'To ask our friend Vector some questions.'

'I'll come with you.'

She shook her head. 'No. I don't need you to do that! You'll only get in the way.' On seeing his expression, she could have bit her tongue. 'I'm sorry, Stephen. But this is something I want to do by myself. It's my job to ask questions.'

He gripped her shoulders and stared intently into her eyes. 'It's your job to ask questions in court, Abby. Let me come with you. This thing is getting too dangerous. Who knows what that man might do? He's obviously out to get you. What if he succeeds?'

Stephen was missing the point. She had to put it to him. 'But why does he want to kill me, Stephen? Why?'

Stephen shrugged and struggled to find the answer. 'I don't know. Perhaps he thinks you know something you shouldn't know. But that's not really the point. As I have just said, what if he succeeds?'

There was genuine concern in his eyes. It made her want

to stay, but she couldn't. On the other hand, he was right. She was now in real danger, but the solution to this conundrum was now in sight, and much as she loved Stephen, she had a yearning to finish things herself. All the same, she nodded her agreement.

'Good. I'll get dressed.'

Stephen whistled with cautious confidence as he sallied forth into the bedroom. Abby was dressed before him, and quietly, while he was still talking to her from the bedroom, she let herself out of the front door.

She looked both ways before leaving the suspect camouflage of the tiled portico. Lance Vector was nowhere in sight.

Cautiously, she glanced again up and down the road. Perhaps Vector had parked a little further down the road. She began to walk. She was feeling nervous. The man with the yellow eyes was still in her mind.

The street appeared empty, the air was damp and gave her cheeks colour. A mist softened the chain of parked cars, lampposts and the red pillar box at the end of the street.

As her footsteps clattered on the uneven pavement, she saw the sleek black car coming towards her. She saw a window wind down. Despite the mist, there was no mistaking the yellow eyes of the man behind the wheel. She turned and began to run.

As her heart thumped against her ribcage, she heard the slamming of a car door. *He's stopped!* The words screamed through her brain.

Eyes wide, hair flying, she glanced over her shoulder. A big man in black was running behind her. She screamed as another car slid to a halt just in front of her.

'Miss Corrigan!'

The passenger door flew open. Saved! There was no way at this angle that she could recognize the driver, but recognition was the last thing on her mind. He had called her name. She literally threw herself into the passenger seat, but not until the car was in motion did she realize that it was Lance Vector who sat beside her.

Chapter 20

Judging by the absence of her clothes from the chair on which she had thrown them, Stephen assumed Abby was in the bathroom. Thinking about the bathroom and what they had just done in the shower made him feel warm and not entirely sensible. But he made an effort to rein in his emotions. After all, this was a serious matter they were involved in. Not only was his career on the line, but now it appeared that someone was out to kill the woman he loved. Loved! Was that really how he felt about her? Then why hadn't he told her more forcibly?

He picked up the book that Abby had risked so much to acquire. Lovingly, as if it were her skin, he ran his hand over the cover and casually opened it. The list of names and sexual preferences danced before his eyes. At this moment in time, they were not important to him. It was her that filled his mind. He then leaned his head towards the closed bathroom door. 'I love you, Abby.'

There was no response. No sound of movement, of running water, or even of the flush being pulled. He frowned, then cursed himself for being so stupid, for depending on her too much. Hadn't she said that Vector had been outside watching the house with his weasel eyes? Wasn't it now time to question him?

He threw the book onto the table and ran out into the street. There was no sign of her. The street was strangely empty and silent except for a lone street cleaner. He was bent over his work, his brush swishing over the cobbled gutter, and his shovel clanging as he filled it with a pile of stiff-looking tissues. *Someone*, he thought off-handedly, *has one hell of a cold*.

Stephen rushed back into the living room. Briefly, he glanced at the open book before picking up the phone. One name above all others jumped out at him. Now, at last, things began to slide into place. Now also was the time for him to save himself and to save Abby too. First he called the police. Not Bennet or any of the other men who frequented the Red Devil Club. He got straight through to Val who was due at the Home Office, but was willing to spare him her time. He told her of what they knew and of the killing at the Red Devil Club. He also told her of the yellow-eyed man and the fear – no, the fact that Abby was in danger.

Val was instantly understanding. 'Stuff the Home Office. I'll send my second along. They can do without my black ass in their plush chair. The whole bloody lot of them get on my tits, Stevie boy. Besides that, you sure have the best white body I've ever seen, and you sure got the tongue of an angel! Wow, you can blow my pussy and my mind any time you like. And I appreciate a pal like Abby. Like minds, her and me. Kindred spirits, you might say, with brains in our heads and fire in our pussies. I've a mind I might know where Archie boy is. Leave me to check it out.'

'Okay. Okay,' Stephen was breathing heavily. He liked talking to Val and on another occasion, he would have talked longer and dirtier with her. But Abby was still on his mind. 'I'll go to the office and see if she's checked in there first. After that, I'll go along and see this Lance Vector. I'll get his address from his newspaper.' He spat the last words. It would be hard not to throttle the man who had written the article about him and taken the picture that had featured day after day on the front page of the tabloid newspaper he worked for.

'Vector? The exposer?'

'Yes. All the people he's exposed are marked with a red asterisk in a book kept at Archie's club. All of them were members of the upstairs elite.'

'I didn't know you were.'

'I wasn't. I presume the others were blackmailed or just their sexual practices revealed for public consumption in a bid to improve circulation. In my case, they had another reason to set me up and broadcast the event, but whoever owns the Daily Sin also owns the club. Do you know who it is?'

'No. Can't say I do, but I'm beginning to understand your problem. You were making too many waves in the Swan and Swallow case; getting too near the real fraudsters, and one of those concerned might very well be this big wig newspaperman.'

'That's right.' Stephen could not prevent his tone from becoming more hurried. 'Look. I have to go. I have to find Abby.' Enough was enough. He promised to meet Val in Abby's chambers around lunchtime.

The roadsweeper was propped against the railings when

Stephen went out. He was smoking and at first seemed to be only gazing into space. A second look stopped Stephen in his tracks. Abby had spoken about surveillance equipment. This roadsweeper had been caught up in the onslaught of technology. What had once seemed futuristic was now commonplace. The earphones on his walkman were almost invisible. What if Archie wore earphones at the club, and what if, on that night he had gone there with Val, someone watching from the surveillance room had recognized him and, through a hidden earphone, had informed Archie. That would explain why Abby in her guise as Carmel, had seen him looking so intently at the woman with the blonde hair. Suddenly, so much became feasible. But who was the man upstairs?

The roadsweeper saw him looking, nodded, then tapped something behind his ear. 'I need the relaxation,' he said, half-mockingly, and half-daring Stephen to pick up the phone to the private contractor who now paid his wages. 'Specially after all the excitement 'ere this mornin'. Like bleeding cops and robbers it is. First one bloke running after this 'ere woman, then this other car speeding up an' 'er gettin' in it.'

Before the man had time to tune back into his favourite music, Stephen stayed his hand. 'You saw a woman being chased by a man? Did he have yellow eyes, you know, like a cat? And a black car? Did he have a black car?' Stephen remembered everything Abby had told him.

The man looked suddenly startled. He eyed Stephen up and down as though what he had talked about now seemed very secret, very personal, and what's more, he wanted to keep it to himself.

Impatient to know what the roadsweeper knew, Stephen grabbed the man by the collar of his crumpled jacket. 'Was it a black car?'

The man grabbed Stephen's wrists. 'All right, mate, all right!'

Stephen's grip loosened.

The roadsweeper took a deep breath. 'A black car pulled up, a big geezer got out and chased the blonde dolly down the street. Then another car came along. She got into that one.'

Stephen stared. 'What colour car?'

'Green – I think. But it might have been blue. Yes, blue. Sporty job, I think. But I can't be sure. It was a bit foggy, you know.'

Stephen let him go. His emotions were in uproar, and although he would have liked to know more, he had a greater need to search for Abigail. First stop was chambers. It was there that the jigsaw might finally fit into place.

Chapter 21

Gradually, Abby ceased to tremble and her breathing returned to normal. She thanked Lance Vector for rescuing her.

'To the victor goes the spoils,' he chuckled. She didn't like to ask him what he meant by it. She was just glad to be able to catch her breath and get her thoughts into some sort of order. However, there were a lot of questions that she had to ask him.

'Mr Vector,' she began.

'Lance. Call me Lance.'

'Lance. Judging by the fact that the more scandalous headlines in your paper are closely followed by your name, you are a very busy man.'

Lance Vector responded to the baited statement. The merest hint of praise brought the braggart in him to the surface.

'I do all the best ones. Uncover all the more lurid cases. They never know I'm there. Never. But I'm always about, spying through keyholes, looking through windows, listening at letter-boxes.' He chuckled again. 'I'm the original fly on the wall. Any fornicating going on between the high and the mighty, and Lance Vector is the one to report it.'

A man truly proud of his job, she thought. Perhaps she could turn such conceit to her advantage.

'I admit to being truly amazed. How do you manage to find out about these people? Where do you get your leads? How do you know where they are likely to be when they indulge in these illicit copulations?'

She saw him smile. Glittering, his eyes lingered on her for a few seconds before returning to the road.

'The governor gives the leads to me, and his governor gives it to him. Or at least, one of the directors does.' He thought of the man in the penthouse suite on the top floor. Directors, owners, managers. They were all faceless, but none so faceless as the one on the top floor. Even now, he had still not seen his face, though he recalled something dangling on one side of his head. He glanced at Abby again and saw the neat silver earring in her ear. That, he decided suddenly, was what the boss wore, but his earring was far from being neat. It bulged like a swinging carbuncle from one ear.

'Does he really dictate exactly how you should approach your subject, or does he give you some leeway to allow for original thought?'

A slight frown creased Vector's brow. Abby still considered him as Vector. There was no way she intended or, indeed, wanted to consider any familiarity with the man.

'They *think* I do it all their way. But I don't.' He smiled and nodded his head as though he were agreeing with himself. 'I do some things they don't know about. I keep copies of some of the tapes and photographs I take. They don't know that.' He laughed, then reached across and shyly touched her hand. 'They don't know I keep the ones I like. I keep ones they know nothing about.'

Abby retrieved her hand from his grasp. He looked hurt, but he kept on talking. 'Sometimes, I arrive early at a shoot. I start filming from the time I get there. Of course, they don't want that footage. So I keep it. Might come in handy one day.'

Abby listened carefully. Some of what he said triggered a reaction in her brain.

'Did you arrive before time in the Stephen Sigmund case?'

Even without looking at him, she knew he had tensed at the sound of Stephen's name.

'Him! He's finished, you know.' He sniggered and shook his head. 'You might as well forget him. They're out to destroy him. And they will. I know they will.'

He looked at her and winked salaciously. Instantly, she raised her hand to her breasts as if she were screening them from his gaze. Remembering his phone calls to her, his offers of lunch brought on a certain coldness. It intensified when she realized that he had been following Stephen and might even have seen them making love. At this moment in time, she had no intention of pursuing the assumption. There were some important questions to be asked.

'Do you still have transparencies of the photographs you took?'

He looked at her and laughed before returning his gaze to the road. 'Copies of the photos, the article *and* a tape.'

He patted her hand again. 'I'll show you it. I think you'll like it. You'll be amazed at the look on his face when he's confronted outside the lavatory – *and* dressed in women's clothes!'

Abby was more than willing to accompany him. At last she could see a light at the end of the tunnel.

Unwilling to disturb his dear mother, Lance drove her round to the yard at the back which was on the same level as the basement.

'Come on,' he said smiling. 'I'll show you everything I've got.'

The double entendre did cross her mind, but she dismissed it and followed Vector into a stone-floored room. Its only light came from the row of evenly placed spotlights sunk into the ceiling.

'This,' he said, spreading his hands, 'is my workshop. You could say it's the devil's kitchen, but don't let mother hear you call it that. She might take it the wrong way. I only mean that I do all the things down here to expose those who do wrong.'

Abby did not comment. She was too busy taking in the banks of computers, video machines and television sets. There was also a pile of note pads, an audio transcriber, and a metal bin full of used tissues.

'So where is the tape you took of Stephen Sigmund?'

Vector, who was bent before his video machine, did not appear to hear her, or if he did, chose not to answer.

Abby looked around her again and shivered. This place might be quite cool in summer, but it was November and the mist outside had not yet shifted. It was freezing.

'Now,' said Lance, 'I will show you the tape I took of Stephen Sigmund. But first, I want you to take your clothes off.'

Abby was about to laugh and tell him not to be so stupid. Then she saw the knife he held in his hand. She took a deep breath. Had she really escaped a dangerous man just to be at the mercy of another? *Be cool*, she told herself. *Think carefully*.

'You wouldn't use that, would you?' She smiled as she said it. He did not react. His eyes did not leave her face. They were glazed and wide. It was as though he had not heard her.

'Take your clothes off.'

Slowly, she raised her hands to the buttons of her neatly-fitted jacket. It was navy, matched her skirt, and had been bought in a Harrods sale from money won in the Cheltenham Gold Cup. It had seemed apt to buy something extravagant from money won on a long shot outsider, and at this moment in time she was loath to let it leave her body. Nevertheless, she continued.

He offered her a hanger. It seemed an odd thing to do until she reasoned he was a fastidious man, a man whose jeans had a neat crease down each leg. Someone, she reasoned, took care of him.

She unzipped her skirt, put that with the jacket, and covered her pubic area with one hand. She was shivering. Already the cold was playing havoc with her flesh.

Vector's eyes were popping out of his head. A lone trail of sweat ran past one eyebrow and over his chin.

Purposely, Abby took her hand away from her pubes. She heard him gasp, knew he was aroused by the sight of her pubic lips and the fact that she now wore only her blouse, her suspender belt, her stockings and her shoes.

Fear was upon her, yet she knew she must retain her

coolness. At the same time, she had to humour him. Abigail,
the blonde, blue-eyed barrister, was taken over by Carmel
acting out her part as Jezebel Justice. Slowly, as her fingers
unbuttoned the cuffs of her white blouse, she began to sway.
Her hips moved hypnotically from side to side. Vector
watched, another trail of sweat running down his face and
mingling with the previous one. He licked his lips and the
hand that held the knife shook slightly.

'What are you doing? Stop it!'

She did not stop it. As she slid the blouse down over her
arms, she turned round and bent over, showed him the firm
cheeks of her behind and the pink lips smiling from between
her legs.

Smiling, she looked at him over her shoulder.

'Is that what you want, Lance? Do you want to see my
pussy close up? Do you want to touch it, to kiss it, to push
your wet tongue inside me and suck the saltiness out of my
body?'

'No!' She saw him wince before he leapt towards her.
Agile as she was, he had caught her off guard. Because the
sleeves of her blouse were halfway down her arms, he had her
at a disadvantage. Quickly, he made full use of her
predicament and tied the two sleeves behind her back, then
pushed her into a chair.

Naked except for her stockings and garter belt, she sat
there, her breasts heaving as he looked her up and down.
Suddenly, his mouth spread into a gruesome leer. 'I've seen
you naked before.' He made an odd noise, a wheezing sound,
a sound like a chuckle being strangled. 'I saw you with him,
with Sigmund. But you didn't see me. You never saw me. But

I saw you. You and him rolling in the leaves, leaning against the rocks, romping naked in the back of his car. I saw everything you did; everything you did to him, and everything he did to you. I saw you in the forest. I saw what you did there.'

Abby felt very cold. This man had a dangerous look in his eyes. Before, she had regarded him as a laughable hindrance. Suddenly, she was very afraid of him.

Stephen rushed into chambers. Frowning, Barbara, the receptionist, told him Abby had not been in. 'I did expect her to be in. She specifically asked me to get two briefs out of the archives for her and wanted them on her desk first thing.' She pouted like a child though she was well past her fiftieth birthday. 'I stayed after five to find those briefs. She said it was important to your case.'

'Really? What briefs were they?'

Barbara flicked at a stray lipstick stain at the corner of her mouth and looked him up and down. He knew she was considering whether she should tell him regardless of the fact that they had some bearing on his case. Her large bosom heaved as she made her decision. 'One is a paternity suit coupled with a charge of GBH referring to a Mr Henry Vector. Plus a divorce and a charge of GBH. The other is regarding a matter dealt with by Mr Probert. I'm afraid most of it seems to be missing.'

'Vector! Can I see that one?'

Undecided, Barbara, who was shared by all six barristers in that particular chambers, viewed him a little suspiciously. 'Well, it is confidential . . . but, perhaps . . .'

Quickly, he unbundled everything, then smiled as he read the contents. Lance Vector, that crusader for moral purity, had been born out of wedlock. His father had been in banking and had also been well battered by Lance's mother when he left her high and dry.

It was all very enlightening, but why had Abby deemed it necessary to retrieve the file from the archives? There was no answer to that. Unless she was going to use such information to force Vector to talk. He made a decision to go along and speak to Lance. Glancing at his watch, he first phoned the paper Vector worked for and was told he wasn't in that morning. He was given his home address. He rang Vector at home. A woman answered.

'He's at work,' she told him sharply.

'I've phoned them. They told me he's not in today.'

'Then phone him on his mobile. They know his number.'

Stephen kept his patience. 'No. You don't understand. They told me he phoned in sick. They assured me he was still at home.'

There was a pause. 'Wait a minute. I'll see if his car's still here. He might be working down in the basement.'

Stephen heard slow footsteps walk hesitantly across what he guessed was an uncarpeted floor. Impatiently, he drummed his fingers on the receiver for what seemed an age before she got back.

'My son's working in the basement. I'll tell him you called.'

The telephone was put down before Stephen could say he would be over to see her son. He swore as he replaced the receiver at his end.

A fear was in him, a worry that was making him think quickly. No matter that posses of journalists were still hunting him, looking for other angles from which they could slant their stories. Abby was missing and he had to find her. First stop was the home of Lance Vector.

'What's the other brief about?'

Barbara shrugged. 'I told you. Most of it's missing. Mr Probert handled it.'

He lifted his hand. 'Never mind. I'll come back to that later.'

He left a message with Barbara. Told her Commissioner Spendle would be arriving shortly. 'Tell her I've gone to see Lance Vector,' he called as he flew out of the office door.

Despite the fact that she was naked and the eyes of Lance Vector were raking her body, Abby stared at the video screen. Anger replaced fear as realization dawned. This man who held her prisoner had been party to a set-up. There before her were three people: Inspector Paul Bennet, rent boy, Carl Candel (deceased), and a woman. Despite a wide-brimmed hat and dark glasses, the sheer sophistication of the woman was instantly recognizable. It was Medina Frassard. But why?

'Bitch!' It was Lance who was speaking.

Suddenly she was aware of Vector's hands upon her knees, his palms prising them apart. She gave no resistance.

'Take no notice of them, my darling.' His voice sounded like that of an amateur actor; as though he were aping someone else. 'Let me see your pussy. Let me see your hidden little treasure.'

As her legs opened, she stared at him. His eyes were closed and he was breathing in her scent, gulping the perfume of her body as his head and his lips came nearer to her. *Be cool*, she told herself. *This is his fetish, his thing. Best enjoy it. That way you might keep your head and your life!*

It was impossible not to groan as his tongue licked over her sex in one long motion, its tip delicately flicking between the sensitive lips. Her legs tensed, her inner thighs trembled as she threw back her head and wished she was somewhere else and it was Stephen's tongue stroking her flesh. *I have to get through this*. She gritted her teeth as the thought passed through her mind. *Pretend it is Stephen*, she said to herself. *Pretend it's his tongue licking you, his palms pressing against your thighs.*

A strange calmness came to her. Imagining it was Stephen made her feel she was riding above this thing, scoring over this man who was moaning long and low as he sucked at her sex.

Different sensations ran over her body. There was arousal, but there was also an odd detachment from it as though she were viewing herself from the ceiling: enjoying it, but not participating.

Stephen, she thought to herself, *would be more gentle*. His hands would caress her thighs, his fingers would lightly tickle the backs of her knees, and his tongue would flick quickly in the places he knew she liked best. Thinking about him made her want him, and wanting him made her wonder where he was.

Gilda Vector, Lance's mother, ached, so she grumbled as she

went to answer the doorbell. Through the frosted glass that was surrounded with alternate panels of bitter blue and ruby red, she could see the outline of a man. *Perhaps*, she thought to herself, *he's the man who phoned just now and asked for Lance*. All the same, she was a cautious woman, so she slid the chain across before she opened the door.

'Good morning,' he said, and looked a bit surprised to see her. Once it had crept across his face, his smile lightened his features and the colour of his eyes did not seem to matter so much. Reassured, Gilda brightened.

'You must be the man who wanted to speak to my son. He's not ill really. He just doesn't like to be disturbed when he's working in the basement.'

'I quite understand.'

Gilda nodded before she began to slide back the chain. Seeing as this man had phoned the paper her son worked for before phoning her, she decided to overlook the fact that he had an off-white complexion and eyes the colour of sulphur.

'He's down there.' The man moved quickly in the direction Gilda Vector pointed. He seemed very light on his feet, and it was only when he was equally quiet when opening the basement door, that Gilda began to nibble nervously at one of her fingernails.

'Are you intending to surprise him?' She said it loudly and intended saying it louder so that Lance was not surprised by his visitor.

Her comment made the man turn quickly towards her. He came close. She could smell him. There was a damp, fetid smell about his clothes, an odd luminosity to his terrible eyes. Cloying, the smell of him made her dizzy as he leaned

299

over her. She saw him raise his hand, saw the flash of metal as it went over her shoulder.

'What are you doing?' Gilda had a loud voice, but today it trembled. Vaguely, she was aware of the telephone receiver passing in front of her face, its coils trailing behind it then pressing against her neck. She saw the knife flash, saw the end of the wire in his hand. 'Oh, God save me.' She closed her eyes and began to pray. 'Protect thy handmaiden, O Lord. Don't let the devil take me. Save me. In thy name, save me.'

Yellow eyes belonged to the devil. She'd told her son that. Why couldn't she follow her own advice? But it was too late for all that now. Slowly, in strangled breaths amid the last words of her prayer, Gilda Vector's life left her body.

'Amen.' The man with yellow eyes said the word quietly, and just as quietly, let Gilda's body slide to the floor. Back he went to the basement door. This time, there was no interruption to warn those below that he had arrived.

Carefully he spread his fingers over the doorknob, and opened the door. Fearful of a stray squeak from a loose tread, he very gently put his foot on the top stair.

Breathless with the image of Stephen in her mind, Abby was slowly beginning to enjoy the sensations aroused by Lance's tongue.

'That is so good,' she breathed, lost in the sensitivity of his touch.

No, cried a voice in her mind. *I can't let this happen. This is not Stephen!*

It was then that she opened her eyes.

There was a figure standing on the bottom step. He was leering, his yellow eyes wide and staring as he enjoyed the scene before him.

She tried to scream. It didn't come out loud enough. Lance never even raised his head, convinced, no doubt, that it was purely an exclamation of ecstasy.

He didn't even have time to take a breath before Charwallah was upon him, his hand clamping Lance's head against her flesh.

Abby cried out as Lance's arms began to flail against her legs, his fingers digging into her thighs. She could feel his mouth sucking for air against her flesh, his nose pressing hard against her clitoris as the man with the yellow eyes held Lance's head tight against her body.

Charwallah was still leering, his eyes and his breath just inches from Abby's face.

'I bet you never had a muff job like this before.' There was cruelty in his eyes, evil in his leer.

'Let him go! He can't breathe.'

The man raised his eyes in mock surprise. 'What a way to go!' He shook his head and tutted in a mocking manner. 'Don't worry yourself about it, darling. Enjoy the attention of his lips and his tongue. That's what he's doing it for – so that you can enjoy it. Look. See how he's enjoying it!'

Abby wanted to be sick. Lance's arms were still flailing, but their wildness was slowly diminishing. A vacuum pulled his lips more forcibly into her body. He was suffocating on her sex, and she could do nothing about it.

She screamed a long, drawn-out *no*! She remembered Lance mentioning something about his mother. She must have opened the door to this man. What had happened to her? The truth made her scream again.

Charwallah laughed. He liked his victims to scream. From screams you could tell how frightened people were, and anyway, there was no one to hear her. The old woman was lying dead upstairs. There was nothing she could do, nothing to be done. He'd have her scream some more before he finished with her – with pleasure and with pain.

Still pressing the dying man's head into her crotch, he kissed and bit her lips. She could taste her own blood and wondered just how much would flow before he had finished with her. By now, the body of the journalist was twitching slightly, his arms lying limp at his sides.

His lips left her and she took a deep breath. If she was going to die, she'd fight all the way. Her eyes blazed.

'Me next, I suppose. Well, get it over with. What are you waiting for?'

Like a shark or a wild cat, his teeth were large and only two or three shades lighter than his eyes. 'Oh no, no, my pretty darling. The delights of life and of death should never be rushed. Be patient, my pretty darling. Be patient.'

All her being cried out for help. Behind him she could still see the tape running. Perhaps something would be gained by her death after all. Perhaps someone would notice the recording Lance had done before Stephen Sigmund had arrived at the lavatories. All it would take would be for someone to put it all together, question Paul Bennet, question Medina Frassard, and save Stephen's career. She prayed it would be so.

'Then get on with it.' Those words she fully expected to

be her last. She said them with clenched teeth, a dead man's nose still flush against her sex.

A sudden rushing of feet made her open her eyes. In a flash, Stephen had smashed his body against the man with the yellow eyes. Vector's body fell softly to the ground between her legs.

Stephen was hitting very hard, but the man beneath him was quick and very professional. He landed Stephen a hard one, then got to his feet. Through narrowed, tearful eyes, Abby saw the glint of steel. She squeezed her eyes shut and waited for the knife to divide her ribs. It didn't happen.

More footsteps, more voices. Scuffles and a call for an ambulance.

Naked breasts heaving, she opened her eyes and looked into those of her lover. Blood was running down the side of Stephen's face, but he was smiling.

'Oh, Stephen!'

He wrapped his arms around her, and as he kissed her, he undid the sleeves of her blouse and released her arms.

'Keep this around you,' he said gently.

Beneath the roughness of a blanket, she put on her blouse, her skirt, and her neat jacket.

As he had once before, Stephen scooped his arm around her back to stop her from falling.

'My legs feel so weak.' Leaning against Stephen, she rolled her eyes, still struggling to take in the scene before her.

The vaulted ceilings of the basement seemed too low and the walls too close to accommodate the many policemen milling around in it. Two of those policemen were laying Lance Vector out on his back. One of them commenced mouth to mouth. She saw him licking his lips between each breath and wondered what he was thinking as he tasted what was undoubtedly the juices of a woman.

There was a sudden choking sound.

'He's alive! Quick, tell that ambulance to hurry. Tell them there's only one dead one now. The other's still alive.'

Abby knew she had been right to guess that Lance's mother was dead. The thought made her shiver.

Stephen held her tight. They both looked at the pale face of Lance Vector. Gradually, he acquired some colour.

Abby kept her eyes fixed on Lance while she asked Stephen a question. 'How did you know where I was?'

'The roadsweeper saw what happened and described both cars. I knew it was Vector's car, so I hoped he had set you down at your chambers. I went to your room and saw the Vector archives on your desk. I knew you intended to use them to get the truth out of Vector. But you weren't there so I phoned his paper and was told he'd called in sick. I rang his home and she confirmed that he was here, and I decided to come over, fast.'

Abby sighed. 'Shame I can't thank Mrs Vector.'

Stephen felt her lean more heavily on him as the news sunk in.

'At least Lance is still alive.' Saying that and feeling the warmth of her against his body made him want to take her to bed, to snuggle down with her in warmth and security as the world outside carried on its own business. The method Lance had almost died by was too bizarre to easily ignore.

Aching and longing now replacing the fear, Abby cuddled closer to him. She looked thoughtful.

'I think,' she said slowly, 'I now have all I need to clear your name. I also think that Val Spendle will win her libel case by a submission.'

The police took the pile of tapes. 'For evidence,' they said. Thankfully, they omitted to take the most crucial one from the machine.

Stephen cuddled both Abby and the tape to him as they left the house, stepped over the inert body of Mrs Vector, and went to give statements at the police station.

Chapter 22

In the cloistered chambers of Lincoln's Inn and the marble edifices of the law courts, men were looking at Abigail Corrigan with renewed interest.

News of the attempted manslaughter of Lance Vector had spread like wild fire. Notwithstanding the method Charwallah had used for disposing of Carl Candel, the visions such an end stirred in the minds of those usually viewed as being musty, strait-laced or past it, could only be speculated upon. And speculation was rife.

Abby bore the renewed interest in her sexual favours with professional fortitude. She also made a point of having her photograph taken with Stephen beneath the headline "Lawyer Rescued by MP".

Newspaper circulation soared and eyes opened wide as the details of Lance Vector's near death and Abby's nudity were read in three different sections of the newspaper.

Charlie Ahmed Wallis was under suspicion for more than grievous bodily harm, actual bodily harm, and outright murder. He was a true professional in that he was not only good at his job, he loved it. He was everything a true villain should be – except a grass. No matter how many hours of gruelling questioning Val Spendle put him under, he stayed silent. The fact that he had been caught in the act of suffocating Lance against Abby's quim was the only irrefutable evidence against him.

Lance had fully recovered, and Medina Frassard had dropped her libel suit against Val Spendle. According to her legal counsel, she had experienced a complete change of heart and had no wish to harm such a shining example of female success.

'Bullshit!' Val spat after she'd said it.

'My sentiments exactly.' Abby did not even look up from her papers. It was mentioned there that a tape had been found relating to the Stephen Sigmund case. Paul Bennet and Medina Frassard must know what it contained.

Val had checked on whether they had links with Swan and Swallow Investments. Neither did. No shares, no director-ships. Nothing. And neither was letting on as to why they should be involved.

Wallis, too, was remaining silent. So was the ultimate head of the Daily Sin who hung out in a glass penthouse at the top of his newspaper building. No matter what happened, he would be safe. He was unassailable, he told Val. His conscience was clear.

Val's fingers drummed impatiently on the desk. Abby tried hard to read the file before her, but it was her ears that were hard at work. She was listening for the approach of Lance Vector.

For the first time since that day in his basement, he was coming to see her.

Their meeting was necessarily brief. She dictated to him

exactly what she wanted him to say in his newspaper. She also told him that she would release the story of his illegitimate birth and details of his father deserting his mother to live in sin with a society beauty. It was enough of a threat to bring him to heel.

'I'll do whatever you want. I don't want my mother's memory besmirched with such things.' He looked sincerely contrite.

Lance Vector, Abby decided, would no longer be lusting after her. He had a memory to protect – a dead woman to worship.

'Do you really think this is going to work?' Val looked doubtful. 'You know I haven't got much evidence to go on. So far, Medina's denied everything. It would have been helpful if she'd given her orders to Charlie Wallis in writing – then they'd both squeal. Unfortunately, felons don't do that!'

Abby ignored Val's scepticism. She was in love and soaring high above such doubts.

She smiled, and for the first time in months, she felt strangely whole and very happy. 'It will work. Trust me.'

On the morning after the news broke of Medina Frassard's involvement in the Swan and Swallow Investment affair, she was on the telephone to Abby.

'Can we meet for lunch?'

Abby agreed to meet her. She phoned Stephen beforehand to tell him where they would be meeting.

Cane screens shielded the two women from prying eyes, though no one could fail to notice the slim, tall blonde in the strict black suit, the white blouse, the satin sheened stockings. They would also have noticed the other woman whose outfit was of powder blue bordered with beige and teamed with tan accessories. Her hair was immaculate, her make-up sheer perfection. No matter what her age might be, Medina Frassard did her best with what she had. She held her head high. Abby assumed that attack would be Medina's only defence. She was right.

'I shall sue if you continue to libel me.'

'It's not libel. I have a tape showing three people meeting near a pretty desperate place. You are one of them. Another is a policeman, and the third is dead. I know a man called Charles Wallis killed Candel, but you hired him. Admit it.'

'No! It wasn't me. I swear it!'

The sculptured face was now contorted with fear. Abby knew she would talk, knew she would do anything to save herself.

She kept her own voice calm. 'All right. So it wasn't you who killed Carl Candel, and it wasn't you who hired him. But who did, and why?'

Medina's bottom lip shook. Black false eyelashes fluttered nervously. Intense emotion strained the tucks where the surgeon had hidden the scars of his art. Suddenly, the smooth facade took on clownish contortions. 'I have my reasons. Believe me, if you have ever loved, you would have done the same. And I love that man. I would do anything to save him from ruin. You of all people must understand that.'

The coldness of Medina's hand permeated the warmth of her own. Oh yes, Abby understood how she might feel about someone she loved, about protecting them. But who was that person?

'Who?' she said quietly.

Medina withdrew her hand and held it to her brow. 'John Humphries. I love him. I didn't want anyone killed. I just wanted to save him and his career.' She looked up suddenly. 'And I would have if you hadn't intervened. John orchestrated Swan and Swallow Investments, and it was his idea to float it offshore once the home housing market had collapsed. It wasn't his fault, it was the middle man. He was recommended, but turned out to be a crook. I love John, you see. I have to save him.'

Abby stared. A high court judge with a mistress was of no particular consequence. But a judge dabbling in a suspect company which robbed a lot of people of their savings was another matter.

'So Hardiman was the middle man. Who hired the killer?'

In the ensuing silence Abby willed Medina to answer. So much depended on it. Medina's voice became very quiet as she said, 'Christopher Probert. He found the man through one of his clients. He had a file on the client. Some misdemeanour he knew of that never came to court.'

'Archie Ringer.'

'Yes. I think that was his name. He runs a club. The man worked for a close friend, so he told me.'

'But why would Christopher want to help you?'

Medina's eyes sparkled with sudden pleasure. 'He was infatuated. I used him. He was nothing to me. I just wanted to help John. I love John. I love him. You must understand that.'

For a few minutes, it was hard for Abby to say anything at all. All the heartache, the danger of the past weeks had left

311

her feeling slightly off balance. But why was that? The reason was clearer than she could admit. People in her profession hid behind their veneer of respectability. And yet, she had thought it was just her and Val whose lives were split in two. Then she met Stephen, and a lot of other people who wore masks in public but let their hair down in private.

It was sickening to think that Christopher Probert had hired the killer who had killed Carl Candel. Indirectly then, he was also the one who had left Mrs Vector slumped on the floor and had almost snuffed out the journalist's life with forcible cunnilingus.

Summer had arrived by the time the guilty had been dealt with and the innocent released.

During that time, Abby had buried herself in her work. Stephen was also working at rebuilding his reputation now his innocence had been proved.

They phoned each other, had rushed lunches together, and Stephen even brought Mr Rheingold to her office to thank her for her part in proving his innocence.

The guilty were all punished. All except the elusive man who ran the Daily Sin.

It was time to build a wall between the past and the future. By late summer, once all the ends had finally been tied up, Abby and Stephen hired a yacht and sailed the Greek islands. Their relationship had taken another turn.

Making love beneath the stars, on the deck of the yacht and on secluded sandy beaches, they found themselves and found each other.

* * *

In London, a man was pouring himself a drink in a high penthouse suite overlooking the City. The editor of the newspaper he owned was standing behind him, wondering what chance there was of being offered a drink too. It wouldn't happen. It never did.

'This didn't go so well, Squires. My friend, John Humphries is ruined. It's a great shame. He could quite easily have made it to the House of Lords. But business is business. The public will want his blood. Of course, we'll have to give it to them. Rake up all you can about his private life. Get that little man, Vector, on it. I'm sure he'll be his usual, enthusiastic self.'

'I'm sure he will, Mr Hardiman. I'll get him on it right away.'

Vector was waiting in his editor's office. The editor told Vector what was wanted. Vector only nodded. There was a strange look in his eyes, a look the editor did not like. Not once had the man blinked as his mission was outlined to him. 'He wants you to go up and see him.'

Vector nodded and got up to make his way to the penthouse suite.

Frowning, the editor watched him go. Vector never looked back. The editor wondered what was in his head.

Vengeance is mine, sayeth the Lord. Lance paced his steps with each word in his head. He had lost his mother. He had also lost the only woman he had ever wanted. It was all the fault of the man up in the penthouse suite. He fingered the knife in his pocket. Vengeance would indeed soon be his.

Adult Fiction for Lovers from Headline LIAISON

SLEEPLESS NIGHTS	Tom Crewe & Amber Wells	£4.99
THE JOURNAL	James Allen	£4.99
THE PARADISE GARDEN	Aurelia Clifford	£4.99
APHRODISIA	Rebecca Ambrose	£4.99
DANGEROUS DESIRES	J. J. Duke	£4.99
PRIVATE LESSONS	Cheryl Mildenhall	£4.99
LOVE LETTERS	James Allen	£4.99

All Headline Liaison books are available at your local bookshop or newsagent, or can be ordered direct from the publisher. Just tick the titles you want and fill in the form below. Prices and availability subject to change without notice.

Headline Book Publishing, Cash Sales Department, Bookpoint, 39 Milton Park, Abingdon, OXON, OX14 4TD, UK. If you have a credit card you may order by telephone – 01235 400400.

Please enclose a cheque or postal order made payable to Bookpoint Ltd to the value of the cover price and allow the following for postage and packing: UK & BFPO: £1.00 for the first book, 50p for the second book and 30p for each additional book ordered up to a maximum charge of £3.00. OVERSEAS & EIRE: £2.00 for the first book, £1.00 for the second book and 50p for each additional book.

Name ....

Address ....

....

....

If you would prefer to pay by credit card, please complete: Please debit my Visa/Access/Diner's Card/American Express (Delete as applicable) card no:

Signature .... Expiry Date ....